Books by Sanora Babb

Told in the Seed and Selected Poems

The Dark Earth and Selected Prose from the Great Depression

On the Dirty Plate Trail:
Remembering the Dust Bowl Refugee Camps

Whose Names Are Unknown

Told in the Seed

An Owl on Every Post

The Lost Traveler

The Dark Earth

About Sanora Babb

Unknown No More: Recovering Sanora Babb

CRY
of the
TINAMOU

CRY
of the
TINAMOU
⌐ S T O R I E S ⌐

SANORA BABB

Introduction by Alan M. Wald

MUSE INK PRESS

www.museinkpress.com

www.sanorababb.com

Second Edition
Printed in the United States of America
ISBN 978-0-9859915-5-5
Designed by Ryan Ratliff

To my good friend Joanne Dearcopp

Contents

Soft Focus:

The Short Fiction of Sanora Babb

Alan M. Wald

For more than five decades, the delicate, lucid, and well-crafted prose of Sanora Babb has appeared in an uncommon range of magazines and journals. From the late 1920s to the present, Babb's stories can be found in proletarian regional "little magazines" such as *The Anvil: Stories for Workers* and *Hinterland;* Communist-sponsored journals such as *New Masses* and *Mainstream;* left-leaning publications such as *Black and White, The Clipper,* and *California Quarterly;* university publications such as *Antioch Review, New Mexico Quarterly,* and *Southwest Review;* mass-market magazines such as the *Saturday Evening Post* and *Seventeen;* and in dozens more that defy such groupings, like the mystery magazine *Ellery Queen's* and the contemporary erotic journal *Yellow Silk.*

This range of publication will surely befuddle readers requiring a label to gain a perspective on a writer's achievement. From diverse angles and at various moments, her possible literary stances include Western regionalist, proletarian writer, multiculturalist, premature feminist, contributor to "slick women's magazines," and other variations. In spite of her consistent literary development and even general cultural project, this dispersion of her publishing efforts came at the price of a coherent audience that is required for the national recognition and critical attention she merits. One hopes that the situation will be reversed by this present publication of her post-World War II retrospective, *Cry of the Tinamou.*

Still, lack of identification with a single subject area and a stable publishing venue are not the only reasons why a writer of such originality and quality as Babb, whose forte is the revelation of the subtleties of character, seems to have fallen between the cracks of literary history. Born in 1907, Ms. Babb is not a prolific author compared to contemporaries Lillian Hellman (b. 1905), Mary McCarthy (b. 1912), Albert Maltz (b. 1908), John Steinbeck (b. 1902), and Richard Wright (b. 1908). Moreover, as a writer who produced during the revolutionary 1930s as well as the repressive 1950s, her work evidences sharp periods. Finally, until now, her short fiction was not readily available nor often cited, although several stories were reprinted in volumes of *The Best American Short Stories;* four were collected in *The Dark Earth and Other Stories From the Great Depression* (1987); and a few have been translated and reprinted in Western Europe.

In fact, while the short story is her preferred genre, Babb is far better known for her sustained prose works. These include the unforgettable, autobiographically based novel of her youth, *The Lost Traveler* (1958; reprinted 1995 and 2013), and her classic memoir of eastern Colorado, *An Owl on Every Post* (1970; reprinted 1994 and 2012). A portion of her 1938 unpublished novel of migrant workers in the San Joaquin Valley, "Whose Names Are Unknown," appeared in a 1990 issue of *Michigan Quarterly Review.*[1] She has also published poetry throughout her life, along with some journalism, and she has edited small magazines and taught fiction writing. How does one locate the appropriate terms and establish the frame of reference to consider such a career?

The confluence of elements producing the artistic vision and style of Sanora Babb flows from the unique pattern of her life experiences. She is, by background, a regional writer of Kansas, Oklahoma, and Colorado, where her unstable, nomadic family wandered, and where she also developed strong affinities for the Oto tribe. Her father's occupations shifted from baker to baseball player to professional gambler, until his marriage broke up.[2] The stories "Run, Sheepy, Run" and "Davy" are inspired by the early and final stages of her parents' relationship.

After Ms. Babb attended the University of Kansas and Garden City Junior College in Kansas, she worked on small-town newspapers and a farm magazine, as well as taught school on the plains. Other stories in this collection, such as "William Shakespeare," "The Wild Flower," and "Tea Party," are derived from her personal experiences of those years. However, as Babb reveals analogically in "Reconciliation," her telling of both the family stories and the regional stories in later decades is not the expression of mere nostalgia for the lost mysteries of youth; the retelling is equally a response to preoccupations of her mature life at the time of composition.

In 1929 Babb changed her life forever by traveling on her own to Los Angeles to attempt a career as a journalist. Here she began publishing poetry inspired by Edna St. Vincent Millay, and then short fiction under the influence of Sherwood Anderson.[3] Southern California and Hollywood settings are evident in "Love Be My Destiny," "Matriarch of the Court," and other stories. In California her career developed by association with the literary and political Left as it evolved from the Great Depression through World War II and into the early 1950s.

Babb's father had talked generally of Democratic Party politics, but in Los Angeles the daughter experienced unemployment and homelessness, causing her to long for more drastic action. First Babb was introduced to political poetry through the work of Lucia Trent and Ralph Cheyney, who edited several collections of revolutionary verse.[4] Then she was invited to attend a meeting of the Communist-led John Reed Club, where she came to know radical writers such as the young Tillie Lerner (now known as Tillie Olsen) and the British-born Harry Carlisle. In 1935 she traveled with Lerner and Carlisle to the American Writers Congress in New York, where she met Richard Wright and many others. She also befriended talented writers on the West Coast more erratically associated with the Left, such as Carlos Bulosan and William Saroyan.

In 1936 Babb voyaged to the Soviet Union with a group of radical writers. She was impressed with what she saw but experienced discomfort over the advent of the Moscow Purge Trials. Remaining in Europe for a year, she worked for the British left-wing paper *The Week*, founded by Claud Cockburn, and married the Chinese-American Hollywood cinematographer James Wong Howe (a marriage that was not recognized in California until 1949).

Back on the West Coast in 1938, Babb made an effort to organize migrant workers, but desisted after threats of vigilante violence. In Los Angeles, she worked tirelessly on behalf of the Spanish Republic and the Anti-Nazi League, contributing to the *New Masses, Daily Worker,* and *New Theater.* One day the Communist screenwriter John Howard Lawson suggested that she might as well go ahead and join the party; Babb agreed. Why not be where the action really was, and where one could be in the company of the most stimulating people?[5] Babb, however, did not see her art as the primary means to fulfill her political commitment. She was an activist in the movement who occasionally submitted pieces to party-sponsored publications, but she never wrote out of an abstract desire to express "social consciousness." Rather, her work always grew out of her own emotions.

Despite anti-Communist stereotypes of the Cold War era, which have deformed much of mid-century United States cultural history, the artistic autonomy Babb displayed was hardly unique on the Left. The Hollywood section of the party contained many inner-directed artists who ignored the advice of Lawson's "Writers Clinic," which often unsuccessfully tried to discourage writers from publishing works that seemed out of the mainstream literary sensibility or lacked explicit social themes. The novelists John Sanford and Guy Endore, and the poets Thomas McGrath and Don Gordon, were typical of such idiosyncratic artistic personalities among Babb's circle of radical literary friends. Although Communist Philip Stevenson, with whom she collaborated on the remarkable *California Quarterly* from 1951 to 1953, produced a series of proletarian novels about New Mexico, he was also an intellectual of broad sensibilities and taste. Above all, life in the Hollywood Left had its social rewards; decades later Babb would recall it as "a wonderful period of camaraderie."[6]

In the 1950s, however, Babb's ties to the Communist Left disintegrated. First, she and Howe, not a Communist, lived in Mexico for a period on location while working on the United States film *The Brave Bulls*. Then, after returning to Hollywood, Babb went back to Mexico alone. A number of Hollywood writers, nearly unemployed as a result of persecution, had established their own colony there. From Mexico, her connections with the party lapsed, as the Hollywood section itself organizationally crumbled under the weight of the anti-radical witch hunt. Although she did not openly repudiate her earlier views, her long-term interests in Native American culture, conservation, natural nutrition, and other aspects of the arts moved to center stage. The party itself underwent a crisis and collapse after the Khrushchev revelations of 1956, with most of the Hollywood Left departing from its ranks as well. So it was not difficult for her to retain contact with many of her old comrades over the years, despite her shift in political convictions toward more conventional liberalism.

Given these fascinating features of her life—her forty-year relation to the world-famous Howe and her decades of passionate political engagement—it may seem startling at first that neither is directly explored in [this collection of] her short fiction. These absences are in sharp contrast to the work of male contemporaries such as John Sanford, who featured both his love life and political life in his multi-volume *Scenes from the Life of an American Jew*, as well as semi-autobiographical writings about radical politics and personal intimacy by James T. Farrell, Thomas Bell, Chester Himes, Edward Newhouse, and others of the mid-century literary Left.

Among radical women writers, the rare examples of such explicit writing are Josephine Herbst's *Rope of Gold* (1939), where the gender of her extra-marital lover is switched from female to male,[7] and Dorothy Doyle's *Journey Through Jess*, on which the author labored for decades before releasing it in 1989.[8] Babb's evasion of direct treatment of Communist politics and her marriage is similar to the legacy of two more famous veterans of the literary Left, Tillie Olsen and Meridel Le Sueur, neither of whom overtly explored their primary love relations or political activism in fiction.[9] The explanation lies partly in the difficulty of the task of recreating the often undramatic details that make up the majority of a rank-and-file activist's political life, and fleshing out portraits of one's trusted comrades in an anti-Communist culture. But it was also problematic for women of Babb's generation to express themselves candidly on autobiographical intimacies without creating the kind of "scandal" that became linked to Tess Slesinger with the publication of *The Unpossessed* (1934) and Mary McCarthy after the publication of *The Company She Keeps* (1942) and *A Charmed Life* (1955).

Nevertheless, the stories in *Cry of the Tinamou* do grow out of the personal experiences of Sanora Babb's life, and the political and personal concerns are more evident than they may seem at first. What is required to see Babb's emotional life as the foundation of her literary landscape is an understanding of her singular outlook and its relation to her literary craft. For example, while Babb was obviously drawn to writing about Latin American culture in "The Larger Cage" and "Cry of the Tinamou," and Chinese-American and Chinese culture in "A Scandalous Humility," "Aslant the Moon," and "The Vine by Root Embraced," her view of cultural difference did not lead her to categorize people according to national "types." To the contrary, after living intimately among people of various nationalities, differences of color and culture seemed to her to recede into the background and her feelings about personalities and character readily crossed such relatively superficial borders. The differences among people fell less along group lines than among individuals. Consequently, while no story in *Cry of the Tinamou* autobiographically depicts the intimacies of her marriage to a "Chinese-American" like Howe, it is fair to assume that she is writing out of her own personal experience in her sensitive depiction of the husband (not identified by nationality) and wife struggling to come to terms with a past marital crisis in her 1947 "Reconciliation," and doing so in the symbolic "shade of the tall Moorish house."

Moreover, the absence of harsh, shocking realism in these stories should not be taken as a marker of political passivity or even nonpartisanship. While Babb in her 1930s period did write fiction of a more "documentary" quality, her craft evolved into a strategy that might be called "soft focus." (Camera references seem especially appropriate in discussing Babb's art; not only due to her husband's career but also because her sister Dorothy, to whom she was always close, became a professional photographer.) Babb's strategy is to evoke emotions through a relatively simple but charged narrative. She aims to write from the point of view of those characters whom she feels she knows best, delineating minor characters clearly without allowing them to detract from the central concerns. But this hardly precludes political astuteness.

The story that opens this collection, her 1953 "The Larger Cage," is an application of this strategy to a complicated situation of social oppression and the temptation to moral corruption under such circumstances. A poor Mexican youth, Rodolfo, has lost his mother and is offered an opportunity to join the family of Maximiano, a street vender of "tame" birds whom Rodolfo encounters in the city. At first Rodolfo is thrilled to become part of a new family, which includes a new mother, Maria, and a brother, Ramon. But disillusionment soon follows when he discovers that the family business is based on a cruel fraud; the birds are not "tame" at all but filled up with small pellets that weigh them down and cause rapid death after they are purchased. Nevertheless, Rodolfo continues in the business for a while, choosing one bird, called Pablo, which he authentically tames to be his companion. Then comes a catastrophe when the police stop Rodolfo and Maximiano, and Rodolfo flees while the weighted birds are crushed beneath the wheels of cars they cannot escape. When Rodolfo resolves to strike out on his own, he is bitterly denounced by Ramon, who declares, "He is no brother of mine!"

Rather than discourse on the social oppression of Mexico, Babb uses Rodolfo's experiences to show the effects and temptations of poverty, rendering these in terms familiar to those outside the culture. Moreover, the other characters dramatize a range of alternative responses to this same situation: the father, Maximiano, is simply trying to survive, while the son, Ramon, is more fully corrupted. Although Rodolfo is attracted by the security of a new family, his character is such that he comes to see how even small pellets of corruption will accumulate in him and weigh him down, trapping him like the birds crushed by the cars.

In these and the other stories, it is the pull of emotion, not the shock of naturalism, or the de-familiarization techniques of modernism, by which Babb aspires to infect her readers with a moral and social consciousness. The prose is heightened by the suggestiveness of certain devices that skillfully prevent the writing from spilling over to sentimentalism. For example, the haunting association of freedom with the unfettered state of birds is evidenced not only in "The Larger Cage" but in this volume's final tale, "Cry of the Tinamou." Throughout many of her stories, Babb frequently employs houses and gardens as suggestive settings and backgrounds. Family relations, especially between mothers and daughters, and the dreams and illusions of courtship and marriage, are strategically employed to reveal the strengths and weaknesses of characters caught in the web of social conventions.

Above all, Babb's stories are replete with the incipient feminism (although she herself might not use the term) associated with her female characters of various ages who transgress socially ascribed gender roles—or who fail to cross such boundaries, sometimes for understandable reasons, at their own peril. This theme, too, is most effectively realized in "Cry of the Tinamou," a haunting evocation of Babb's youthful sojourn in Costa Rica. The autobiographically based character of the North American writer, through her independence and self-reliance, defies the constraining customs of her own country and more cautiously negotiates those of the mountain region she visits. In this writer's quiet gift of the Zuni necklace to the Central American Indian girl, who has been betrothed against her will to the aging chief, Babb establishes a female bond against patriarchy. This act also suggests how Babb's own art is itself a gift to her readers, a gesture of solidarity across cultures expressing her sympathetic recognition of the slow and painful process of human self-emancipation.

[1] See "Whose Names Are Unknown," *Michigan Quarterly Review* 29, no.3 (summer 1990): 353-71. [The book was published by the University of Oklahoma Press, 2004.]
[2] See Douglas Wixson's fine introduction to the reprint of *The Lost Traveler* (Muse Ink Press, 2012), pp.xi-xxiii.
[3] Wald interview with Sanora Babb, Los Angeles, July 1989.
[4] Wald interview with Babb.
[5] Wald interview with Babb.
[6] Wald interview with Babb.
[7] See Paula Rabinowitz, *Labor and Desire: Women's Revolutionary Fiction in Depression America* (University of North Carolina Press, 1991), pp.157-71.
[8] See Alan Wald, "To Live without Hypocrisy," *The Responsibility of Intellectuals: Selected Essays on Marxist Traditions in Cultural Commitment* (Atlantic Highlands NJ: Humanities Press, 1992), pp.119-22.
[9] Despite the fact that Constance Coiner's *Better Red: The Writing and Resistance of Tillie Olsen and Meridel Le Sueur* (New York: Oxford, 1995) is based on primary research and interviews with both women, relatively few details on such matters are disclosed in this substantial work of scholarship, either.

The Larger Cage

It was evening and the light had gone. Rodolfo waited for the policia to come for the body of his mother. She lay on the straw mat in their jacal, a sheltered corner of high brick walls over which they had made a roof of odds and ends. Two sides were open to the weather, and Rodolfo lingered at the boundary of this room dismayed by death.

He had cried all day, and he had not eaten. He might cross the street to the modern apartment building and ask a servant to permit him to empty the garbage. With luck there would be a bit of food half-eaten and still unspoiled. The city-wise Indian criadas saved la basura for the children who nightly came to their doors.

He turned to look in his mother's basket for a tortilla. Then he saw her like an alien stone in the grey dusk and his hunger sprang away.

Sometime in the night she had died. Rodolfo had accepted the death chill of her body as part of the long night's cold.

For a moment he thought of his mother as the Sleeping Lady of snow, unknown and legendary, high and far, atop the volcano. He sat beside her and watched the dark grow up around them like a sorrowing field, and listened to the unconcerned and living city-sounds, clear in the delicate air of the high plateau.

Street lights bloomed on the tangled vine of night like tropic flowers. And no one came for her.

His shirt that she had washed flapped in a melancholy way on the quiet wind.

Suddenly vibrant in the night street, the auto by its very sound of hesitation and authority seemed to be searching. Fearful at having no money and knowing that everything in life depended upon it, he leaped up and ran to the end of the wall. From there he saw two men discover the jacal and take his mother away as carelessly as if she were a dead dog in the streets. The auto roared away.

Before he could move, a man, a woman and three children came out of the shadows and took the shelter. They must have been waiting, watching and waiting.

Rodolfo grabbed his shirt that wavered like a ghost on the wire, and ran as if he were a thief.

Under the trees of the Paseo de las Americas he felt diminished by the whispers of lovers—the servant girls and young workmen sitting together on the stone benches. He turned into the avenidas named for the world's great writers, feeling lonely and afraid. The ponderous Spanish Colonial homes, guarded by white walls crested with broken glass, or spike-topped wrought-iron fences and gates with heavy chains, rose up on either side of him like uninhabited canyons impervious to his grief.

Ahead three men were sitting around a fire protecting the wealth of wood and bricks for a new house. He plunged a tough bare foot into a hill of sand piled ready for cement.

"Do not molest anything, hombre," a workman said. "This man has received a fortune from heaven, perhaps, and he builds a castillo and pays us honest men to see that no one steals." Satiric laughter circled the fire and reached out to enclose Rodolfo, but he walked on slowly, counting the ways of earning his living. He had carried and run all his remembered years. When he was five he had sold lottery tickets in the Avenida Juarez until dawn. He had bargained over la lena from door to door, but now he had no burro to carry the wood. He was eleven years old, he reminded himself proudly, he did not wish to beg.

He brushed the grass from his clothes, washed his face in a fountain and wet his black hair. He put the clean shirt on over the old one, and then as an added inducement for someone to hire him, he washed the blue volcanic dust from his feet. He went to a supermarket.

"How much do you earn?" he asked a boy just inside the door.

"Five pesos a week, hombre. And tips. At this pay the tips are very necessary. Have you a family?"

Rodolfo sternly held back his tears and shook his head.

"You're lucky," the boy said. "I have a mother and a small sister to support. Adios!" He directed Rodolfo with his eyes to the manager.

Before Rodolfo could speak, the manager waved him aside impatiently. "No more boys! No more!"

Outside, imitating other boys, he politely accosted the norteamericanas who carried their own packages. The manager came out and thumped his head sharply. "Go, pronto!" He swung his arm at all the boys. "Get!"

Rodolfo fled into the dusty street where he wandered among the native food stalls more disconsolate than the bony, resigned dogs.

He begged when he could not endure his hunger. He slept in doorways with other children and shared their schemes for survival. He loitered in the narrow busy street of Madero with its fine shops and spending foreigners and the well-dressed people of his own kind. But suddenly he hardly saw the people. He was looking at a most beautiful and wonderful sight. Four small birds on a stick held by a man who was selling them to passersby.

Birds he had seen, but these birds had black feathered bands across their eyes like the masks worn at a masquerade ball! They were tame and they sat sweetly on the stick, permitting strangers to caress their sleek backs with tender fingers. Their wings were not clipped; they were *tamed,* and the wonder of this would not leave Rodolfo's mind or heart.

Rodolfo watched the jilgueros chinos, and when women bought them and took them away, he imagined himself having the four or five pesos and gladly exchanging them for a bird.

Late in the day something happened that was even better than buying a bird. The man, who was used to his hanging about, asked, "Hombre, how would you like to catch birds with me and sell them?"

"Los jilgueros chinos?" he asked eagerly, using the name he had overheard.

"No," the man laughed. "Los jilgueros chinos are only in the state of Guerrero! I have to buy them."

Rodolfo's black eyes saddened.

"Ah," the man boasted, "There are jilgueros chinos in Chihuahua and Oaxaca and even in the Desierto de los Leones near here, but they are not the same as I sell!"

"Our country is filled with beautiful birds," Rodolfo said quickly, fearing that he had made a mistake by preferring the little masked birds.

"Do you want the job?"

"Si, senor!" he said, and then more cautiously, "If we can agree on the money."

The man laughed again, and all the while he was speaking and considering Rodolfo, his dark eyes were searching for likely customers. "A wise one! From the streets, or perhaps from Monterey?"

"I am a Mexicano and a man of the city," Rodolfo stated proudly.

"We'll agree," the vendedor said easily, and then his eyes pointed at Ro-dolfo as sharp as spikes and his soft lips hardened and warned, "Do not cheat me! Not one centavo!"

"I am no ladron!" the boy said angrily and moved a few feet away to lean against the iron fence of an old church crowded by shops. This man was very cunning. He had watched him sell the birds. First, the vendor selected one person from the crowd and that selection was seldom wrong. At times he spoke to no one and then his quick eyes found someone, and his low voice and appealing, innocent looks began their magic. To a man who was not young, Maximiano would say delicately, "Ah, senor, perhaps there is someone—and these two birds would please her." Even if there were no one, the man would buy the birds and go away and it could be seen in his face that he was making a plan.

The vendor pretended to have forgotten Rodolfo and concentrated on selling the birds remaining on the stick. Rodolfo appeared to be interested in the man who was selling puppies. He caught the bird-seller watching him. He waited and when the man walked casually by striking the palm of his left hand with the empty stick, Rodolfo as casually joined him and they walked together, discussing the terms of employment.

"You like the birds very much?"

"Si!"

"Remember, this is a business. It is not easy to keep alive. A man makes a living the best way he can."

"Claro! I have to have food and a bed."

"Meet me here in the morning at ten o'clock. I'll have a stick of birds for you to sell."

"I'm not to catch them then?" Disappointment glowed briefly in his dark eyes, but he quickly concealed this childishness.

"Later."

"Muy bien."

They parted and Rodolfo went along feeling the emptiness of his pockets. The streets were filled. Tourists pressed and hurried to their hotels. The Mexicanos walked more slowly. Cars moved end to end, honking wildly. The sun was gone and dampness came up from the muddy floor of the ancient lake upon which the city was built. The massive statues of Greek goddesses and Indian heroes, generals and liberators, and the bronze worker shone boldly in the evening air. Spicy hot food-vapors drifted from open cafes into the avenue. Lights and the advertising signs came on and music played softly in a carpeted cocktail bar whose elegance Rodolfo glimpsed briefly through a swinging door.

As they worked in the narrow street of Madero, Maximiano watched Ro-dolfo closely.

"That is not my way of selling," he observed, "but you sell, so?"

Secretly, Rodolfo chose the kindest looking women walking in Madero, and sometimes he urged a man to give this alive gift to a woman. If Maximiano were out of hearing, he advised professionally, "The little birds are happier in a large cage, and they do well in the sunlight and fresh air."

When Maximiano took him to his adobe hut on the edge of the city, and Rodolfo saw Maria, the wife, he could not smile enough, wanting her to like him. That night she placed a straw mat on the earthen floor of the kitchen and he slept near Ramon, the son.

They arose while the night was still on the land like black moonlight, revealing only the dim shapes of things in the shapeless air. Maximiano, Ramon and Rodolfo went silently over the pathless hill and entered the Desierto de los Leones, a forest of pines that held the still dark body of the sleeping night.

The melancholy daybreak was like the glow of a smoky oil lamp turned up slowly in an old room. A bird awoke and twittered. Another and another. Then the forest was filled with the waking eager conversation of birds!

The hidden sun dissipated the eerie mists and brightened the air with the shadows of far away fire. Rodolfo was lost in the magic of morning and the forest and the singing of birds.

Maximiano nudged him. "Watch closely!"

The sharp whisper gave Rodolfo a start.

Maximiano loosened the dirt with a heavy stick and spread the net over the ground. He and Ramon pressed the net into the earth and covered it with loose dirt and twigs. A part of the net remained outside but it lay brown and deceptive on the forest floor.

"Watch Ramon scatter the alpiste!" Maximiano whispered.

Ramon took a folded paper from his pocket and from it carefully threw the bird seed over the covered net.

They sat down at the foot of a tree and waited. No one spoke. For a long time no birds came. Then one lighted and pecked at the seeds and flew quickly away. Soon, five birds, alert and wary of danger, were eating the grain.

With a swift movement Maximiano swung the uncovered net over the birds. One escaped. The others beat their wings wildly against the imprisoning threads. The muffled desperate flutter of wing-sounds gave Rodolfo a feeling of helpless pity.

"Quick!" Maximiano commanded. "Now, you will begin. Reach under the net and toss out that pajaro pulquiento!"

"Free?" Rodolfo asked, on his knees by the net.

"Si! That kind is just good for the lice to live on."

Rodolfo reached into the mass of terrified, struggling birds, and the pity in his heart was joined by another and surprising sensation of pleasure, the two feelings equal and side by side, confusing him. It was very difficult to catch and hold the common unwanted bird but at last he clumsily and gently extricated it from the others. Its frightened pulse beat furiously against his fingers and when he opened his hand the bird sat stunned, then faltered into the air, gaining swiftness with flight. The others still moved blindly against the trap.

They spread the net twice more, placing all the birds together in a covered basket.

On the way home Maximiano said, teaching him, "Some days we will use the trampas. Each of us will sit in a different place and catch birds under a trampa. Ramon will show you how to make your own with some small boards and a mesh."

"A long string and a peg!" added Ramon importantly. Then he asked with a strut of authority. "Do you like it?"

"Si!"

"Well, then," Maximiano continued. "You will learn the next step now, and we will all be in the street selling pajaros before noon."

Maria gave them a sober nod of approbation when she saw the birds. Ro-dolfo looked shyly into her worn young face. She gave him a smile, tight-lipped to hide the loss of her teeth. He watched her move about with the baby heavy on her back concealed in her rebozo. She was going to town to sell the little wooden flowers she had made.

"In the evening I will help you with the work," he said, wanting her eyes to rest on him again. He had seen mischief in them when she played for a moment with Ramon. Her face remained closed. She is wondering, he thought, if I shall eat very much. It is important. "Now that I work," he said, "I will pay to live here."

"No importa." She gave him a push and he saw the flash of mischief across her face like the shadow of a bird flying swiftly out of the net.

He turned toward Maximiano feeling gay as he had not felt for a long time.

"You will only watch today. Watch Ramon. He is very good with the birds. His hands are better than mine."

Ramon spread his small brown hands before Rodolfo. "The secret is to hold them well without hurting them."

Rodolfo gazed at Ramon admiringly. "To tame birds is an art like the painters, maybe better."

Maximiano winked at Ramon and Ramon smiled.

Rodolfo went on eagerly, "I would rather learn how to tame birds than to win the lottery."

"Tonto!" Ramon chided him.

Maximiano brought a can from the house and sat down near the baskets, one with the birds and another empty. Ramon dropped to his knees and beckoned Rodolfo to do the same. Ramon reached into the basket and brought out a bird. Rodolfo could see the throb of its heart making a quick rhythm on the feathered throat. The fragile feet curled. He rubbed its head gently with the cushion of his forefinger, but the wildness of the bird would not change so quickly.

"Now!" Ramon announced.

Ramon's left hand held the bird in such a way that his fingers pinioned the wings, leaving his thumb and forefinger free to touch the bird's tiny beak. He dipped his right hand into the can and brought out a number of small black balls. He opened the resisting beak and carefully rolled the buckshot into the throat of the bird, closing the beak quickly and holding it for a moment, forcing the bird to swallow. The bird gasped, and strained its body to escape, spreading and curling its toes in astonishment and fear. Ramon ignored the struggle in his hand and repeated his task. Then he set the bird on the ground. The terrified creature lifted its wings, fluttered them helplessly for a moment and as if surprised beyond all protest folded them quietly and stood still. In a moment the bird tried again briefly to fly, and failing again, gave forth a bleak note of overwhelming dismay.

"Perfecto." Ramon nodded with professional satisfaction.

"At least his belly is full," Maximiano laughed.

Tears stung in Rodolfo's eyes. Disillusion weighed him down like the shot in the body of the bird.

"Just enough and not too many," Ramon declared, lifting the bird into the empty basket and dipping into the full one for another, "—so that the bird will not fly away and yet not be so heavy that it will fall over."

"After a bit, he will sit quietly on the stick or wherever we put him," Maximiano said. "His belly is very heavy, and he is smart enough to know that he can't get away."

Rodolfo took a deep breath in order to control his tears. Maximiano nudged him to pay attention. He counted the buckshot in a whisper partly in sad fascination and partly to impress Maximiano. This is a real job, he told himself. But the pride of selling the birds was gone. He might not find another job for a long time; there would be months of hunger and sleeping in doorways. He had no shoes and his trousers were ragged and he needed a coat, an old coat, an old jorongo.

He watched Ramon forcing the buckshot into the throat of another bird.

He could beg until he found another job. There were many children begging, many much younger than he with no other way to survive. Begging was no way to live, a starving, creeping life.

"An easy job, no?" Maximiano asked, encouraging him.

"Si, senor." He glanced at the helpless bird. "Si, senor."

"Bueno. Now you see why the birds must be sold today."

Rodolfo looked at him, unable to understand all that he meant.

"They will live only a few days. The people who buy them will then think the bird is unhappy or sick, but that it is not our fault."

Rodolfo nodded.

"In a few days you will be *taming* the birds yourself, hombre," Ramon laughed.

"At first it bothered me a little," Maximiano admitted. "I was sorry for the birds. But who is sorry for a man? I said. I got used to it. It is a good business."

Rodolfo stared at the little adobe hut, a better place than he had ever had. "Si."

Maximiano shrugged. "It bothered me at first but it never bothered Ramon. He grew up in the business. He 'tames' the birds and dreams of tortillas."

At this, Rodolfo's ignorance occurred to Ramon again and he sat back laughing. He mimicked the other's idea of taming by stroking the bird he held, speaking in a soft voice, "Pajaro lindo, pajaro lindo."

"Pajaro, you!" Maximiano said angrily, then he added morosely, "Already my son is a man of this world. His heart is like a nut."

Ramon looked up and smiled appreciatively, and went on with his work.

"Thank you for teaching me—a business," Rodolfo said politely to the father and son.

"Por nada."

They closed the basket and went into the city.

Rodolfo learned to "tame" the birds. Now and then, Maximiano bought the little masked birds, los jilgueros chinos, from a man who caught them in the state of Guerrero. When Rodolfo had saved enough money, he bought one from Maximiano, giving him more than the cost so that he would not complain of the time

spent with the bird. Then, in the evenings and on Sundays he began to tame the bird with stillness and feeding and kindness. The
jilguero chino was very wild. Maria became fond of the bird. In
time, the jilguero chino perched on Rodolfo's shoulder, his hand
and even the top of his head, which made Maria laugh.

Because of the bird, called Pablo, and the alpiste seed and the
money paid to Maximiano from his wages, Rodolfo had managed
to buy only a pair of second-hand trousers and a shirt.

Because of the bird, the responsibility of the bird, and the
necessity to keep his job, he thought less and less about "taming" the little creatures he caught in the forest and sold each day
in the street. And after a long time he hardly minded it at all.
He consoled himself with the knowledge that in a few days they
would be dead, freed of their misery, but—and he was troubled by
this—freed of their life too.

Ramon taught him certain sly tricks, tricks that did not please
Maximiano. Rodolfo kept to his own ways, but all these other
ways were in his head like the seeds of the devil's claw waiting for
the season.

He began taking his own jilguero with him into the city. Pablo
remained on his shoulder and did not interfere with the sale of
other birds. In fact, Maximiano believed this was an attraction
and proved the genuine tame-ness of all the birds. Pablo was, of
course, more active. He lifted his wings slightly, he nibbled his
beak against Rodolfo's cheek, and except when he was advised
against it, he got into Rodolfo's shirt pocket where he knew the
alpiste seeds were kept. The other birds appeared more shy but this
could be explained. Many people wished to buy Pablo.

Maximiano urged him to sell the bird and tame another, perhaps even tame others for occasional sale, as a form of protection,
a proof of the legitimacy of their business.

Rodolfo caught a centzoutle in the Desierto de los Leones
and tamed it for Maximiano's "protection," but because people
liked its mocking songs, Maximiano sold it at once for a high
price. As a gift, Rodolfo tamed a canario from Sonora for Maria.

When Maximiano wanted to sell it, Maria went on with her work not looking at her husband, but she said *No* with such finality that he was offended. Rodolfo then bought two cardinales from a man who had been catching birds in Durango and tamed them for Maximiano. When these were sold in one day, Rodolfo refused to tame more and Maximiano struck him. Wishing to keep his job, Rodolfo accepted the blow. Maria was silent but later she gave him a fruit she had been saving for Maximiano.

In such a great city it seemed to Rodolfo that one could sell birds endlessly. People might pass by all the silver vendors and the leather vendors with their wares spread temptingly under the gaze of the touristas; all the small vendedores selling pencils, chains, blouses, rebozos, kittens, puppies; all the children selling lottery tickets, all the beggars, even the armless man who wove little baskets with his toes; and still stop to watch the tame birds and thinking them no trouble and seeing that they were so cheap, only a few pesos, end by buying one or two. He saw himself with a job that went on year after year. He forgot to watch for likely purchasers.

A well-dressed woman stopped to inquire pleasantly about Pablo. He explained that some days he left him at home. Then she asked Rodolfo his name and admired the birds on the stick he was holding. She ran a finger caressingly under the beak of one and the poor creature toppled off onto the sidewalk and sat stunned and waiting. Rodolfo quickly picked it up and placed it on the stick. He was surprised by the old pain of sympathy he felt for the helpless, docile bird, and he stroked its small back.

"He is the one!" the woman shouted, startling him out of the tenderness.

Two policemen who accompanied her hurried through the crowd and stood near Maximiano and Rodolfo so that they dared not move.

The woman opened a small package of crumpled paper and in it lay the dead bird slit open so that all its inners were exposed. There, too, were the small black shots.

"My son wanted to see why the bird died so quickly," she explained to the police and the people who had gathered.

A man said, "What's the importance? She had a few days pleasure, didn't she? She had her money's worth."

The two policemen looked as if this small case were of little interest and yet they attended the woman who obviously had more money than the bird-sellers.

"Arrest them!" the woman demanded.

One of the policemen took hold of Maximiano's arm. Maximiano sneered for all to see. The other grabbed for Rodolfo, but Rodolfo without thought or plan, whirled into the street and ran, darting among the moving cars. With his first violent movement, the birds fell, scattered in the street beneath feet and wheels, unprotesting and helpless. He tried to gather them up hastily but the cars sounded their horns, imprisoning him. He ran on, gripping the empty stick. In a shadowy side street he threw it from him, feeling sick and grieved for the birds, trying to push his imaginings of their squashing deaths from his mind.

After dark he went home. Maximiano was not there. Maria's eyes were somber with worry. Ramon had already guessed the truth before Rodolfo gave them details.

"You did right to escape," he said professionally.

This Rodolfo was relieved to hear. "Gracias," he said in a low, ashamed voice.

Ramon laughed. "The policia will let him go. He will get out of it."

"How?"

"A small case. There's no money in it. Perhaps on the way there, Papa gave the two men a few pesos while the woman was not looking, and he got away. Quien sabe?"

"I have never heard that the police were kind," Rodolfo said stubbornly.

"Son brutos!"

"Ramon!" Maria cautioned, and glanced about fearfully.

"But—" Ramon continued, giving his mother a look of wisdom, "—the policia are poor men."

"Ojala!" Maria whispered.

Rodolfo gave Maria the money he had made, taking his wages from it.

Ramon's bright eyes slid over him with triumph. "Afraid?"

"Brother!" Maria shamed him.

"Honesty is very dear," Ramon warned.

"Maybe I am no more honest than you," Rodolfo replied, "but I cannot kill the birds any more."

Ramon spat on the earth floor as if to say he had always known what Rodolfo was.

Rodolfo's eyes snapped angrily at Ramon, and then he turned to Maria. "I am going now to see about Maximiano."

"No," Ramon said.

"Be careful, Rodolfo," Maria said, "you do not know how these things are. Someone must sell the birds tomorrow in another street."

"No to everything!" Ramon shouted. "He is better off without you."

Maria stared at Ramon who stood now as if he had taken command. "But—you are like brothers," she whispered.

"He is no brother of mine! The *bird tamer*," he said with contempt. "My brother, the *bird tamer!*"

Rodolfo looked with proud love at Maria and then he went out, closing the door quietly and firmly. He was trembling.

He whistled softly for the jilguero chino. Pablo was asleep in the tree and after a second whistle, he flew down onto Rodolfo's hand, protesting drowsily.

"Of course, amigo, as Ramon says, I was afraid of the policia," Rodolfo said to him, "but it was really the birds under the wheels. *They couldn't fly.*"

Pablo murmured and settled himself for sleep.

Rodolfo took the small bag of alpiste from the tree and put it in his pocket. He moved the bird gently into the bend of his arm so that Pablo would not fall in his sleep onto the long dark road.

He felt like a man of the world, a citizen of the city, and life was before him like a threat. But the earth, grand and beautiful under his bare feet, promised him something. The hidden power in the night, the grass, the sleeping people, the silent volcanoes, all one, ran like a gathering underground stream through his eleven years.

"Pablo," he said, stroking the bird, feeling his warmth, feeling not alone in the vast dark. He began to walk steadily. He could not see the road but his feet went with familiarity, without fear.

A Scandalous Humility

This afternoon, as all afternoons, Mrs. Tsiang sat in the small open square of Chinatown letting the western sun warm her old bones. She was very small, sleek as a blackbird with none of its boldness. Her simple Chinese dress was of black silk brocade, and her hair still black was pulled tight from her forehead into a thin knot. In her ears were little gold rings and on her wrists she wore three narrow jade and gold bracelets, the yellow gold of the Orient. Her dark alert eyes, when not looking down in old-fashioned modesty, contained a seeking light; they shone like gems in the high mounting of her face bones clear under the skin patinated like old ivory. Her perfect teeth were not her own. They appeared to wait under her flat mouth to come forth in a large smile, but as there was no one to accept her smile, they hid in dignity, while the eyes spoke and searched and waited.

She had waited while the hasty American time went by, year after year, but now every day was crucial.

"Not one, but two cruel problems to solve before I die," she said in her mind. "They are separate—one here and one *there*—and yet they are both together like two feet upon a path."

In the time that was left, she must get face within the community of her people, that face never won, its lack shutting her out, isolating her in loneliness, humiliation and subtle dishonor. Though she had lived without face, she must not die without it, not alone for herself but for her unappreciative sons and most of all for her grandchildren whom she was allowed to see only by chance.

Money, she thought with keen pleasure, I will leave them money, more than anyone knows, and it may be when they are grown, they will have the good sense to consider it more important than the other legacy. I will leave my sons money so that they will want to show their respect at last. They will ache to thank me but my ears will not hear. Mrs. Tsiang's mind was folded tight like a green bud enclosing this bitter hope. She moved her head slowly back and forth as if denying herself, appearing to doze, but painfully awake.

At the splash of a coin in the wishing well, she sat up with a start. Two young lovers leaned together on the wrought iron fence, tossing pennies. She watched them until she saw beneath their ease and familiarity the age-old symbols of the magic current in which they were caught. They could never be aware of her as young, but aware of them, she saw herself and Tung-shu circled, all but suffocated by the inexpressible eloquence of their first feelings of love. She saw herself, in the blue silk dress embroidered with birds and flowering branches, his favorite, and she saw him proud of her beauty, deaf to the cruel words that stung her and left their sting, even then. Her beauty gave him arrogance but she had considered it her bad luck until her marriage to Tung-shu. Tung-shu, long dead, came into her memory now as a young man.

A door clicked. Mr. Lee, Mr. Wong and Mr. Sui emerged from the imposing entrance of the Harmony Association, conversing in Cantonese. They switched abruptly to English. In this square she could overhear much of the Chinatown business and gossip. If English excluded her, she had but to wait; others would soon repeat it in *toy san*, the popular village dialect. These three leaders of high moral standing passed her by without a sign of recognition. Her heart beat hard in expectation and yearning and the usual disappointment. They pretended that she wasn't there. If one spoke or even nodded, she would be given face, and others would follow their example. Alone, one might speak, but he would have to be certain that no one observed him and spread the word. In Chinatown it was unlikely that no one observed, so no one spoke.

Restaurant workers appeared in the square on their way to string snow peas, shell almonds and walnuts, wash cloud ears and prepare a variety of Chinese vegetables brought in that morning from Chinese farms; then to eat their early meal before the evening rush. Some entered The Three Crested Mountain, owned by her son, Hong. They nodded or spoke and she accepted their routine greetings, but they held no special value; they did not give her face. She listened from habit.

"Boy! That big-screen close-up four times in one picture! What more do you want? The customers will be asking for your autograph."

The waiter only shrugged. She knew him to be very *old-China*. But he was a part-time actor as well.

"You going to buy yourself a $50,000 house in the hills? Like Hong Kong."

They could all speak English perfectly well but they were speaking *toy san* which caused her to listen with affection for these young men.

"When you going to give up this waiter job?"

"When I get a TV series," the waiter replied at last. "Why should I give up a steady salary and good tips?"

Mrs. Tsiang nodded her head in approval. But a shudder went through her; *she* certainly would not risk being photographed and losing her spirit, having it caught on film, snatched out of herself, as these young people did so carelessly.

The appearance of the waiters was a sign for her to go to her apartment and take a nap. She lifted her handsome quartz-headed cane from under her cashmere sweater and walked slowly home, her furious old pride straightening her back and lifting her head. She knew she was observed and she knew as surely that they would never see her humbled, no matter how her thoughts ached for face.

Across the square, along a row of shops, glancing secretly into one window crowded with a large bronze lion-dog, jade and quartz figurines, teak-wood furniture inlaid with mother-of-pearl, and other treasures of Old China, past this window, she unlocked a heavy door, climbed the stairs and was some time turning the keys in two foolproof locks. She sat down at once to rest, hearing her son, Wing, moving about in the antique shop below. He was her Number One son, her favorite, and the most friendly of her children, nevertheless he would not permit her in his elegant shop. When he went to Hong Kong on buying trips, he asked her to care for Lo-Fu, his cat. She did so with love, bringing dainty tidbits from The Three Crested Mountain and holding long conversations with the cat. It was a great pleasure to speak with the cat who understood only Cantonese. She asked him questions about her son and replied for him, expertly interpreting his replies and aloof silences. In this way she invented a whole life for Wing that was utterly unknown to him.

"Lo-Fu, does Ah Wing speak of his mother?"

"Now and then." Lo-Fu was evasive like Ah Wing.

"Do you think he will ever forgive me?"

"Perhaps. Perhaps not."

That was the sly way he answered her when he had no grapevine gossip to pass on.

She eased her tiny feet out of the western slippers and into her soft silk ones, and shuffled about the dark and richly furnished Chinese room. In one corner was a little altar with a graceful white jade Kuan Yin. The old woman took an incense stick from a bowl, lighted it, held it in both hands while she bowed three times before the Goddess of Mercy.

"Let me have face," she prayed humbly, "and the rest will follow."

It seemed to her that the goddess required something more of her but did not reveal it. Patience, patience, she advised herself, taking the words from the fragrant air around her, feeling her lips tremble in a moment of weakness before her hope and strength were restored. She lay on her narrow couch, asking herself and Kuan Yin the familiar question. "What is required of me?"

She had raised her sons according to custom and they were honorable and hard-working. She had given large sums of money to them, to the Benevolent Association, the Four Families, the Chinese Evening School, the Buddhist Temple and the Christian Churches; to all Chinese charities, to the Red Cross, the Community Chest, and so on and on. She had bought government bonds when she could have invested at much higher interest. She had donated a beautiful fountain to the Chinatown Square. She had acted as a stand-by mother for a homeless boy from China, adopted him and raised him as her seventh son. He had loved her, but perhaps because of her, he had saved his money and gone to Malaya where he bought a coconut farm. In ten years three letters announced the number of children, and one of them, to her hungry joy, contained photographs, which she studied with a magnifying glass. She sent him a thousand dollars when he did not ask, and prayed that in Malaya the spirit had not such a tendency to escape as in China and America.

"What is required of me?" she prayed. "I will do it. There is not much time."

She fell asleep, and when she awoke she knew the answer had come at last.

"Humility," she said aloud into the dusky room, adding a word of gratitude in the direction of Kuan Yin. "But how?" Confronted suddenly like this, a state she had taken for granted became evasive and mysterious in application. How? When she had ceased to grumble at the ill-treatment by her children, was not that humility? No, that was an acceptance of moral debts she had created in this and past lives, her unknown karma. Besides, she had to admit the element of cunning: she had hoped to win her children, even to shame them.

Mrs. Tsiang rose, put on a blue crepe dress and a blue coat, and went down into the square where the late afternoon sunshine was lying on the stones like old silk. Walking slowly, considering the vagaries of life newly compounded with humility, she passed in front of a modern-designed restaurant, along its side wall into an alley. There she entered the brightly lighted stainless steel kitchen, and went straight to a small table out of the way of the activity. The steamy air was fragrant with a blend of ginger and duck, honeyed squab, almonds and oil of sesame. When she had a good appetite, she preferred to eat with the men because there was more variety of food. She saw that she was too late, and one of the waiters came over at once to ask what she would like. The men, accustomed to her presence, hardly let up in their joking and bickering, but they treated her with respect and kindness. Her son, Hong, came into the kitchen several times, and on one of these trips, gave her a perfunctory nod. Other nights he spoke, or ignored her. Tonight he mentioned to the chef a fresh fish steamed in black bean sauce, a dish she especially liked; and Ah Hong reminded him not to forget her Moon Festival cakes to take home. She flushed with embarrassed appreciation and was about to call out to him in her delight but he was gone into the spacious, fashionably decorated dining room forbidden to her. She had seen it before the restaurant was open and had decided on a secluded permanent table, but Ah Hong had told her in the direct American fashion (not even bothering to observe the courtesy of passing his message through someone else), that she was not allowed to enter or sit in the dining room. His spoken reason was that she was too old-fashioned. He gave her a space and a table in the kitchen.

She drank her tea and remembered that first humiliation. She could eat in other restaurants; several small ones had far better food; but that would further injure their family face. Besides, in this submission there was no self-abasement: a dignity of philosophical proportions was required, and she had earned that dignity through pride and suffering and the daring to find joy in life, rather than hide in shame. This was what her children wished, what Chinatown expected—shame. Kuan Yin suggested humility not shame. She would begin in the only ways she knew and surely a part of its meaning would reach their Christian understanding.

II

This evening after dinner, as every evening, she sat on the bench in the square thinking about her bones. She thought a great deal about her bones. People crowded through the streets looking, shopping, dining. Now and then a group of well-dressed Chinese, respected persons of business and professions, passed on their way to a dinner party. She watched their eyes avoid the bench where she sat, and thus knew they had seen her enjoying the gaiety of the evening, taking the air, retired on her means. When the coolness penetrated her silk embroidered coat, she went back to her little apartment which smelled of incense and precious things; made tea and refreshed by it, considered taking a taxi to play mahjong with her two old friends. They were poor, had no standing in the community but they were from her village near Canton.

While she was taking money from her small hidden safe, a secretive scratch on the door made her start. It might be Ah Wing's cat, Lo-Fu, paying a call, but when a knock sounded, she closed the safe and asked who was there. As soon as he spoke she opened the door, suppressing a smile of relief.

"Ah Chek, you have returned in time!"

He ignored her implication. He had been gone a month, this nephew of her husband's who could be trusted when paid well.

"I came straight here. I'm tired from the long flight, and Hong Kong is a madhouse. You can't count the refugees. Not all of them poor." He smiled and she knew that smile, and just then noticed the package.

She pretended not to see it and made tea, and they endured the manners of small talk until he opened the package and showed her the old jewelry he had bought cheaply from rich refugees. Her face darkened.

"Sell them to Ah Wing downstairs; he'll know if they're real. I'm not interested."

He began to speak of price. Her eyes grew hard, her voice cold and sharp. "You know what I want. Why are you delaying? Did you fail? In a whole month, did you fail?"

He rewrapped the jewels and held them on his knee.

"Don't sit there waiting for insults to raise your price," she said, thinking what a duck-egg face he had.

He protested and hesitated.

"Did you or did you not arrange to have my bones smuggled from Hong Kong back to my village?"

"It's old-fashioned," he said. "Very hard to arrange."

"Then you've arranged it," she said with a shrewd laugh. "How much?"

He named a rather large sum.

"Hong Kong or U.S.?"

"U.S."

"Too much."

They bargained for some time, and reached a compromise price that each knew was the necessary amount in the first place.

"I will want proof."

He laughed. "How can you have proof afterward? And ten years afterward at that?"

"Before then," she said and began to laugh with him. "You are like my husband. He used to make me laugh when I was too serious."

"I will have to make arrangements here too. It will cost something."

"Only to prepare my bones. I know all about that. Ten years of the customary rest here, then—"

"Ten years of interest on a small sum would—"

She ignored his crafty remarks and continued, "With a new government in China that does not approve the old ways, we must use bribery. So far, you have done well."

She noted that he tried to bow in the old way to please her. An awkward, false bow. What had she been thinking of to trust him? And yet, there was no one else; she had no choice.

"When my bones are ready, they will make the long journey home," she said, her voice eased and calm. "And they will lie in peace in the soil of my ancestors, in the village of my childhood. They could never rest in foreign earth."

"It is old-fashioned," Chek said softly, without criticism.

"I want to become the dust of my own hills." The utter abandon with which modern Chinese bones were left in American cemeteries was one of the puzzles of these times. She said so.

"We're Americans, American bones."

She looked at him with distaste and delight.

"I'm tired," she said, not wanting to appear more eager. "Come back to-morrow night at this time with your plan."

"A plan for ten years is not easy."

She brushed the air with her hand as if to clear away *gong sei*, the business of death, and stood up, wanting to be alone, all desire for mahjong dissipated.

He left.

What proof could she rely on? She made fresh tea and sat up late, thinking, heavy with distrust. In the old days of her youth, when there were more workers than businessmen, the Chinese grocery stores had mail racks, and even now, a few of them still received mail for working men without permanent addresses. Under one such rack she had seen and never forgotten the gunny sacks of old bones labeled with the names of their long dead owners, ready for the journey home.

Of course, her own bones were only one part of her problem, but an urgent one. Many lifetimes were required to enable a human spirit to flower and fruit, but in each it was important not to burden the next any more than one could help. Unfortunately, in youth, she had thought very little of this and had created a terrible mountain of wrong, so monstrous that she had lost face forever, or at least her lifetime here.

Lo-Fu, the cat, appeared as if from nowhere. He liked to hide in her place and sleep away the afternoon. As he stared at her, she seemed to hear his thoughts: "There is time enough for the long evolving journey of the spirit through an eternity of selves," he pontificated silently, "but on earth there is almost no time left."

"Impertinent cat! But you are right. Only last night I was called by one of my ancestors in a dream." She stroked Lo-Fu.

How many more nights could she sit waiting on the bench in the damp evening air, waiting for a witnessed sign of recognition and acceptance? How else, after all other ways had failed?

After letting Lo-Fu out, she went to bed with a new plan, but the memories of her dishonorable past kept her awake. She saw herself as a very young girl in Canton, fresh from the village, without parents but with beauty, so that it was easy to become a picture bride and to go to *gim shan*, the Golden Mountain of the United States. She was arranged for in honor, but something went wrong, and the group of young girls on the long cruel trip by sea were not delivered to husbands but to an old woman with straw hair and blue eyes, a foreign ghost, who paid for them and owned them and set them to their tasks. After a few years she managed to escape, and not by innocence to make her way until she met Tung-shu, a gambler, famous in his way. After they were married, she behaved as a proper wife, but the respectable families of the close community would not accept her in any way. The children came, six sons, reason for honor. Tung-shu was rich in sons. She was a strong and affectionate mother. Then Tung-shu, who was much older, died, leaving her a great deal of money which by then she had learned to manipulate into more. At last an ambition could be realized: she went into legitimate business, and later she financed her sons in business. She was honest, and generous with her money. But nothing she did won her face in the Chinatown she loved. And, gradually, as her sons heard the old story, as they understood the harm she had done to their own face, as they grew successful without her, they turned away, keeping up the least of pretenses. Four moved to other states, and two remained. She saw their children by accident in the street, and they knew her as an 'old auntie' or someone else's 'old grandmama.' She could have returned, rich, years ago, to her village in Old China although the grapevine had spread her story even there; but the real reason was in herself, this aching need for face right here.

These thoughts kept her awake until the new plan soothed her to sleep. As she had come to some wisdom through the years, she realized that it was a poor and shaky plan but it must be tried as there was no other remaining, and perhaps it was after all the meaning of Kuan Yin's answer to her prayer.

III

She chose Moon Festival to appear in the square wearing old clothes. This was not easy. She was vain. Her wardrobe tempted her. She ran her fingers over the long gowns and robes, handled her jade jewelry, thrilling to the pleasure of their adornment, and the material success that had made possible their purchase, silks and embroideries from the Orient, sewed here by old dressmakers who had learned in China to work their needles with a delicacy unknown in the West. One silk coat with a hidden fur lining was especially hard to ignore because it added comfort to her pride.

At last she took the rich coat and a pale brocade dress from the closet and folded them into a box not even showing them to the old woman who sat on a severe teak chair, waiting. Her old friend, Pear Blossom Woo, with the village still showing in her manner and dress, opened her hooded eyes in amazement, and said, "How can I wear such fine clothes?" in a tone that inferred Mrs. Tsiang had lost her mind.

"Just wear them!" Mrs. Tsiang commanded, knowing the clothes would give Mrs. Woo added face as coming to call on her, a rich woman with no face for herself, had done. She noted how uncomfortably her old friend sat here, and thought how gay and gossipy she behaved in her own poor rooms.

Mrs. Woo unwrapped a package she had brought and placed a plain black cotton Chinese dress on the couch, adding with caution a baggy worn coat of cheap material.

"I washed and ironed them this morning," she said. "They are clean, but very poor. You wouldn't be seen in them."

"Oh, yes, I will," Mrs. Tsiang said, her voice wavering only a little.

"But, why—?"

"That is between Kuan Yin and myself."

The old woman closed her eyes in respect as much for Mrs. Tsiang, her rich friend, as for Kuan Yin.

"Will you be down Monday night as usual?" she asked, all dependable things made uncertain by Mrs. Tsiang's new behavior.

"I'll be down Monday night as usual," Mrs. Tsiang replied, already looking forward to the evening with the two old women from her village.

"Then, I'll be going," Mrs. Woo said, holding the precious box at rest on her little round belly, her face alight as if with a vision of herself in clothes such as she had never worn.

After the door was closed and locked, Mrs. Tsiang stood for a moment wondering about her nephew, Ah Chek, who had not returned with the proof that her bones would be smuggled into New China and buried near her village. He had not devised a proof that would pass her judgment, but he would come soon with a lie if nothing else because he wanted the money. A lie would not do.

Struggling to feel only love and humility, she failed and whispered bitterly, "Seven sons and I have no one to trust."

Changed into her old friend's worn clothes she stood before the mirror, her mouth puckered in distaste. Slyly, as if being observed, she removed the coat and placed it in the closet, selecting one of her own.

"That old coat is too warm for Moon Festival," she said without a glance at Kuan Yin so that the change admitted no vanity. Then with an appreciative look at her ebony cane, she drew an ordinary wooden cane from its new wrapping, and went out. She settled herself on the bench, permitting her silk coat to fall away from her knees revealing the poor material of her dress. The cane of a large and awkward size lay across her lap in plain view. No one appeared to notice her, but she knew well enough that puzzled comments would be exchanged over the gay dinners.

The true first night of Moon Festival she wore the shabby coat of her old friend, and while eating in the kitchen of The Three Crested Mountain, her son, Hong, came in and actually sat down at her small table. After a waiter had brought him tea and poured it, Hong spoke to her in his direct American fashion as if he had no time to waste on pleasantries.

"I know you haven't lost your mind—not you! So, what is it?" He indicated her faded clothes. "You have made bitterness for us all to eat. Now, do you make more?"

She drank the burning tea to stifle one pain with another. Ah Wing was not coarse in his manners as was Ah Hong; nevertheless, Hong knew well enough that she loved him.

She thought of Kuan Yin and remained silent.

"Have you gambled all your money away?" Hong asked.

"Gamble! I don't gamble!"

He shrugged. "Well, don't sit on the bench in that outfit. You make me ashamed. I've got a good business. Do you want to ruin me?"

She sat letting his words fall upon her like gentle rain, humility called forth in this unexpected encounter, bitter and sweet by turn. No sooner had she become aware of this opportunity than she became aware of pride in her humility. How treacherous was human nature, or, was it simply her own nature? Her discouragement also released several sharp words in her defense, but reminding herself of Kuan Yin's compassion for her, she offered compassion to Hong. He thought it was a trick; his expression became wary.

"Bring her dinner," he called out.

Mrs. Tsiang knew that even with the support of Kuan Yin, she could not eat alone this night. When Hong had gone into the dining room, she rose and made her way through the furious traffic of the restaurant kitchen, through the familiar and terrible din, through the fragrant steam until she was beside the chef. He was from Old China, the Chef of a Thousand Dishes, who knew the health-giving and medicinal values of all foods. She spoke to him with respect.

"I'm going to take dinner out tonight."

"For three." He smiled at her.

"Yes, for three."

"Very good dinner," he said. "Special."

When Mrs. Tsiang went out she stood for a moment looking up at the moon, shining more brightly than on any other night of the year. Feeling still uncertain and even a little dizzy from Hong's harsh words, she went through the crowds to the Chinese bakery where she bought gaily decorated moon cakes in the shape of the benign goddess herself, in the shapes of pagodas, fishes, horse and rider. Steadying herself with the awkward cane, she returned to the back door of The Three Crested Mountain. One of the waiters had called a taxi for her and after he had helped her in, and placed the food, he bowed several times in the old way which lifted her spirits.

Her two old village friends were not expecting her. The three of them clucked and laughed in high quivery voices, and Mrs. Hoy pushed the evening rice to the back of the stove, put the water on for tea. Then they saw Mrs. Tsiang in Mrs. Woo's poor clothes. For a moment their faces were blank with astonishment, then each covered her mouth and giggled.

The two seamstresses lived together in a shabby room in a shabby building in the old part of the city. Colored silks and brocades cluttered a sewing table, and a finely hand-sewn *cheongsam* hung ready for its owner. The room had no balcony; they could not eat their cakes in the sight of the Moon as was a proper honor for the goddess.

So, all three went to the open window and looked worshipfully at the Moon, and then at the Seven-Star Mother in the Great Bear Constellation. They exchanged the little gifts they had been saving for one another, and sat down to their sumptuous festival dinner. Afterward they nodded drowsily in their chairs, at last succumbing to sound sleep, their flutterings of breath and faint snores making a rough embroidery on the silence of the room. They awoke almost at the same moment, each pretending she had not been asleep. Restored, they cleared the table for fresh tea and moon cakes; the cakes too rich for them, they nibbled in order to make their offerings to departed spirits.

Old Mrs. Hoy wanted to play mahjong. Mrs. Tsiang wanted Mrs. Woo to try on the silk dress and the fur-lined silk coat, but

Mrs. Woo refused. She had already sewed the elegant clothes into a cloth bag and placed them on the closet shelf sprinkled with aromatic leaves.

"What for?" asked Mrs. Tsiang disappointed.

"For my coffin, what else?" smiled Mrs. Woo, and the other two then nodded approval, Mrs. Tsiang making a mental note to select a suitable outfit from her wardrobe for Mrs. Hoy. For herself she longed for the strength and humility to wear the dress she was wearing this very night.

"How are your sons?" they asked her out of politeness.

She replied as politely, but a dark passionate sense of her mother-place and their unnatural denial, even hatred, was suddenly almost more than she could bear alone. She began to speak too animatedly of some trivial gossip, and her two old friends, aware of her sorrow, gently led her into their favorite talk of youth in the Kwantung village. Mrs. Hoy, frustrated that there would be no mahjong this night, absent-mindedly began to hum.

"Oh!" exclaimed Mrs. Tsiang, restored in her memory to a time before the terrible events of her life, the cause of her grief and loss of face. "Do you remember just before Moon Festival how we climbed the highest hills and burned incense to Heaven and Earth?"

Mrs. Hoy started up. "I forgot the incense!"

"We'll not be climbing any high hills at our age," Mrs. Woo laughed.

The incense filled the room with a mysterious persuasion. They were silent for a moment, unable to believe they possessed so many years. A diaphanous, radiant being danced within each of them, ageless, joyous, unending; and they were filled with longing for some far realm of spirit where these bright beings that they felt were truly themselves hidden in old flesh and unwilling bones, could emerge.

Mrs. Hoy began to hum again, and the other two caught at the tune with thin, reedy voices trembling into the words of an old village song, an innocent song of wind and flowers and southern sun on the fah-nim trees. As memory absorbed them, they heard themselves as long ago, Precious Dove, Pear Blossom, and Whispering Willow, young in their hearts and far away.

This song reminded them of another and another until they were overcome with pleasurable exhaustion. Mrs. Woo telephoned for a taxi. Mrs. Tsiang went into the night street, unaware for the first time of her poor clothes; and, with a kind of tough strength with which she always came away from her old friends, she climbed into the car, gave her address and sank back in a doze.

IV

Mrs. Tsiang awoke from a noble dream: the visit of two amiable ancestors. Aside from a slight uneasiness, she felt that their manner was one of welcome and partial approval. But this visit also meant that time was growing extremely short, as she herself recognized from certain other signs: the simple flight of stairs gave her the feeling *sheung san*, of going up the mountain; or the overwhelming desire to remain in bed forsaking the day.

The thought of Kuan Yin's guidance and compassion gave her strength, and Lo-Fu's scratching on her door provided the immediate impetus to rise. She let the cat in and they engaged in their usual conversation.

It was only when Nephew Chek came with an elaborate lie on which he asked for a down-payment that Mrs. Tsiang was harshly brought back to critical earthly demands. It pleased her to pretend that she believed him. The cat, Lo-Fu, had reminded her this morning of Ah Wing's cruel remark on their parting: "You cannot *buy everything*, Mother." She had replied, "Almost." She had thought to buy Ah Chek's loyalty, but she saw now that she could buy only his treachery. It was worthless as such, but a fairly large sum might in time weigh heavily on his conscience and awaken a spark of honesty in him. She gave him a little more than he asked.

When he had gone, she made a small bow to Kuan Yin and said, "That is finished."

There was not one way left, not one person to help her make the urgent arrangements for the smuggling of her bones. She had no more face in Chinatown than she had had all the years past.

Her lips began to tremble and her eyes ached with reluctant tears. She groped her way to the little altar and lighted a stick of incense.

When the despair had passed, she telephoned her attorney to come at once, to bring his secretary and a portable typewriter. They did so, and worked all morning changing her will, which was signed, witnessed and sealed. She cut each of her sons to the legal token of one dollar, not in animosity or revenge, but in order not to burden them with self-recrimination. She was generous with the innocent grandchildren. She remembered her old village friends, Mrs. Woo and Mrs. Hoy. Their family associations would not find it necessary to pay for their funerals, and the attorney was to notify them at once to ease their concern for the future event. Her income property and the bulk of her cash, *on one condition,* would go to the Harmony Association that administered Chinatown's educational charitable activities, contributing to the Chinese community's self-sufficiency. She wanted responsible sons and daughters to go into the common world with some memory of their heritage.

After resting until mid-afternoon, she dressed in the old dress, the shapeless coat, and supported by the crude wooden cane, went slowly down the stairs. She was trying to convince herself that it was a part of her efforts toward humility to eat her evening meal at Hong's Three Crested Mountain, but as the loss of her old fierce pride had not yet been replaced with tranquility, she felt empty and defenseless, shaken with dread.

The glare of the August sun, the intense light from the big western sky sent little black wheels whirling and spinning before her eyes so that she did not see Ah Wing open the door of his antique shop and hurry to overtake her.

"What is it, Mother? What has happened to you?" He was staring at her clothes, appalled.

She thought she could distinguish genuine concern in his voice. She kept walking and it was true that he followed her into plain sight of anyone who wished to look.

"Mother! Do you need money? Have you lost your own? Answer me. Why were Bong and his secretary there? Do you need me to help you?"

She was faint with joy. "No, no." She waved him away. "Go back to the shop, the door is open." She imagined someone taking the precious jade and quartz and ivory, which seemed to her now only trifles.

Wing turned back, saying in his gentle voice, "I'll be up to see you later."

She went on, mumbling her thanks to Kuan Yin, and sat in the sun's warmth. After a while she shuffled calmly into the kitchen of The Three Crested Mountain, and the staff, as yesterday, carefully revealed no surprise at her clothing. The chef made her a light cleansing soup to balance yesterday's feasting. Ah Hong appeared only once and when he ignored her presence, she tried to remember Ah Wing asking to help her.

Back on the bench, Mrs. Tsiang observed the evening people. Mr. Wong and Mr. Lee and Mr. Sui passed by and they did not see her, as usual. She had overheard that they found her humility embarrassing, almost scandalous. She smiled a sly secret smile, and she felt a great patient waiting infuse her whole being.

V

In a few days the infallible Chinatown grapevine was alive with a startling rumor. In a few more days, Mrs. Tsiang received in the mail an invitation to an important social affair, the annual banquet of The Harmony Association, headed by Mr. Wong, Mr. Lee and Mr. Sui. The invitation was marked Formal and RSVP.

Next, her son Wing came to see her, carrying a large box. Lo-Fu, the cat, came too, looking on wisely.

"The most beautiful dress of anyone there," Wing said, lifting a traditional richly embroidered heavy satin gown. "Specially flown from Hong Kong. You will look like an empress."

Mrs. Tsiang studied her smiling handsome son in an effort to discern how much of his solicitude was joy for her sudden achievement of face, or shame for her humble appearance. She allowed him both, and thought surely tears would come to her eyes with her thanks, but none came. She had waited so long that she could feel only like an observer of an unreal scene.

"My son," she said, stroking the dress as if it were the back of Lo-Fu. "Ah Wing, my son." From a great tranquil distance, she looked up at Ah Wing and saw the tears in his eyes.

With a discreet murmur, she turned. "Lo-Fu," she said tenderly to the cat, "No needle has two points. Isn't that so?"

VI

That evening of the banquet, she dressed in the finery specially flown from Hong Kong. She wore her most valuable jade, and emeralds shone from her ears. The reflected glory of herself in the mirror did remind her indeed of an ancient empress. The other women would be wearing *cheongsams,* or even western dresses, but Ah Wing wished her to be distinguished from all the rest, perhaps to be easily identified so that many would speak to her and bow, giving her an abundance of the face she had longed for all the years of her life in America.

When Wing entered the room he exclaimed in admiration. Elated, she began to laugh, feeling free, giddily and somberly free of the long years of isolation, and, of grieving for her favorite son. Wing began to laugh with her as if he too had shed the weight of another time.

"Are you ready?" he asked uselessly.

"Yes, yes," she said, and then she began to sway a little and sat down on a hard chair.

He was alarmed and rushed to her, asking questions.

"Ah Wing, don't be so upset. This is just a little weakness of my age, nothing more. I am not used to all this excitement and—" she lied, "not used to being up late at night."

He insisted she lie down.

"No, no. I shall have a cup of tea."

While he was making the tea she said in a strong sensible way, "Ah Wing, you must go to the banquet without me."

"No! The banquet is not important. I will stay with you."

She soared on a great wing of happiness. "I am an old woman and it is better that I go to bed. But it is important that you go there before all those people and give my excuses so that they will know *I* was invited."

"As if they didn't know already!" That was Lo-Fu, the cat, again. She could swear she heard him distinctly, but he only sat staring straight into her eyes. His eyes said, "How well we sly ones understand each other."

"Scat!"

Wing gave his mother a long look of understanding, and promised to report to her over breakfast. "And then," he added, "we're going to the doctor for a check-up."

She made an ungracious little snort of disagreement. When necessary she would go to Dr. Fong, the herbalist.

As soon as Wing was gone, she shed her pretense of illness and hurried to the window to watch the men and women going into the brightly lighted building where the banquet was being held. She saw one of the officers who had ignored her for years accost her son, saw him shake his head in disappointment. She smiled. She supposed that after the banquet Ah Hong might even prepare a table for her in the public dining room of his fine restaurant. She smiled again.

"All purchased," she said aloud in amusement. Then, tenderly, "When I am gone, Ah Wing will not be humiliated with the memory of my attendance at this banquet."

Others were greeting Ah Wing as if he were one of them. She felt his happiness and knew it was not alone for his business but for himself accepted at last. "In time, for him, the acceptance will be real."

She came away from the window and called out, "Lo-Fu, let us talk." The cat ignored her. "Lo-Fu, my humble self asks your forgiveness for offending your dignity and intelligence."

"About time," she spoke for Lo-Fu, as this was clearly his attitude. "Have you forgotten your bones?" he indicated cruelly.

"Ah Wing, appointed by my will, will have the privilege of taking my bones to Hong Kong and arranging to have them safely smuggled." Her attorney had telephoned the British Consulate and learned that such bones would be permitted to accompany the bearer as excess baggage. She did not mention this to Lo-Fu. "The people who are giving me face tonight will learn from my will that they cannot have my money until they officially prepare my bones ten years after my death, according to old custom. They will have time to grow wiser and even kinder."

"And you aren't even ill," Lo-Fu suggested. "Furthermore, there will be other banquets."

"I have no further need of banquets." She went to the altar, lighted an incense stick and bowed, almost overwhelmed by this fact, by gratitude and new understanding. Tears of purest joy came from her heart. "Kuan Yin," she whispered, "Great Mercy, Great Pity, Goddess of the Southern Sea, of pure and compassionate regard, who listens to the sounds of the world; O, Sun of Wisdom whose light pierces all shadows, Charity who covers all beings like a kindly rain, I thank you for the return of my son! You gave me face just as I asked, but you illumined its worth. How mysterious are your ways, Kuan Yin! I bow before you."

She did not even glance at herself in the mirror as she removed the silk clothing and put on Mrs. Woo's familiar and comfortable dress and coat. She dropped her emeralds and jade into a jewel case and left it without securing the lock. Next she folded the beautiful dress into its box, thinking how well it would look on Mrs. Hoy at the proper time.

The stairs were easier to descend than for some time. Lo-Fu ran ahead into the busy evening streets and disappeared.

A porcelain God of Longevity in the lighted window of Ah Wing's shop made Mrs. Tsiang pause. She stood there sensing the power within her of long years ahead.

In the taxi she settled herself and the box, and sat back in anticipation of the evening of talk and singing and tea with her old friends in whose love her money or her other self of the past had no significance or place; in whose acceptance face was understood by the harsh reality of their lives to be a mirror of true honor or a mask.

She pictured Ah Wing at the banquet wearing his new face, which he had earned and which he enjoyed, and she was glad. She imagined Ah Hong greeting his customers in his new smiling mask. These are poor gifts to my sons, she thought, but time will reveal their purpose.

She slipped into a doze suffused with an intense and tranquil light that shone on and yet dimmed her two old problems that were like two feet upon a path. The path led to a far distant horizon and beyond. She awoke with a humbling sense of knowing that she had a long way still to go, and was somehow pleased. She looked out the window and saw the moonlight on the dirty stone of the street and could not remember ever having seen it there before.

Reconciliation

The two of them sat on the back step in the afternoon shade of the tall Moorish house. The woman was delicately friendly, almost arrogant. She glanced at her husband's face, seeing an instant of grief pass slowly into resentment and slowly back. An urgent feeling of warm concern erased her arrogance.

The February sun lay on the steep side of the sumac-rough hill and hot on the white wall of the big house on its crest. The Southern California winter was moving imperceptibly into spring. The man held a garden hose sending a long, thin spray of water far up the wild and unkept yard. As if it were an unusual pleasure, he danced the spray over the geraniums, the tall cacti, the low succulent floor, the narcissus, the banana tree. The water plopped gently on the great papyrus leaves and the fiery poinsettias. He pointed the hose upward into the pepper trees and down carefully over the tender sorrel and the shaggy grass. The slope was a designless mass of color. Purple lantana and cerise bougainvillea dropped over the low rock wall, which separated the level strip from the hill. In odd places a strange plant had risen from a hidden bulb, bloomed, and disappeared.

"A wild man must have planned this yard," she said. "Or perhaps the wind dropped these seeds in the neglected years when the house was alone."

"The yard went crazy while *you* were gone," he said significantly. "It's all right with care." She ignored him. He wants me to feel guilty in every way, she thought.

The heat came delicately into the shade. The woman pulled the long silk dressing gown above her knees and slid her bare feet along the cool tile walk. The man looked at her feet.

"Small, but strong and even," he said quietly, reminiscently, as if they were lost to him.

She was still, listening and feeling the spring coming up subtly through the warmth of this ever-flowering land.

A radio symphony, low and soft, suddenly mounted loud into their silence.

"Tchaikovsky," he said.

"Yes. Turn the radio off," she said gently. "I like it but I want to listen to the little things here."

"The Fifth," he said as if to change her mind, but he got up.

When he came back a fat rusty-rump thrush was drinking from a big leaf near the wall. The bird sat boldly on until he was full.

"I wish I could smell a creek," she said. "Run the water along the wall again. Sometimes in the evening when the hill is cooling, there's the odor of a strong plant out there, and something about it, just a trace, of that wild place."

"What wild place?"

"You know, the one when I was a little girl, that strange, wild place. It's my grandfather, and a lot of things I don't even understand."

She broke a twig and started a design on the damp ground. He looked at her and she was far away, farther away than when she spoke of any other place.

"You lived so many places. I don't know about this one."

"Really?"

"Where was it, now?"

"Colorado. The plains. Except that this place was below the plains like a ragged edge below the rim of the earth. My mother used to say it was the jumping-off place of the world. It was a lonely spot and she hated it. But Konkie, my grandfather, and I, we loved it, and it was like a secret between us of which we never spoke. I understand it now. My mother was a young woman, my grandfather was old, and I was a child. We were on the edges of her kind of loneliness."

"You understand that now?"

"Do you?" she asked cruelly.

She drew a long straight line on the bare earth, and parallel to it a curving one.

"The rock precipice was like this. It must have been a hundred feet tall. Over its face were the little pocket nests of swallows. Here was the creek winding between the wall and the cottonwoods on its other bank. The wide bed was white sand, and the stream was only a few inches deep."

"I'll bet you used to play there," he said uncomfortably.

"Yes," she said dreamily. "I would slide down the steep bank holding onto the willow roots, or leap off into the sand. No one ever came. We were many miles from anyone, so I often wore no clothes, only a sunbonnet. I made dams and caught minnows, or hunted anything, or lay on my belly and pretended to swim. In the evening the kildees ran along the creek bed like arrows. They made a plaintive call." She was silent for a moment. "That cry—wild and lonely—in that desolate place . . . it's. . . . "

"It's the way you feel now," he said, and his eyes, as she looked up, said, "with me." But there was no accusation. She could not even touch his hand now, feeling withdrawn and unrelated.

Her thoughts held him, the other one, in an intense moment of solitude for her lost desire. Only tenderness remained and she would not defile what had happened by denial of its meaning. These two did not conflict; one took nothing of her from the other. But pride, humiliation, possession, and a thousand other tendrils of instinct and custom made resolution necessary. Still that resolution now was little more than her self-contained presence, so because she must not humiliate him with guilty kindness. How could there be guilt without shame or ugliness? Only the participant was free to understand this. There was only sorrowing regret in her to hurt someone loved.

"What else was it like?" he asked impersonally.

She drew her thoughts back to the place and time which were rising from her memory in unbidden, urgent force. She made new lines on the map, and after a bit she spoke again.

"Up on the narrow ledge which was our yard there were many places to play. There were three levels, you see, the creek, the yard, the prairie. A steep road curved down from the plain, which was really all the rest of the world, and into our yard. The far end of the yard curved into the high wall so that we lived on a shelf. Around the house like a narrow collar ran the edge, and we could get into the yard ten feet below only by a path at the front and back. The path was almost straight up and down. Everywhere was shale, the yard had no grass, only rocks and snakes. But along the creek we had planted a patch of alfalfa. It is a lovely plant, tender and green, and its purple blooms perfumed the air for miles."

"Why are you so full of memories? Are you telling the old ones, thinking the new ones?"

She saw his eyes cruel for a moment with jealousy. He directed the water hard against the wall and a fine spray came back upon them.

"Between the house and the barn near the wall"—she drew more lines across the narrow yard—"were a small dark canyon, and a perfect rock room with a red berry tree at its door where the mockingbirds sang, and a narrow path leading up to the plain. This path climbed in the only place which was not a precipice, and it was hard to get a footing even here. On the prairie above was our garden. It seems absurd to have had a garden there. Why didn't we have it in a corner of the alfalfa plot? My father was not a farmer, but he was intelligent."

She drew a fence around the garden.

"Anyway, we had a garden there and could never raise anything but potatoes and squashes and watermelons. I shall never forget the wonder of going each morning to see the growth of a melon in the night. Konkie and I would climb the path every morning and push the leaves aside and look at the melons. I could feel his excitement and I know he felt mine. In the evening we would carry buckets of water up to the plain."

"Had you no crops?" he asked.

"Oh, yes, we had broomcorn and kaffir and maize and cane in a field upon the plain. The field was two miles from the house and all of us worked there. We would take water and food, and work all day, resting at the ends of the rows. In the summer we worked with large knives chopping the stalks and laying them in bundles to dry, then shocking them later. The shocks were like tepees and in the autumn I played Indian in them."

He looked at her delicate-boned wrists and slender legs.

"Walking in a field, swinging a heavy knife."

She smiled at him now.

"Why didn't you make money?"

"Because those were the dry lands. There were magnificent storms winter and summer but almost never any rain. Only the irrigated portions owned by the big farmers could raise crops successfully. Usually, our crops burned up in the fields. Much of that country is irrigated now, but when we lived there we were pioneering the margin lands."

"Well," he said, "it sounds like a very dramatic place, and I imagine life was more interesting then than now."

"Oh, no, but it was interesting, if you can call it that while it's happening. We were terribly poor. Life was hard."

"But it didn't seem hard then, did it? I mean to you?"

"Yes. When people are that poor it seems hard even to children no matter how full of imagination and pretense they are. Hunger is a hard thing, and we were almost always hungry. Memory doesn't enhance that."

"Really hungry," he stated to himself. He could never believe it and somehow he resented it.

"I remember a kind of final day when my mother sold her wedding ring for flour and lard."

"Did she ever get another?"

"No, but there was a white band on her finger for a long time. She used to laugh sometimes and call it the shadow of her marriage."

"Did she mind very much?"

"Well, I suppose she did, but we never carried on about any of the things that happened to us."

"Why was that?"

"Because, I suppose, getting voluntarily upset was a luxury we couldn't afford. No telling what would have happened if my mother had ever let go. My father was a spendthrift of energy and emotions. He had a violent temper and he let it loose often. It used to pounce upon us at unsuspecting moments like a savage animal. He couldn't stand the pressure of our lives."

"You wouldn't say that of your grandfather, would you?"

"He couldn't stand the pressure of responsible living."

"Oh."

"My father kept at it."

"Your grandfather was a very handsome man?"

"Yes. He was tall and brown with long hands and fierce black eyes that seemed strangely to conceal their fire."

"Perhaps his appearance explains some things."

"Perhaps, though only a little," she said. "I believe there's some pressure attached to being so alive and handsome. More distractions from the hard duty."

"Yes, for a beautiful woman as well. It would have been easier for me to have a homely wife."

It seemed to her he was sincere, perhaps forgiving her. "There are many beautiful women," she said. "You should not take it so seriously."

"Well, you are other things too, good things. That's the trouble."

She was silent.

"Well, go on," he said. She hurried into the first memory brought up by the sight of the water running in the lines she had drawn on the ground.

"When the snow melted in the Rockies which we couldn't even see, suddenly one day we would hear a terrific roar and see a high wall of water rushing through the creek bed, tearing at the banks. Each spring a little more of our yard was torn away. When the well went we had to leave. But that was a long time after."

She returned to filling in the map she had made on the earth.

"My father was like that water. Without warning he would terrify my grandfather and me. I used to think he hated us both, but perhaps not. One night he stormed and threatened so much that Konkie and I went up on the plain. That night I felt he would kill him, and Konkie felt it too."

"Surely not!"

"It is hard to know. We were afraid. We walked for a long time on the plain. The air was like a pearl with moonlight and every star was showing in the tall sky. After a while the beauty of the night came into our minds and there was no space for the trouble we had carried out of the house. My grandfather was a sensitive man, and very quiet. We spoke in odd ways, seldom with words, but there was a warm understanding between us."

"I'm sure of it," he said rather sharply.

"That night I remember how his long shadow leaned on the plain, and how he would glance far down from his tallness to me and nod quick and sidewise. In that nod was all the sorrow he felt for the words and the hate from which we had fled. He would lay his long bony hand on my shoulder and leave it there for a while as we walked. 'Don't tremble,' he would say gently. Just for a moment I would see his black eyes in a tender caress, and then he would lift his head and his eyes would be looking far away, secret with the thoughts of his own world. It seemed to me then that I understood the essence, if not the words, of every thought he had."

"He must have been an unusual man."

"He was, in himself, but he had his weaknesses. In his youth when his wife died he almost drank himself to death. And all his life he suffered the defeats of not trying rather than come up hard against the world."

"You are sentimental about his weaknesses. Perhaps they seemed picturesque?"

"No!" Her heart beat hard with a flare of anger and in a moment of silence quieted again. "No. But I could never hold them against him, not knowing the cause. He may have been miserable with them, and I could not help him then."

He adjusted the nozzle and set a fine round spray against the crooked fuchsia branches. The little bell flowers with their long stamen ding-dong-ing in the shower clung briefly and fell to the ground. She retrieved several and put them in her hair. He handed her two more for earrings.

"Once," she said, "when my feelings were hurt, Konkie suggested we walk to the nearest town. It was a store and post office in a shack seven miles away. My father was in the field on the prairie, walking in the deep furrow behind the plow. It was like a betrayal to go to town as he worked, but I washed my feet, put on a clean dress, and we walked."

He looked at her feet again.

"Oh," she smiled, "my feet were hard then from going barefoot. It took a long time and there was no shade all the way. We got a cold drink at the artesian well. My grandfather asked for the mail and bought a little flour. It had to be charged till harvest. He wanted tobacco for his pipe and I longed for candy, but we had a rule that those luxuries were bought only with cash. While he visited with the old store-keeper, I hung over a bean-barrel and gazed into the candy case. When my grandfather could think of nothing more to say, he did not call me to him but walked to me. The grocer walked along behind the counter. I was ashamed that my desire had been so urgent as to make me forgetful of my manners."

"Are you often ashamed?" he asked with a crisp and intimate smile.

"He knew I was hungry, and yet he reached in the case and brought out a small hard piece of candy, the smallest there. I felt my grandfather's sharp finger against my shoulder blade. 'Thank you,' I whispered in a terror of shyness. The grocer waited for me to eat it, he waited to see my gratitude again, and as if that weren't enough, he said, 'Eat it!' I'm sure he meant no harm; it was a small event to help along the lonely day. I whispered, 'No,' and put the candy, already sticky from the heat of my palm, into my pocket.

"By the sun it was after four o'clock when we started back. We drank from the artesian well again. Konkie had a letter in his pocket for my mother. It would be like a gift. The bag of flour he attached to a thin rope and flung over his shoulder. Outside of town he decided to save his shoes and tied the strings together to saddle them over his other shoulder."

She rested her chin in her palms and spoke as if she were thinking aloud. He sat listening now as if he must hear what she had to say.

"We felt happy because we were moving. Konkie sang a little song about tramping over this wide, weary world. 'I've been nearly all over the land,' he said, '*afoot*. America is a beautiful country. It's a shame everybody can't see it.'

"'Is it like this?' I asked. 'Well,' he said, 'this is it too, and a lot more besides—all kinds of people and all kinds of scenery.' I tried to imagine it but all I knew was the flat plain like a round plate with a sky for the lid. I looked as far as I could see and tried to think about America. It was the first time I had thought about America; it was like hearing your own name in a new way. He looked down at me and said, 'Now, don't let it confound you. There's a whole world. Whenever your dad can get near a school or move to town, you'll learn. Meanwhile I aim to teach you what I can. Last winter you learned to read the papers on the walls. This winter you can read my book, and I'll tell you things. This book isn't much but it's all I have; so I read it over and over. It's called *The Adventures of Kit Carson*. But it's summer now!' he said.

"We walked in silence for a while and then he said, 'Half my life I've wanted to go to a place called Costa Rica. There's a river there named Reventazón. I read it once somewhere—"the wild Reventazón"—and I've never been able to get it out of my head.' 'Will you go?' I asked him, taking it for granted because my grandfather disappeared and reappeared several times a year. 'No,' he said, 'I can't tread water. If I worked and saved for the trip, I'd die before I'd saved enough; if I don't work, I can't go. That's life, but, mind you, it's not the way it should be. So, I work a little and walk.'

"It's a shame," she said, "that he never saw the 'wild Reventazón.' It *is* wild, and strong, and it rushes along the feet of great mountains softly green with moist grass, and coffee and banana trees."

Her husband turned his head and looked at her for a long time but he said nothing.

"Konkie was silent all the rest of the way. When we came in sight of our field, the sun was going down, sending a fan of colored beams all over the west. My father and the horses were little black figures against the sun. We watched him come to the end of the row and unhitch the horses. He picked up his water jug, and stopped to look at a snake he had hung over the fence. Holding the lines, he walked off behind the horses toward home. We were still a long way off but in the clear desert air we could see all these things well.

"'In my time,' my grandfather said, 'I have had many dreams. It always seemed to me I was patterned for something, but I could never make it come out.' When he spoke in this way I knew he was speaking to himself, so I watched my father walking over the plain. Often I did not like him because we were strangers, but for all this and his wild anger, there he was, tired and perhaps lonely, after a hard and sober day working to get our food and the rent for the farm. Perhaps he had his dreams too, but there was no room in our world for this other part of him, and he was angry. I thought if I could plant these two men I loved like seeds in another soil they might come up one beautiful plant, one person. Then, I should not be divided and neither should they.

"The summer dusk was rising up around our feet when we reached the edge of the plain where we went down the precipice to our yard. The unharnessed horses were going into the alfalfa with their mouths dripping water. We splashed water on our faces at the well and washed our feet.

"In the house, Konkie gave my mother the letter, and I tried to break the sticky candy in two. I wanted to give my father a gift for the sight of us going to town."

"How silly."

"Perhaps."

"The point is," her husband said abruptly, "you really like a man who will go out of his way to give you some rather foolish emotional satisfaction better than one who works hard to give you the more important things."

"Sometimes," she said, "I think such a man would work the same to give *himself the important things*. Don't you?"

"That's hardly the point. And it leaves out love—his love."

"I was speaking only of my life."

"I realize that," he said meaningfully.

"Well, it is past and my grandfather is dead."

"Your grandfather is never dead! He is the universal fascinator!"
She wanted to strike him.

He waved the hose over the grass without interest. She looked at his blonde head and the reddish Sunday whiskers, the cool face turned away, the emotion hidden, controlled.

The long, Moorish shadow of the house had crept up to the top of the hill. Suddenly a mocking bird sang from a eucalyptus tree near the street and flew into the tree above them. Others sang wildly.

"That's their dawn chorus," she said. "They've got mixed up."

He turned off the water and went indoors. She had wanted to put her hand on his arm, against his loneliness, but she could not. It would be like a further betrayal. Sometime, perhaps, not now.

She could hear him faintly, her ears long familiar with the sounds from the house. He was searching through the record albums. These were his refuge. Suddenly she felt irritated with her easy, thoughtless conclusions of him. Had her love been his music? Perhaps the music was his expression for that part of him submerged to silence, as the story she had been telling was her discontent, her loneliness, her plea. They had found no way to be friends and could not speak directly.

The beautiful and disturbing music of Scriabin's "Poem of Ecstasy" disquieted the dusk.

She had needed him; she had shown him only in a cruel way, thinking of herself, and he had gone into the house consumed with his own need. She drew the stick across her drawings on the earth, and listened for a long time, as if she were hearing the words in his heart.

The music moved into the "Poem of Fire." She stood up and walked through the deep grass to the end of the yard that dropped steeply into a narrow canyon. Some radiant energy, long bound by the weight of confusion and opposing desires, demanded release. Not in flood, but in a long full stream, beginning now, flowing through their relationship and beyond it into many things. It would not be easy. She hardly knew how to begin. Perhaps only a little thing at first and then on and on until this enmity of strangers had dissolved between them, freeing them, as much as one is ever freed, to tend their lives. This waste of self-absorption in a world of many needs was shameful, and yet shame was unknown or forgotten in that aching void between them. A carelessly abandoned hope came softly into her thought of him. Some day he would listen to his music in fullness, not in desolation. And she would not be speaking of her loneliness, or hiding it.

Like an inverted sky the city far below in the valley was bejeweled with street-lamp stars. A low wind smelling of the sea came in gently to the great hills. She turned back toward the house. Under the desperate music and the quick winter dark, she could hear the foolish frogs singing as if nothing great or small would ever be changed in the world. She hesitated a moment thinking of flight. The frogs were singing of eternals, innocently, blindly. She opened the door and went in quietly, wanting to be known, and to know him whom she had not fully known before.

The Meeting

From the bus stop Cass walked along the wide clean street shady with pepper trees. Old mansions, relics of wealth that had moved west with the city's change, sat with an air of insult and injury on neglected lawns. Under no obligation to fashion or the lack of it, flowers bloomed along walls and circled trees, as bright for the has-been houses as for any hacienda of other years.

The young woman walked slowly studying each place. A Southern Colonial, alien to the historically Spanish tradition of California, displayed the sign ROOMS in a front window.

When the landlady opened the door, she said to Cass, "Well, dear, you've come about the room."

"May I see it, please?"

The mansion's interior was far from the original. The life had gone out of the drapes and furniture and carpet; they seemed dead, unlived with. The landlady wore a simple expensive dress of another decade; her ruined hair had no will of its own, but her eyes were direct and sympathetic, her movements lively and a little harried. The room was small, and although it was upstairs, it was over a low first story to the back so that the one large window opened upon the very top of an orange tree bearing and flowering at the same time, filling the shabby place with its fragrance. The rent was cheap, the lock broken, being held with a wire and the woman's promise of repair.

"But we're all like a big family," she assured Cass. "They all leave their doors open. All except the lady harpists. Twins. Never married. You'll hear them. Their music gives the place its old refinement."

"In case I... where do you. . . ?"

"Oh, I have the apartment above the garage. Geraldine has the other one. This was her home."

"Was?"

"Yes, dear. I bought it for back taxes years ago. She lost everything in a tragedy. I've been noticing, you have a lovely aura." She raised the blind with a snap, explained the domestic rules while surveying the dismal furniture. "This is a perfectly beautiful room, the orange tree and all."

"I'd like to have the lock fixed right away," Cass said, wondering about her aura.

"Oh, indeed, yes. Now, next to you, that's Haakon, a big strong tall fellow, Scandinavian descent, about your own age, a beautiful soul. And so clean it's pitiful. You'd never know he's in his room. He has his troubles, but he'll get back into life again someday. Now, dear, what work do you do?"

"Newspaper."

"A dying trade."

"I hope not," Cass said. "Anyway, I'll find a job soon."

"I know, I know." The landlady opened the closet and a musty smell came out. She fished into her pocket, brought out some cloves, and tossed them onto a shelf. "Are you from far away?"

"Only up the coast a ways. San Luis Obispo. I worked on my hometown paper."

"You look incredibly innocent, my dear." She tossed more cloves around the room.

"People are always saying that," Cass said, annoyed.

"No offense, my dear. It's just so unusual these days. Now, how did you find us?"

"I was looking for a room near downtown and a bus line, and when I saw this house somehow I knew it was the place."

"Well then, you were directed here. We all follow the thread of our destinies."

"I hope to make my own."

"That, too," the landlady said. "In the long view they are all one."

Cass was silent. She wanted to make a new life in a new place; to *be* new. She moved to the window and looked into the tree. Sparrows and linnets hidden among the leaves were chattering and singing. She would stay. The mingled fragrance of orange flowers and cloves filled the ugly little room. A narrow bed, a heavy Spanish chair. Pushed against the bed was a desk with a lamp. She could read in bed.

The landlady dusted the desk with a tissue. "One thing more, dear. In the living room you may have noticed that beautiful old screen in the corner?"

The antiquated screen was like the rest of the landlady's treasures.

"Well, there's a young man, Leroy, sleeps on the floor behind the screen. He used to rent this room. I couldn't put him out. I gave him a quilt. He has no skill or trade, poor lost soul, but he helps me around the place. Two nice elderly gentlemen and a working man live in the bedrooms downstairs. They all pay their rent promptly or I couldn't make ends meet. But, back to Leroy, he's harmless."

"I'm not afraid," Cass said, smiling at her.

Downstairs the woman said, "You will come back?"

Cass was reading a printed note thumbtacked to the door: "I do not know how God will judge my handiwork. During the last three weeks I have written fifty pages of *Parsifal* and saved three young dogs from death. We still have to wait and see which lies heavier in the scales. Richard Wagner."

"You know," the landlady said, watching her, "you can even help bees. And, not only by fishing them out of the birdbath. Sometimes you see one so worn out, wings getting ragged, grounded. I take a toothpick and put a small drop of honey down. That little hard-working honeybee eats and flies away."

Cass rather liked this woman. She opened her purse and held out a week's rent.

"Bless you, dear. We must bless this money—yours and mine—and we'll have enough."

"We'd better," Cass smiled. "Now, I'm going to get my bags from a locker at the station."

So quiet was the upstairs that Cass seemed to be alone. On her daily trips out and in she saw the old men talking or one playing solitaire, the other reading Emerson. The landlady was about her chores and once Leroy was watering the lawn. Cass kept to herself and made plans, and the plans included her snug room with its bird song and orange flower air, and the bright touch of her few good books on the shabbiness.

Then, one night she came wide-awake; the clock face shone in the dark: three o'clock. The air was dense and heavy. All the house was quiet, and outside not a sound, as if the night were holding its breath. The hush itself was like a sound. Cass lay motionless in animal alertness and caution.

The darkness intensified as if with a palpable presence. She felt her flesh tense over her bones. A sense of something near was strong. She tried to doubt herself but instead she was filled with loathing of whatever was in the room. "All right now, Cass," she thought. "Here's an experience. Observe." With the sheet pulled up under her chin, she strained her eyes into the dark, held her breath, listened, and aimed her cool reason like a weapon against her fear. "But reason isn't everything. I'm just whistling in the dark."

"Wild feeling," she said to herself. "This is only a wild feeling." She tried to reach for courage. Her impulse to thrust her hand into the malevolent air and turn on the light was balked; her arm would not move. Perhaps she was in a nightmare and knew she was in it: a dream within a dream?

Ill-assorted as they were, the roomers gave Cass no reason for fear, not even Haakon who padded in and out all hours of the night in his bare feet. She wished she could hear him now, but the rooms were silent in sleep. The depraved heaviness clung to the air; she could hardly breathe. She thought of leaping from her bed and running down the stairs into the clean night, but the tightly wound wire on the door would detain her an exposed long moment that could not be borne. Just as it seemed she would call out against her will to any stranger, and the roomers were still strangers to her, there was a marvelous occurrence.

A ripple of sound, a tentative plucking of strings, and the two harpists in the front bed-sitting room began to play. The unfamiliar music was very soft as if they played for themselves, mindful of disturbing others, but in the silent house it vibrated pure and clear. It dissipated the sense of evil and the fear, and as Cass listened she fell asleep.

In the next day's sun, walking in the crowded downtown streets, Cass doubted her impressions of the previous night. As she entered the house, the voices of the old men discussing politics, the landlady whistling in the kitchen reassured her.

Upstairs in the dusky light, Haakon was leaning against the frame of his open door. She had not seen him before and felt shy, almost overwhelmed by their meeting and his arrogant, smiling assurance, as if he were mocking himself.

"Hello, Cass," he said, "I'm Haakon."

She felt as if he and she were within a slowly whirling circle of intense awareness.

"Hello," she managed.

He was carving a small head from what appeared to be a large bar of white soap. The emerging head was that of a girl with long hair lifted softly by the wind, her delicate face lifted too. She was poetic in the way of another time, and yet without fashion, so well made that Cass saw her whole, walking perhaps in a spring meadow colored with wild flowers bending in a gentle wind. The wind was bringing a shower that would fall through the sunshine, and the girl had tilted her face upward to see the cloud. There was something strangely familiar in all this, almost as if it were her own experience. Cass could not look away from the small sculpture, and to disguise her sense of memory she said, "It *is* soap! It's too beautiful to be carved of soap."

"It was all I had. I started it a few months ago. I never did anything like this before. I was here in my room and suddenly I had an urge to carve this head. I couldn't finish it, but now I've started again."

"It's alive," she said.

"Yes." A natural gaiety came into his face, a face open and clean with eyes full of hidden things. He smiled as if he had been restored to himself. His own powerful aliveness seemed about to break out of him. Cass felt assailed by his magnetism, and dismayed by her acute awareness that it concealed a demand of her, a demand for recognition of some sort. Confused by her own tangled perception and her impulsive resistance, she turned into her room.

"Afraid?" he asked.

"Of course not." But she was trembling, not in fear, not in desire, not in any way she understood. Before she closed the door and before she could turn on the lamp, she heard a woman's voice calling her name.

"That's Geraldine," Haakon said.

The woman's voice was filled with malice. Why? She had not even met Geraldine. Cass wound the wire to secure the broken lock. Geraldine was at her door in an instant; she knocked with possessive authority and tried the knob. Cass felt cold and afraid, and then she heard Haakon's door open—he must have closed it quickly at the sight of Geraldine—and with an equally possessive authority, he said, "Get away from there, and don't come in here, either."

"Says who?" Geraldine replied with startling venom.

The tone and cruel familiarity of the brief exchange made clear one of the landlady's remarks: "Geraldine has a gift for bringing the worst out of others, the poor lonely thing."

Geraldine spoke through the door in a taunting, intimate way, "Little girl, there are certain people around here not fit to associate with."

Cass bristled at "little girl" but remained silent.

Haakon laughed. "You'd say anything, wouldn't you, Geraldine? Explain why *you* are always trying to associate with me. We'd both like to know."

"Leave me out!" Cass said angrily.

After that, Haakon was not to be seen; his door was closed, but there were times as she went down the stairs she felt him watching her. Geraldine subsided. Cass imagined her busy with schemes to color her drab and loveless existence.

Ignoble and savage and sometimes even sordid, the life of the house had benevolence above all else, contributed every day afresh by the compassionate landlady who worked about the place finding something "perfectly beautiful" at every shabby turn.

When Cass came in early from an interview, the Emerson man stopped her, saying, "Don't disturb Mrs. L. She's having her little siesta reading Ma-dame Blavatsky. That's hard going. We don't see eye to eye."

Cass had never heard of Blavatsky, but before she could ask, he said, "Young lady, are you aware that Emerson had a large Oriental library?"

"No."

"If you'll read the Oriental philosophers, you'll get a lot more out of Emerson, you'll get his real meaning."

"Will you suggest some books?"

"Another day. We have company."

Leroy came in and, seeing Cass, rushed behind the screen and reappeared holding a sleeping bag. "She gave it to me for my birthday!"

Cass praised the gift and Leroy beamed.

The working man had moved out suddenly, and his room was occupied by an ex-convict from San Quentin. Leroy gave Cass that brief news.

The landlady hadn't mentioned him, but one evening when Cass came home late from the library, she heard him pacing the floor of his room, cursing quietly and steadily to himself. She hurried upstairs and seeing Haakon's door open and that he was not in, she felt drawn to look more closely at the small head carved of soap. It was almost finished, and again, Cass was conscious of a subtle familiarity, an informed sense of someone or something all too swift to grasp.

"You!"

Cass turned at Geraldine's voice and the cruel tug of her long hair. Cass was angry, and her first impulse was to strike back. But Geraldine had got away and was nowhere to be seen or heard. Cass went into her room, impatient with the broken lock, and wound the wire tightly. She pushed the heavy old Spanish chair against the door, resolved to move as soon as she found a job.

The lady harpists were playing, and Cass realized they had been playing for several minutes, even while she was looking at the carved head, and that perhaps was why she had not heard Geraldine. Taking advantage of their soothing influence, she went at once to bed and read until she fell asleep.

She awoke in the dark with the hairs standing up on her cold arms and her scalp tight and prickly with the sense of something in the room, some enormity in the atmosphere of the night itself. A plane passed over, and beneath the distant throb of its engines she heard Haakon's door softly open and Haakon going on bare feet down the stairs like a nocturnal lemur into the nighttime jungle of the city.

Silence returned and the air was furry black. The watering truck came by washing the streets, a reassuring sound, but its swish and sough were lost in the dense portent.

No moon, no sheen of stars burnished the dark or glowed in the stillness of the orange tree. The night was black against the window like the pulsate hide of a great brute. The lamp made it blacker; she retreated again into the dark, her eyes avoiding the window or the wraith of its curtain.

A bird uttered a *cheet* and was quiet. From a farther tree a mockingbird sang out its lyric songs, repeating itself wildly like a mechanical toy. It stopped abruptly as if turned off.

Cass lay thinking how the room seemed more in the tree than in the house. A ripe orange falling plopped onto the ground. On moonlit nights she had visualized a luminous descent; tonight the orange fell hidden and secret. Those first nights here the atmosphere had been beneficent, mild, or quick with that beauty so imperfectly perceived. She had gone to gentle sleep to dream of the next day's search and her imagined future. She had felt rather like a letter in passage, filed in its numbered box for a little while, separate and unrelated to the letters in other boxes, sure of the journey and its destination.

Morning must surely be near, yet the night was a marvel of unillumined shade. The silence began again, ominous, weighted, even more suggestive and vile. Cass drew the sheet over her head and curled her body into a snug ball. She began to tremble, unable any longer to disclaim her dread.

Would all in this house, however separate their ways, be connected and marked in some way forever by this malefic and baleful night, which must draw them together in its spell as no joy ever could? Each one in his bed in his waking or sleep was unaware of the drama that would involve them all, a drama perhaps so secret they would lay no blame, or a drama so loud they could never escape its voice.

Cass gave herself up to this knowledge, trying to trace and touch the threads of all her living that had brought her to this house in this city, her life to mingle with theirs so unknown to her and yet so deeply felt. She heard them in their stunned or timid or vicious voices unknown to themselves; she heard them like noble music unplayed and waiting to utter their songs in some faraway day of another time.

And then she heard Haakon coming up the stairs, his bare feet cautious on every step, her own senses purely attuned to his presence. She uncovered her head and waited.

A stifling, amorphous weight fell upon her mouth and pressed hard against her breast as if the very air of the room had become malevolent. She gasped and struck at the shapeless force, and it seemed to her as the air cleared that she must be emerging from a hideous nightmare. But at that moment she heard a faint, distinct rustle of silk in the hall, moving toward the head of the stairs. Geraldine was waiting, predatory, on the top step, as Cass had heard her all the nights before.

A sudden hiss of discordant whispers ripped the stillness. From the indistinguishable words a miasma of rancor, spite, rage filled the hall and seeped into the room. A struggle. The whispers stopped. A struggle among several persons. Silence. A silence of hatred and cold fury. The whispers began again. Fast. Faster. Explosive. Then a furtive grasp, a blow, a stab into flesh. The covered scream, and the sickening grunt of final surprise. The silky, helpless thump and thud of Geraldine lurching dead, surely dead, down the stairs.

Cass felt as if she herself must die of terror.

In the long hush that followed, the house itself seemed to be listening, as voiceless as its roomers.

Then Cass heard the slap of bare running feet to her door. She was stiff with fright. Haakon jerked the lock free of the binding wire. Without conscious decision or movement, Cass found herself at the window pressing her violently trembling fingers on the hook, pushing at the rust-embedded screen, to leap into the orange tree and let herself down onto the grass to run in the street to the nearest safety of any house that would take her in.

But Haakon was there before the screen broke away. He spun her around. A great fiery energy rose and struggled against his enormous strength, but he held her as if she were a tiny creature in his grasp.

"Stop it!" he whispered. "I'm not going to hurt you."

When he took his hand away, she pulled free, but she could not control her trembling alarm and loathing of all she had overheard.

"What did she do to you?" he demanded.

"Nothing."

"She meant to. I saw her come out of your room."

"No. No."

"Yes."

An obscure dread nearly overpowered her. The first forlorn light of morning came into the room, and she saw Haakon's face, white, anguished, his eyes burning deep with an experience all his own.

"She meant to kill you," he said.

Cass could not absorb this injustice.

"That's why I came back. She would be more careful tomorrow night. She—"

"But why?"

"Cass and Haakon," he said low, in irony.

She ignored this, and yet a sense of exquisite joy rose in her, like something almost but not quite remembered. The terrors of the night became vague. The exaltation seeped away. She looked at Haakon and would have turned aside except for the wonder that had passed between them.

"You've killed Geraldine," she whispered, and began to tremble again.

"I didn't kill Geraldine. *He* did. The one downstairs. Her husband. He killed..."

"Oh, I don't want to hear any of it! I just want to move out of this terrible house."

"Go today, Cass. Geraldine hates you—the purity in you."

"But I'm not pure."

"Not all. But enough. It's your purity released me."

"How? What are you talking about?"

"I recognized you that first day. Remember? But you didn't know why you were here."

"I still don't."

"You will."

Haakon shook his head as if to shake free, to stand before her in another self. The ruin of this night slid away. His grave eyes changed, touching with love, taking, all in an instant of time that was already gone, lost in futurity. In that spelled hush was recognition of their strong and secret groping for the essence of each other. This desperate hunger drew upon all that she was until now, overwhelming her, extending her and lifting her into his desolate exaltation. Not by themselves, themselves forgotten and put aside, they moved toward each other's merciful embrace, sorrowful and reverent, mystified beyond thought.

He looked at her and she at him, this omened stranger that she knew as he knew her on that first day, and waited.

"Strange how I came to this house," she said.

"Before that I kept waiting."

She was startled that she believed him.

"I live in another country," he said.

She only half-understood what he meant; he was unknown to her and yet known, but she sensed this had no importance. Her breath drew in as sharp as a paper edge; she thought of the bare-foot excursions in the night and felt sad and cold and bewildered.

"I went out to get away from Geraldine. She was always here at night. Even after her husband... Even after that, she kept on. I couldn't get away until you came."

"I?"

Haakon smiled at her. "I'm free. I can go."

A morning sweet stillness came up to them from the streets. A rising tender awe encircled them again.

"Cass and Haakon," he said, and this time his voice was full and quiet.

"Cass and Haakon," she repeated in dismay.

He smiled. "You said that."

"Yes. I don't know why."

With the first faint sun the blossoms released their fragrance into the room. She heard his door close softly and his steps moving to his window where he must be seeing and breathing the same bright air.

Then she saw her own door with the lock wired, and the heavy Spanish chair where she had placed it last night. The small sculptured head supported by the slender young neck and shoulders stood on her desk. It was she, but in some other time. Not now. For a long, stunned moment she thought she could not bear her knowledge. She began to pack her clothes, shaking so hard she could barely hold them.

The landlady was knocking on her door, announcing herself. Cass pulled the chair away and unwired the lock.

"Haakon's gone," the landlady said, smiling. "Where he belongs. I feel such joy for him. I knew you'd be going, too."

"Will the police come now?" Cass sensed this was wrong, but she had to say something hard and clear to try to make sense of this terrifying night.

"No, dear." She put her arms around Cass. "You're trembling, poor child." She smoothed Cass's hair back from her face and released her.

Cass gave up packing and fitted her portable typewriter into its case.

The landlady began to pack the clothes. "That's all there is to it, just the commotion."

"You call it commotion!"

"Well, dear, I do. The murder itself happened years ago. I worked for that evil Geraldine. Managed her affairs. She corrupted Haakon, who, of course, was corruptible, but he was innocent, too. She hated that. Her husband killed them both one night when she was waiting on the stairs for Haakon. The husband was executed."

"But, Haakon?" Cass did not want to believe that Haakon had simply disappeared from her room.

"Haakon isn't one of us, dear."

Cass began to cry. She sat on her bed and sobbed.

"Every spring," the landlady went on calmly, "*he* came back at this time. Her husband—that convict. They were bound to relive the murder until one or all of them could raise their consciousness to a higher plane. I know Haakon was trying."

Cass was staring, uncomprehending.

"He sent for you." The landlady nodded toward the sculptured head. "It's the way you looked then. You released him."

"How did I do anything?" Cass said desperately.

"Just by being. At times being is a form of doing."

"I don't understand. He was so real!"

"He had great energy, and you and Haakon were very close in some other life, I'm sure. It's a pity you can't remember, dear. A few can. But it's too much. We'd be burdened beyond endurance. But sometimes we recognize others, as you know now. Maybe just a fleeting awareness on the street, a glance and they're gone. Sometimes, well, like Haakon. Hand me your clock, dear; I'll put it between these dresses."

"Oh, who is real and who is not?" Cass demanded, wondering even at her own state.

The landlady laughed. "We're all real, dear, although I know what you mean. Leroy and I are still in our earth bodies, and, of course, you, if you doubt it. And the elderly men downstairs. They'll be moving if they heard, but I doubt it; they have very small incomes and are happy here. The convict has gone—poof. Until next spring. I have to advertise for new roomers nearly every year. Otherwise, we are a rooming house of ghosts, you might say."

"How can you live here?"

"Well, dear, I try to understand."

"Aren't you afraid of Geraldine? I am."

"Fortunately, I know how to protect myself. Her vibrations are very low and she hangs onto them. But I'll keep trying to help her. The lady harpists—beautiful spirits—are trying to help us all, trying to clear this house."

"I never did see them."

"No need. Just listen. They manifest only in their music."

"I never saw Geraldine, either," Cass said, "but I know now I felt her."

"She's around half the time. Restless. Geraldine is so untidy, but she always dresses up for the murder. A silk dress. The one she had on. Maybe Geraldine will settle down a bit now Haakon's gone for good. But it's best you're leaving."

The two women closed the bags.

"When you find a room, call me, and Leroy will take your bags to you."

"Thank you," Cass said, all her confusion bandaged for the moment by exhaustion.

The whole morning shattered with bird songs. Cass picked up the sculptured head, holding it close, and went to the window watching the sun sparkling the grass and the leaves and the white orange flowers. Everything in the world seemed new except her own renewing which was dark with pain. She strained back to the knowledge of an hour ago, trying to hear again the renewal in Haakon's voice, to understand the revelation in their pure embrace. But in all this morning splendor, she could think only of Haakon and how their lives had touched again for a moment and gone their disparate and separate ways together.

Aslant the Moon

We three good friends shared a small house and an abandoned wary cat we had named Brooke. Although the city surrounded us, an adjoining vacant lot was yellow with wild mustard each spring. An old bearing apricot tree graced our tiny back yard. Around the house was a narrow collar of soil, once dry and weedy, now colored with a variety of flowers and vegetables. We had shaken together the seeds, scattered them on loosened soil and were rewarded with a garden as diverse perhaps as the three of us.

We had jobs, we had our dreams, our troubles and delights. It was a good time in our lives. We had little money, but enough, if there were no emergencies, and if there were, emergencies were simply new experiences in the flow and rapids of our days. It is true that Sui-Ping had more money than Kwei-Yin and I, and had recently quit her job in a bank because she wished to work in importing. Kwei-Yin designed wallpaper and I worked at Sotheby's. Our natures were such that we lived in more than less harmony and were free to go our own ways.

One day a letter from Singapore, an unusual love letter, threatened our happy menage and drew us into an intense sharing that we still possess in our now separate lives. That letter lying so innocently alone in our mailbox that day, that letter that initiated all the rest, left its particular mark on the three of us.

It was for Sui-Ping from someone by the name of Fan Teh-Wah. Sui-Ping read it aloud to us, wondering how he knew her address. She replied politely, briefly, after the three of us came to this decision. The exchange began.

Mr. Fan's letters were beautiful, poetic. They were learned too in their wide range of knowledge and casual references to the world's classic literature, in apt quotes, in thoughtful comments whose originality made us exclaim. They were not effusive or we might have made quick judgments from the dubious heights of our contemporary vernacular standards.

We listened to Sui-Ping's eager, musical voice. Her thirty-five years were hidden in her lovely glowing face and small slender body. She was more of a beauty now than at twenty. But her husband's desertion years ago had left her doubtful of her qualities as a woman. She had been brought up to please a man, to ignore her own feelings, and even though her marriage had been an arranged one, and she had not thought herself unhappy, she was hurt and troubled that she had failed.

"I've been lonely for a long time so I mustn't be silly," she said. The loneliness had been for Barton, not her husband. Barton was an English archeologist she had known in Egypt. Their long serious love affair had ended when he suddenly married a colleague. It seemed another failure. He had died soon after that and had left her a small legacy with which she could live a few years without working. Her husband had gone away and left her nothing. At the time, because of her grief over Barton, she had continued to work, and only now had decided to use the money toward a new career.

In the midst of these plans the first letter came from Mr. Fan. It told how he had traced her through several countries and now to this American city. He had hired detectives, but he urged her not to be offended since his love had prompted his desire to see her again.

"Again?"

"Yes. It isn't as if I don't know him," Sui-Ping said. "He was fourteen and I was twelve. Our families were close, and when my parents were killed in the war, I lived with his family for a time."

"Do you remember him? What was he like?"

"Actually, I remember him rather well, but as a child, I didn't know him well. He was terribly serious and quiet and was always reading. He was tall and somber, and I used to try to make him smile. We sat in the garden and he read to me. We felt a young love but were too shy to express it."

"Imagine! He has been in love all these years!"

"Well, I haven't." She laughed. "But circles have great meaning."

Kwei-Yin opened her notebook and began drawing circles in a modern design. "He says he has never married, that you are the only one in his heart. Oh, Ping, I wish someone would tell me that, though I probably wouldn't trust him if he did."

"Someone will, Yin."

"He must be rich hiring all those detectives."

"I think he is. He comes from a wealthy family. His mother was English, his father a wealthy Chinese publisher."

"Doesn't he work?" Kwei-Yin asked. "I have the Chinese work ethic."

"It seems he is simply a scholar, maybe a recluse."

"Should we trust a recluse?"

"Perhaps he is just unmarried, Joanne. Perhaps he is one of those persons who can love only once."

"That is suspect," I said.

"Very small of him," Kwei-Yin added.

Sui-Ping laughed. "You girls are so much more worldly than I am."

"Actually not, Ping," I said. "None of us is really worldly even though we have seen a bit of the world on foreign jobs and running around on a shoe string, hard class."

"Remember our pact?" Kwei-Yin said. "Here we were each alone and we kept meeting by accident, first in London, next in Alexandria, then in Bombay. Our destinies were to be together, and here we are."

"There are no accidents," Sui-Ping said. "But we have choices within the larger pattern. You always chose risk, Joanne."

"Still do. I like the adventure of risking."

"We had a lot of unworldly adventures, didn't we?" Kwei-Yin said.

"Sui-Ping has had the most."

"Yes, but I don't know what she does with them. She just quietly accepts everything as karma, her old debts paid. And that's it."

"It is," Sui-Ping said. "We must see them as lessons. But there's good karma, too."

"We want you to have some. It's high time, Small and Peaceful."

"That brings us back to Mr. Fan," Kwei-Yin said.

Brooke came in with a superior air, allowed us to admire his self-reliance, then leaped into Sui-Ping's lap and purred loudly. We discussed renaming him Evinrude.

Fan Teh-Wah sent a small picture. We examined it through a magnifying glass. He was a genuine combination: a long English face, fine nose, black hair, and eyes that in spite of being rounded appeared Chinese. His expression was intelligent and mournful, his mouth sensuous. Even though we saw only his face we knew he was tall, and weighted with knowledge. We were impressed.

"Why didn't the young love continue?"

"His family moved to Singapore. We were in school. He sent me poems and I was too shy to reply. Soon, or so it seemed, my marriage was arranged and we began to travel."

"I've always wanted to ask you if you loved your husband," I said.

"I grew fond of him. We were rather like friends. He was a restless person, and, as you know, abandoned me before we had any children. That was a disappointment. I learned to support myself, and you know the rest."

By the seventh beautiful letter from Fan Teh-Wah, a letter revealing such generosity of spirit, we could say only, "What a wonderful man! Letters tell best. Ping, how can you help falling in love with him?"

"I am afraid I am."

"Afraid?"

"Yes. Just as I was feeling in total balance, these letters are making me lonely."

"We're most alive when we're not in balance, when we're trying to get in balance," I said, not knowing what I was talking about.

Sui-Ping was impatient with us, said we were romantic, which we admitted, but her protests were more in fun than censure. She read the letters over and over, shared them with us, but did not share the ones she wrote to him. Soon, it seemed that most of her time was used in answering.

The letters grew more beautiful, more appealing. We said they should be in a book. Unlike most love letters, they could be read by others with aesthetic pleasure. We could hardly wait for the post. While Kwei-Yin and I had our own lives, we were all three in love with Mr. Fan, save that our love seemed to be a part of Sui-Ping's; we were adding ours to hers, and more and more she began to feel that a great and tender and reliable love had come to her at last. It was meant to be. The other experiences had enriched her in their own ways in order that she be ready for this.

In three months he proposed marriage. Immigration quotas prevented his easily coming to the United States. Since both he and Sui-Ping held British passports, he suggested they meet in Canada, marry at once—he wished her to know his feelings for her were honorable—then he would return to Singapore, she would return to the U.S. and soon join him.

The three of us discussed it. We urged her to say yes, when she had already said yes.

After a flurry of buying new clothes, she left. We saw her off, happy to witness her new joy. She looked young and vulnerable and innocent, as if she had been transported to the time and the garden of her youth.

A blissful cablegram arrived, then brief daily notes of their sightseeing and browsing in bookshops. A wedding picture was in the next post. How handsome they were together! Next came a note mentioning the first known flaw. "He spends a great deal on books but is very thrifty about everything else. I may as well say it: stingy. He is a wealthy man, but, listen to this: he has suggested that we share the honeymoon expense. I cried in embarrassment for him and disappointment for myself, but he explained it all away as a playful test of my love. Perhaps it was. In all other ways his treatment of me is as beautiful as his letters."

A next letter said: "Teh-Wah has gone to a rare book dealer's so that means I have time to write you and to bathe and dress for dinner. I shall wear the jade he brought me. Wait till you see it! Last night he said he does not want me to forget the best in our ancient heritage. He read to me from the Tao Te Ching this passage from Lao Tzu: 'There is something which existed before heaven and earth. Oh how still it is, and formless, standing alone without changing, reaching everywhere without suffering harm. It must be regarded as the Mother of the Universe. It appears to be everlasting. Its name I know not. To designate it, I call it Tao.'

"Teh-Wah said that in the teachings of Lao Tzu it is a joy to experience the human form, but that since there are transitions of birth and death into eternity, there should be no fear or sorrow at death. He wishes me never to fear death. Teh-Wah is not upset by the non-belief in the modern world. He says we must understand it as a transitional experience of man; that it, too, has a purpose.

"These ideas are familiar to me, but it is so good when we talk of them together."

In another letter: "He is interested in books on many subjects and I am proud to have such a brilliant husband. But he is obsessed with books on old murder cases, and buys every one he can find. He has made a list of others he wants us all to search for when I get back. I could never enjoy reading such books and he says he doesn't expect me to. This is his hobby, his relaxation. It has been years since I have heard Chinese poetry in Chinese and he reads it beautifully. I feel as if I am in a wonderful dream, and I don't want to wake up."

The next letter: "This is the beginning of our second week together. Today he bought some fine Canadian wool blankets and he wants me to send them to him from the U.S. I think it is because he wants me to pay the huge mailing cost. I am ashamed to write this. After all, that is only one fault in a man who seems to be as perfect as it is possible to be. He may be observing my own faults. He says I am everything he has dreamed of all these years. I can learn to understand his thriftiness. I have long noticed that many wealthy people love their money to the point of obsession."

Sui-Ping loved to spend money giving gifts. We decided that we should advise her to keep her legacy in a private account. That would eliminate or, at least, lessen a prime source of difficulty for both.

"After all those things I wrote, he bought me an elegant, expensive pair of shoes, but he wrote the date in them with indelible ink. This amused me so perhaps I am growing in tolerance. Also he bought me flowers. I love that. Sometimes, as you know, I rest in the hotel while he browses for books. In these times I write in a diary of this almost enchanted experience. When he came in today he brought me the flowers.

"We are not going anyplace tonight. I am glad. He said. 'We must make the most of every moment; we will soon be apart. I will be very lonely until you settle your affairs and come to me for the rest of our lives.' I know I shall be lonely too. This is all so strange."

No letter came from their last week but that was understandable. Then, "Finally, I have a chance to write. I am enclosing my diary. Please meet me if you can. I have all these blankets and part of his books, so I am taking the train. I need some time to myself."

We taped the date and time of arrival on the refrigerator door. We loved trains and even though current rail travel was poor compared to that on the great trains of recent history, we appreciated her need to be alone and were pleased that she should enjoy a train trip, which was now almost as much an oddity as the nature of her courtship and marriage.

"I can't get over it," Kwei-Yin said. "Compared to Mr. Fan, our dates are so dull, I feel lonely just thinking of them."

"Now, Precious Swallow," I teased her. "Remember all the persons in cities unknown to one another, seeking to mate by computer, meeting in single bars, matchmaker clubs that cost from ten to five hundred dollars . . ."

"That only proves that class has no corner on loneliness."

"Or love," I said. No one believed in romance but most hid some longing, some ache, some desire for its magic. False, impersonal words gave it new names, rather high-sounding names that helped cover the emptiness.

"That reminds me," she said, "Where's my little radio? I don't want to miss Dr. Glasser and all those calls about how to find love, how to live with, even how far to go sexually. I like to listen to the callers more than the doctor."

"I always thought people knew such things naturally, but maybe not." Such a plethora of yearning and loneliness in so much freedom! And here was Sui-Ping as yearning and lonely as the rest, who had made not one move to visit an astrologer, a psychic, a private orgy club, a non-denominational church, and she was privileged to be given a fairytale romance. She had just worked, made acquaintances, gave them gifts, dodged certain parasitic young men; and when she read that women far outnumbered men due to wars and homosexuality, she felt herself fortunate to have loved and been loved twice, and prepared to concentrate on a new career. We admired her adaptability and self-sufficiency, and rather thought of her as one of the new women, lonely down-deep perhaps, but new. She did not care a thing for such descriptions, she was simply living her life. She was vulnerable as we all are, and the letters had tenderly and steadily shattered her defenses. Perhaps defenses is not the right word for her self-sufficiency, a misnomer in itself.

We spoke of all these things and more while Sui-Ping was coming south on the train in what we imagined to be an ecstatic, dreamy state. After work we cleaned the house, picked our best flowers, bought her favorite Scotch shortbread cookies, and a bottle of sparkling burgundy. We changed her bed and sprayed her pillow with Caron's Rock Garden before we put on its case. We had a laughing good time with all this silliness and added to it with a last year's Valentine heart placed on her pillow. It was not only that we wished to give her these light pleasures to show her our own, but under the lightness to tell her our love when she would be far away.

"Not to spoil anything," Kwei-Yin said suddenly, "but can two of us manage the rent where there were three?"

"We'll give up meat, expensive shoes. We'll give positive thought to a raise."

"I like this little house and the vacant lot with its wild mustard in the spring."

"We'll manage. We'll be right here for as many springs as we like."

"Oh, you've received a telegram from heaven?"

"No, but Sui-Ping's diary came by air today, and a separate note."

"I wonder why she sent it instead of simply bringing it? Does she want us to read it?"

"I shouldn't think so. No, we mustn't."

"Let's make some tea and read the note. It's thick."

We settled down with our tea and muffins. When I opened the envelope a miniature book fell out. Shakespeare's Sonnets, inscribed with love to Sui-Ping from Teh-Wah. It had the charm of all miniatures; we could not resist reading one sonnet aloud. The note was brief and appeared to be written by a hand that trembled. "Read the diary. Love, Ping." My own voice trembled though I did not know why.

"That's odd. I don't think I want to. Do you?"

"No. But it's a kind of command. It's something she wants us to know that she can't say."

"It seems going a bit far."

I decided to read it to myself. Yin could refuse if she liked.

The book was new and small. In those first days in Canada, Sui-Ping must have bought it to record the unexpected magic. I read a few lines: "We are shy together. He is so serious. But today in the park when we were feeding the ducks, he laughed and I remembered the young boy. At dinner we were much more at ease." Another page: "Teh-Wah keeps saying that I am like someone from an ancient book, that I am innocent and accommodating. An odd term. But am I? He is pleased."

A dated page with the date underlined. "We are married! I had a sensation of having been through it before, exactly. It was as if had I wished to turn back, I could not. As if some numbing power were moving me along. That passed rather quickly. I began to feel very happy and secure. It is not the overwhelming love I felt with Barton. This feels permanent. It is what I need now."

I glanced through a few pages, skipping. "He is so considerate, not rushing me. He says he wants me to learn how happy we can be. Does one have to learn that? Perhaps so. I am not a philosopher. I do not have his intellect. But I have my own ways and I am not stupid. It has never occurred to me to 'learn' men. Seeing Teh-Wah again reminds me that I was brought up to serve them. It has left its mark, I suppose. But taking care of myself has left its mark, too. My mind lives in two worlds, and two are more interesting than one, but I shall keep this to myself. I am content. I think I am happy."

A single entry. "My life now is truly beautiful. Teh-Wah is a gentle, wonderful husband. I trust him and believe that he has loved me all his life, as he says."

All the pages I had just read were crossed out with a big X, the last entry bitterly slashed so that the paper was torn.

I was afraid to go on. A few dates were missed, then the writing resumed, but here the firm Hong Kong script trembled.

"I am writing in the bathroom in my only moments of privacy. I have found a hiding place for this little book. We have not left the room for three days. Our meals are brought up. At such times I am sent to the bathroom, thank God. My life has become a nightmare. I watch for ways to escape but he is always here." The writing was hurried. The abrupt endings and breaks revealed the fear of interruption. "I do not think I can bring myself to write down what has been and is being done to me. Not every hour, of course, but many hours of the night. He tries to soothe me in the days but even in this he knows so many ways to hurt me. Yes, hurt me physically, and that means in every other way, too, because of the intimate nature of these horrors. In the next pages I shall try to be clearer, but I cannot, cannot describe them. If anything should happen to me, I want it known that I am not a party to these torments. He says nothing will happen to me. How I loathe him. I must stop."

The next date: "I still cannot put down what is happening. I am too nervous. I feel weak and dizzy, not only from the pain but the terrible experience that I cannot understand. My suffering gives him pleasure, every kind of pleasure. My tears excite him. I try to cry out, to call for help, but he binds my mouth. I wish I could explain. None of this is violent or brutal in a common way. It is far worse. It is refined as if it is an art he has perfected. I am terrified of this because it is all so subtle. I hurt, hurt, hurt, especially *there* and my breasts. Yesterday he rubbed Tiger Balm on the small cuts and I thought I should faint from the burning. I have not been fortunate enough to lose consciousness. Anyway, I am afraid to."

The next day: "How can such a brilliant man be insane? No, he is not. He does not deserve such an excuse. Besides he never appears insane. In the crudest times he looks at me with such love that I begin to believe *I* am insanely imagining his eyes and face. I do not know how much more I can stand. Since I cannot escape, I long for death. It calms me to remember those words from Lao Tzu. But Teh-Wah will not kill me, especially here."

Another day: "He says he will teach me to enjoy our love. He speaks with great admiration of a Frenchman and his writings. I forget his name and his title. I am not very good at world literature. Teh-Wah says his library will lend me knowledge and wisdom. Lend. (I do not believe wisdom can be learned from books.) He speaks of our quiet future together. He does not care for any social life at all, and I know no one in Singapore. No one would know I was there. It seems because he is a respected scholar, his old friends leave him to his chosen seclusion. He has servants who live in cottages on the grounds, and, of course, I shall have an amah. I..."

I stopped reading. My stunned mind was trying to perceive Sui-Ping's thoughts. My own were saying over and over, "Dear God, she is going through with this marriage."

The next day's entry was in a firm hand. That shocked me still more. "I have just had my bath and a little time to myself. I feel better. I was afraid I was going to break. He is reading. He has read aloud to me all afternoon from an old legal book of terrifying murder cases. He says he is a frustrated barrister. In this way he is able to explain away his fascination with unusual murderers. It seems to me sometimes that he considers they have a special gift. When he hinted at this I could not control a violent trembling. He held me so gently and tenderly, saying, "It is only an old book on one of the dark sides of life. All life is interesting. We must try to understand it all. My little treasured love, you are so innocent you enchant me." He suggested I take a long leisurely bath to feel better. And I do. Oh, why can he not be kind all the time?"

The final entry said: "Teh-Wah's plane left today. He said I must rest here a day before leaving. He hurt me only a little last night. When I cried he said he is going to change and that when I get to Singapore I will see that he has become the man I love. He begged my forgiveness for misjudging my own ability to change. He was very convincing. One of me wishes it were true. One of me gives eternal thanks for immigration difficulties. Teh-Wah reminded me that we are married."

When I closed the book, I gave a long shuddering sigh as she, too, must have done.

"Is that a sigh of vicarious love?" Kwei-Yin was busy making what we called our Eurasian salad.

 "Yin, I can't eat. I'm sorry. Maybe later."

"Well?"

"All I can say is that it is a vicarious experience." I placed the diary on the table beside me. If she wanted to read it it was in sight.

Sui-Ping arrived on an evening train with great packages of Canadian blankets and books. She looked older and her eyes glittered with fear that had not yet worn away or withdrawn into her secret mind. I could see that Kwei-Yin had read the diary; her own eyes were hesitantly observing. She did not need to look hard for signs. Sui-Ping's smile was tense and a small tic appeared at one corner of her lips.

At home we made tea and we did serve the shortbread cookies that she would consider an affectionate welcome. I had put the sparkling burgundy out of sight. While we were speaking of the train, I remembered something I'd forgotten. I went to her bedroom and seized the terrible red Valentine heart as if it were guilty of all the wrong and corruption in the name of love. I could not think what to do with it, and quickly in giddy relief, placed it under the mattress at the head of her bed as if it were a coin for childhood's winged fairy who would take away the ache in exchange for this symbol of romance. To excuse my absence, I turned back the covers. The Rock Garden cologne had faded enough so as not to suggest celebration.

From her bedroom door I said, "You must be tired from the long trip, Ping."

She stood. Kwei-Yin carried her bag, left it unopened and lifted fresh night clothes from a drawer.

"Thank you," Sui-Ping said as she entered. Her voice was pinched as if the small kindnesses were undoing her control. "I want to give you your gifts."

"Tomorrow, Ping."

We hugged her goodnight. Her body was like the stem of a sculptured iron flower.

If her return had been joyful, we should have sat around her room half the night, talking. I knew she was grateful for her benign and solitary bed.

"Tomorrow," she said, "we must wrap the blankets and books and send them to him."

"I'd give them away," Kwei-Yin said.

"No," Sui-Ping said very quietly. "He paid for them. I want to make a complete end."

She was waiting for us to leave the room before she undressed.

Run, Sheepy, Run!

Laurie sat very still in the plush seat and looked out the train window at the low wooded hills of Oklahoma. She had watched every daylight mile for two days and at night had shaded her eyes and pressed her face against the pane trying to see what lay beyond the lonesome dark flying by like a black wind. This was her first journey and the strange earth marked a separation from all that was home, the landscape of Kentucky, her sisters and brothers and friends, her mother and the gravestone of her father in the garden. Now was a new life.

She looked at Clete, asleep, relaxed in his graceful masculine strength, handsomeness all over him, and all the ways she did not know flowing quietly somewhere in him. A great rush of love saddened her. She loved him too much; there was no way to reveal this inexpressible feeling. She watched and listened to be sure that he was truly asleep, then she turned to the window and with a childish young-girl finger wrote in the dust: Mrs. Clete Starbuck.

Clete's hand swiped across the name. She jumped.

"Stop that kid stuff! I told you yesterday if you did that again, I'd—"

She began to tremble and her gray eyes, tender and worshipful, shone with tears. Clete observed her for a moment before a smile began.

"I'd kiss you if we weren't on the train."

"Please, anyway," she whispered.

"What would your mother say?"

"But we're married."

"We're not putting on a show," he said with a finality that scolded her.

At the home wedding her school friends had gazed at them with wonder and affectionate envy, and secret curiosity. This exciting, tiresome journey was their honeymoon. They were going to one of Clete's towns where he had a job and friends, where a baseball manager had hired him as a pitcher. He was already a week late because her mother would not give her consent to the marriage. Clete was a stranger, and an orphan besides, and Laura...

"Hardly sixteen! And young for her age at that! So little, too. Like a child, until you came. She isn't at all grown-up like some girls. Do you know, young man, that she still plays with dolls?"

"Only one," Laurie had ventured. "My favorite."

"She'll soon grow up and stop that."

"I've no doubt," her mother said, cool and resisting.

Clete spoke then with a passion that Laurie relived again and again. "If you don't give your consent so we can get married, we'll run away! I'm taking Laurie back with me!"

"Oh, horrors! I'll not have that disgrace!"

Clete had taken Laurie's hand, pulling her after him. "I hope you'll forgive Laurie, Mrs. Reed. You don't need to forgive me."

Her mother concealed her humiliation in a rush of commands, and won, having lost. The days following she sewed long hours making Laurie a small wardrobe to wear in the "terrible wilds" of Oklahoma. Clete forgot his foolish pride and was openly happy. That first night on the train Laurie cried for her family, cried and couldn't stop; and Clete was furious and shook her. That was a long time ago, two days and two nights ago, and she was still Mrs. Starbuck.

She glanced at the smear of name across the dusty window.

"I've probably made a mistake," Clete said. "What does a man twenty-three want with a child?"

That hurt. She was not a child. She couldn't recall the feelings she had before Clete. She said nothing. Her love was outraged; it ached like an injury. Without interest she saw a ploughed field, the earth rich and brown; and a river with woods on either side. A memory quivered, of embracing sun shafts, of finding violets in the woods, walking and dreaming in the twilight of trees, smelling the damp fallen leaves.

"What are those trees?"

"Wild pecan." He did not even look out the window.

Clete was full of all kinds of knowledge learned in the country and supplemented by reading anything handy. She could ask him odd questions, and she felt proud when she heard him talking with others. He knew the population of cities, the history of wars, facts about weather and crops and animals. He had even talked politics with her mother and they had disagreed about the President. Laurie disliked argument and she didn't care who the President was or what he did but she kept still about it. She might change. She hadn't even got the giggles *once* since she was Mrs. Starbuck. Clete said she had to stop that now and it was almost the hardest thing to do, except that there weren't nearly so many funny things as there had been only two or three days ago. She thought about this without reaching any conclusions, stood up and excusing herself, stepped over his legs and lurched along the bucking aisle to the *Ladies* at the far end of the coach. Inside she studied herself in the mirror to see if she looked married. But how could she? The thought of living in a place of their own made her blush all over and feel a little bit afraid. Keeping house, of course, would be like a game. She splashed water on her face, wished for a bath, and brushed the dust from her dress. Next she unpinned her long blonde hair and twisted it up again, pushing it high above her forehead to add age. Satisfied, she stuck her tongue out, making a "face."

"That's for you, Clete Starbuck! Child! But I know you love me."

When she got back, Clete was over his sulk and his eyes were anxious. "You mad at me, Laurie?"

"No, silly." She thought he seemed disappointed, and she wondered what she had done wrong.

"What's your name, little girl?" he asked in a low, intimate voice.

"Laurie Reed Starbuck," she said coolly.

"From now on, no more of that Southern stuff, just Laurie Starbuck."

She began to cry and before she could turn her face away he smiled. But his smile, his sudden good humor, delight even, confused her terribly. She longed to fall hard into his arms and be comforted and praised and treasured until she didn't mind that Laurie Reed was gone. The imagined wonder of all this soothed her and she fell asleep.

A long shudder and sighing of the train, a screech of brakes, the quick steady rhythm of the wheels slowing, slowing, the whistle dying, the bell ringing, all came into her sleep. Clete's hand touched her awake.

"We're here, Laurie, wake up! Look out the window!"

She obeyed and saw twenty or thirty Indians sitting on horses, all quiet. The Indians wore their long hair in braids, and it was black as a horse's tail. Bright blankets were drawn around their shoulders and moccasins were on their feet. Their faces were dark and impassive, their black eyes were like blackthorn plums, and they were tall strong men.

Laurie felt stiff with terror. She flung herself against Clete and whispered, "What will they do to us?"

"Nothing. They rode by to see the train come in." Clete raised the window and called out names, and two young men rode over, their horses moving along with the train. "Outfielder and second baseman," Clete said to Laurie, and then to the Indians, "This is my wife, Laurie. Ben Good Bear and Lester Crazy Snake." The young men looked at her solemnly and said, "Ho." One of them touched his hair and gave her own a shy glance and said to his companion, "Corn silk." They laughed in embarrassment, and Laurie struggled up through her fright as through a nightmare, and floated free on a wave of giggles. The Indians watched her with interest, and Clete with terrible shame. Seeing his face through her tears of laughter, she called out helplessly, "Oh, Clete, I'm sorry! I've got the giggles!"

"You rob cradle," Crazy Snake announced seriously to Clete. "Maybe twelve years old."

"Heck, no! She's sixteen."

The train stopped with a jerk and Clete carried their bags onto the wooden platform and went to see about Laurie's trunk and hope chest full of linens. Calm now, she drew in a long breath of new and drier air and looked up at the people staring at her. Almost everyone smiled in a friendly way, and a fat man, late it seemed, climbed onto the platform and came over to her.

"Must be Clete's wife." He patted her cheek. "You're no bigger than a trout and just as pretty. I'm McCleary. Doc McCleary. We'll make you happy here." He shouted when he saw Clete and they embraced. "Come on, now, we'll walk up town." He signaled a boy hanging about. "Haul all their belongings to my place, right away."

As the three of them stepped off the platform onto the dirt street, leaving the breathing, hissing train behind, Doc spat ten feet for pleasure.

"Glad you're back from your wanderings, boy. We need you here. Got yourself a nice little bride." He flipped Clete's city hat off and laughed, quaking like a huge mold of jelly. "You been keeping that right arm in shape? We'll work out, easylike, tomorrow."

"No, I'm in shape. I'm ready to go." Clete was laughing and strutting.

"We'll see. That Crazy Snake can hit a ball a mile. You pitch to him you'll be ready for the enemy." He remembered Laurie with words crossing over her. "You'll have to learn all about baseball, little one, and go out Sundays, dressed to kill, and root for our team. A scout looking over the bush leagues tried to get Clete away from us but Clete told him he'd throwed his arm away. Didn't want to leave Oklahoma."

"That was your idea."

"Well, now, it didn't make you miserable, did it?" Doc laughed.

Laurie was staring in amazement at the main street of Indian Feather. High above the dirt streets were board sidewalks and along them were gray unpainted stores and shops. In her own town the grass grew between the bricks of tree-shaded walks, and painted houses were everywhere. Swings kept time in gardens, and horses each of one color, sorrel or bay or white or dappled or black, drew buggies and carriages.

All around her the wild raw face of Indian Feather was bare and strange. She saw one scrub tree far ahead in the street, although woods lined the river outside town. Horses were tied to railings and riders trotted their painted ponies in the little canyon of wooden walls, raising the dust. The Indians rode by going home to the reservation and Laurie noted with relief their many bays and blacks. Clete and Good Bear spoke together in their language and she listened in astonishment.

Ahead, Doc climbed wide splintery steps to the boardwalk above, and all along the way Clete was greeted and Laurie introduced, and nearly everyone joked with Clete about her being "a little girl." An Indian family passed in single file, the man ahead. Laurie stared at the papoose strapped to a board on the squaw's back. The sight of the baby gave her a sudden yearning thrill.

"Look here!" Doc was speaking to her and she had to look away from the baby. "This is the bank. Run and owned by an Indian, been to two or three colleges, smartest man in town. Every week you make Clete give you a little of his money and you put it in there. Understand?"

Laurie smiled up at Doc and said an eager "Yes!"

"I'll handle my own money and give her what she needs and nice clothes."

"Remember what I said, Laurie. Clete spends his money."

"You're damn right I do!"

"Hold your temper, boy. I'm only saying being married will change a few things."

"A few."

"Well, here we are," Doc said to Laurie as if no words had passed between him and Clete.

McCleary's Cafe was painted across the window. The place was small with a counter and oilcloth-covered tables against the wall. Every stool was occupied by men and the two waitresses were busy. Clete spoke to them and followed Doc into the kitchen, and Laurie thought how she was walking behind him like the squaw. The kitchen was steamy hot; two pale sweaty men nodded to them and gave Laurie a cautious glance. The smell of frying grease almost made her sick, and she was relieved when Doc opened a door and they passed into a long narrow hall. At the end they entered a large room and although it was quite removed from the cafe, the odor of stale grease lay in the air. Clete began raising the windows.

The room was raw and ugly like the town, and in it Laurie saw the two men as strangers and herself alone and separate longing to be in her mother's house. Doc left them, and the boy Boze rumbled in with the luggage. As soon as Clete had paid him, Laurie fell on her knees and laid her cheek against the curved top of the trunk and smiled. Clete pulled her to her feet and kissed her and kissed her until she laughed and begged him to stop. When she looked at the room again, she began to see at once how she could change it and make it pretty. She would burn cloves against the invading odors, sew curtains and pillows and take things from her hope chest to make this their home and to remind her of the one she had left.

"When baseball season's over, we'll get a better place. I'll start a small business then."

"Where's the stove?" Laurie whirled around in a dance. "I can cook. There's only that little oil heater."

"We'll have to eat up front till we move. But I don't want you in that cafe except at meals."

"I don't want to go there. But how shall I get out to the street?"

"There's a back door here, locked, but you won't need to go out much. Wait till you get well acquainted."

"But, how, Clete?"

"Oh, at ball games and around."

"I could tell that everyone we met thought I was too young for anything. And they do seem a lot older."

"You'll grow up. You're just right for me. Who else do you need?"

"No one, I guess."

"You guess?" He picked her up and held her in his arms as if she were a baby. "You're such a little thing. I want you all to myself."

"Oh, I like that!"

"Unpack our clothes now."

He brought hot water from the cafe kitchen. "You can take a bath and change while I go to the barber shop for a bath and shave. Then I want you to dress up and we'll go walk around. I want to show you off." He took his best suit and fresh linen over his arm and went out the back way. She heard the key turn in the lock and felt protected.

The room was comfortable with her handiwork. Clete had built a shelf and she had turned it into a dressing table with a gingham flounce. She longed to write home describing her achievements but her sisters might remind her of her old room. She omitted the cafe also from her letters and wrote mostly of the Indians, a Pow Wow they had attended, of once seeing a dead brave's clothing in a tree, of the meadows white with daisies and the river running through the hickory and pecan woods. She mentioned the fine family of Whartons who owned the hotel and of her new friendship with their daughters.

The evenings were long and lonely. Clete sat in the street and talked with the ball players and businessmen. When he went out to practice by day he locked the door and carried the key. The two waitresses were rough young women and made fun of her innocence, and they told Clete when she went out the street door to visit the Wharton girls, making him jealous and angry. At home he was affectionate and they were happy. His possessiveness that had thrilled her at first was bewildering but she defended him in her thoughts, sure that he did not understand how she felt, seldom being with anyone else.

A month had gone by since she had dared visit the Whartons. Kit, who had become her close and confidential friend, must feel betrayed. But she would have to wait. Today after lunch in the cafe Laurie had gone hurriedly to the dry goods store and bought white batiste and lawn and lace and ribbons. She had made up her mind over the tasteless food: she would secretly make baby clothes, and show them only to Kit. Clete promised to open a bakery in the autumn; they planned to work together; there would be less time to sew. To prevent a rumor she told the clerk the material was for doll dresses for her sister's birthday. When she blushed over the lie, the clerk smiled her share in the secret.

Laurie came back flustered and as she passed through the empty cafe, the waitress whom Doc scolded for picking on Laurie stopped her and gaped into her reddened face. "Such school-girl blushes! Flirting with a little boy your own age? What will Clete think?" She lowered her voice. "Really, how old are you, midge?"

Laurie was too much startled to consider the words; she jerked away and bolted as if guilty. She hid her purchases and sat in the new rocker embroidering and listening for Clete's steps as she waited every evening. She imagined him talking with other players, going over every play in last Sunday's game and all others since he had first pitched a ball. He was a good pitcher and one Sunday at the end of the game in Ponca City, the people in the grandstand had gone wild and started throwing silver dollars onto the diamond, chanting his name. She thought her heart would burst with pride in him. The players had picked up the money and filled their caps. The next day Clete treated his teammates to a big celebration, and bought her a sewing machine.

"You won't have to do your sewing at the Whartons any more."

The hall door from the cafe slammed and she ran to look at herself in the mirror, moistened her full lips with her tongue and patted the bosom of her dress under which she was wearing a fluff of small ruffles made that very morning.

Clete's steps were fast and staccato. He flung open the door and as she ran to him in greeting he pushed her away, his face pale with fury. Before she could explain about the batiste and the clerk and his finding out last, he shouted at her and she backed away to stand behind the rocker, her eyes wide and dry, a small flare of rebellion lighting them in a way Clete had not seen before.

"That proves it!" he shouted again. "I should have had better sense. Serves me right."

"I couldn't tell you because it really—"

"No! Somebody else had to tell me. How do you think I felt?"

"Clete, I went to the store to—"

"Lying on top of it!"

"It isn't lying." She felt helpless to explain her impulse so that he would understand.

"Listen here, now, Laurie. You're married to *me*. You belong to me. I've tried to protect you until you grow up a little more." His voice was husky, almost tender.

She stepped from behind the rocker. "I don't need all that protecting, Clete. I'm a married woman." She felt proud and sure, almost grown up.

"Woman? You think you're a woman!" He was angry again. "From now on, you stay out of the cafe and out of the street, unless I'm with you."

"I'd rather just have some fruit of my own."

"From now on, *this* door will be locked too. And don't ask old soft Doc to let you out. I guess you'd better promise that."

She looked down at her feet in the pretty beaded moccasins Clete had bought for her from a squaw. No promise came.

"Promise, I said!"

What did it matter? she thought. "I promise."

"That's more like it. Now, we'll go eat supper."

"I don't want anything to eat."

"Why not?" Clete was impatient and surprised. Then he reached for her hand. "You have to eat, Laurie girl."

"Go on," she said very low.

"All right. I won't beg you. Not after what happened this afternoon. After supper I'm going to play cards with some of the boys."

"Don't send her back here with any of that old greasy food!"

Clete was halfway out the door and he turned and looked at Laurie with new interest. "Well, I'll be—! So that's what a little flirting does to you, puts you on your high horse." He closed the door, turned the key and withdrew it.

Suddenly Laurie realized they had been speaking of two different things and she called out to him to explain.

"Go to bed!" he commanded.

"All right!" It was all the same, no matter what, the door would be locked. "I won't ever tell you," she said aloud in the silent room. Anyway, there was no baby on the way, but there would be in time and she could hardly wait. She would make the clothes in secret.

Slowly she moved to the window, dreaming out into the summer evening, soft and warm and inviting. Moist grass and flower fragrances came from the pastures beyond the town. Someone nearby was hoeing a garden and the fresh rich smell of upturned loam drifted on the air. Dogs barked idly to dogs. The road sounds, the outside sounds of horses' hooves and wheels and the rhythms of leather came muted and melancholy. Supper sounds and voices, too, of fathers, and the long undulating calls of mothers, and children answering, running home.

Laurie turned away from the window and kneeled by her trunk, unlocked it and raised the curved lid. From beneath her clothes and a crazy-quilt she was piecing, she lifted out her big doll. Then she sat in the new chair and rocked back and forth, singing softly for a long time.

The secret noise at the window came through her memories and her singing and her altering dreams. When she heard it finally, she knew it had been going on for quite a while. First, there was a small quick knocking on the wood, next, a small quick pecking on the glass, and whispers and silence and then an urgent whisper of her name, "Laurie, Laurie!"

She rose with the doll in her arms and went to one side of the window, keeping out of sight. Dusk had fallen, the room and the outside were one.

"Hey, Laurie!" A girl's whisper.

Laurie pushed the half-open window as high as it would go and leaned out. Kit Wharton's face loomed in the dark. Laurie heard cautious movements and low titters along the wall.

"Come out and play."

"I can't."

"Come on out, Laurie!"

She hesitated.

"Clete will be out late. He and our brothers and some Indians are running foot races, and I heard them say they're going to play cards tonight."

Laurie held the doll tight against her breast and the doll was alive with her own heart beat.

"Come on."

"I don't want to."

"You do, too," Kit said. "You know you do."

"No, I don't." The doll was warm like a baby. "I have some sewing to do."

"Sew tomorrow."

"What will people think?—me, a married woman."

"No one will know, *woman*," Kit said. The others giggled.

"Well—" Laurie felt sad enough to cry, but she wanted to go. "Give me a minute." She flew to the trunk, locked her doll away, and ran to the window and leaped out into the midst of boys and girls, shadowy and unknown.

"We won't tell on you," a boy said from the dark. "But we got to change your name because we'll be calling. It'll be Whitey."

"We're going to play *Run, Sheepy, Run*. Do you know how?"

"Of course!" Laurie laughed, and peered through the deep evening shade to identify her friends.

"Come on, Whitey!"

Still she hesitated, yearning toward the children and the pleasurable game, yearning back toward Clete and his foolish misery that made him cruel. As if from far away and yet within her a small glow of new wisdom began. She felt old, older than Clete and as young as herself. She could play as a child with the children this night and never again. Her woman's young heart sprang its lock, trembling into new awareness.

"Come on! Play!"

They all turned together and ran fast across the weedy vacant lot. Laurie's long hair fell free of pins. She laughed. She felt her body lifting, parting the silky wind, her legs leaping in hunger and delight, her feet flying, flying through the summer evening. And all around her, laughter darted this way and that like the white-barred wings of the nighthawk gleaming in the dark.

Love Be My Destiny

This morning I fell in love, literally, but it might be more apt, the way I feel, to say I am threatened with love. I am a sensible man. As most people encounter love later in the day, especially at night, I am forced to trust this love for no other reason than that it occurred in the morning, a time when the head triumphs over the senses. This is a logical presage of substance, of a love that could last a lifetime. Is there anything more cruel? More calculated to deprive a man of his true estate? Or mine, at least. If this situation continues, I shall likely be at my wit's end. And, *there is no escape.*

I do not know her name, I have never seen her. And yet she will walk beside me one day soon. Her footsteps are there empty and waiting.

Now, in the evening, I am walking along the deserted beach of this western ocean, thinking of her, thinking of every detail of the morning. When I come to the end, my memory presents me with another run-through, and so on again and again. When shall I see her? Where? An omen of lifetime love and all this uncertainty! This is one reason I came down to the ocean. I had to be alone in the presence of its enormity so that I might recover my sense of proportion, feel puny and logical and clearheaded. I intended to come here in the first place to rest in the sun. Now I cannot rest anywhere, and this is the first day of my vacation from the post office.

The sun has gone down, the sky fiery a moment ago is now like an opening fan of radiance. A small cloud is mauve with the last colors. Far out, there is a shining pool, the high breast of the sea silvered with light. I stand looking out and I cannot feel puny or logical but I feel clearheaded, though not in the way I sought. I feel aware of the great tender sky, the enormous water, the rising tide, and they do not belittle me; they take me in, include me, reassure me that I am a part of this unknowable grandeur. I am child of the ocean, brother to the sun, I am at once identified and blended with all the rest. Isn't that love? Without the addition of that woman? The mere thought of her—well, it isn't like me; I've suspected such ideas. I've never been taken in by any sort of wildness.

The light has gone. The water is leaden, and the sound of the waves is heavier. The foam dashes harder and runs faster and farther up the beach. I walk closer to the cliffs now. In the sudden dark I feel small and fragile; the black ocean is ominous. I try to run up the precipitous path, my feet slipping, my body drawn as by a magnet down toward the dark water, animal-alive now and in pursuit.

Halfway up, I stop for breath, as I'm no boy, and I see Venus all alone, high in the western sky, big and brilliant, and so beautiful that I ache because I'm earthbound.

The moon shows up high and thin; suddenly stars appear and Venus no longer has the sky to herself, but she's the crown jewel. Contemplating these nightly wonders, I forget my tenuous footing in the decomposed granite of this cliff and slide back nearly to the water's edge. Night at sea is peaceful, but there is something terrifying about black primal water in its relentless crash on land's end. I climb again, uneasy with this mystery.

Thank God for light! As I reach the top of the cliff, cars beam their mundane eyes on the coast highway, street lamps are coming on like welcome worldly stars. Thank God for urban mediocrity!

Ugly signs flick the news of their wares: gasoline, beer, fish and seafood cafes, hot dogs and hamburgers. A billboard picturing a steaming cup of coffee as big as a room reminds me that I haven't eaten since morning. Perhaps food will restore my sanity. If not, I am lost. Shall I be lost in that glowing daytime relativity or on that night-ominous water's edge? I must eat! I must search for that cursed house again!

That means I'll not go to the library tonight. I guess I can skip one evening, but I hope no one disturbs the slip of paper I left in that new book because I've forgotten the page. *The Key to Life* or something like that. I just happened on it. I supposed it to be one of those how-to-live books, so popular among our people who are always seeking formulas. I know the key is love, all kinds of love, but knowing is one thing, so I carried *The Key to Life* to the table, trying to conceal the cover and my need, only to find that the subject was the latest laboratory attempt to reproduce life, plain, simple, elusive breath. It would interest me if science would try to make a seed, any seed, from its chemical analysis, and plant it, see if it will grow. I am all for such experiments.

It's a good thing I like to read anything and everything. This turned out to be a fascinating book. I feel a foot taller—mentally. Without any education to guide me (oh, I've been to school), I doubtless make mistakes, but that's half the fun. I respect books. I was born with this respect. I feel sorry for all the people who cannot go to the public library at night; they don't know how it is there, the soft sounds, the quiet people all around you reading at the big tables. I know a lot of people in novels. When I get back to my small apartment in downtown Los Angeles, my thoughts are filled with them. People in the flesh have never been so revealing. In fact, they have eluded me.

Well, I must eat. This place looks clean.

Finished, I realize the foolishness of continuing my search through unfamiliar night streets. I walk along the Palisades under the tall palms and relive the odd experience of the morning. If anyone had ever said.

I don't know where I was, one of the beach towns. I'd been walking and they sort of run together in places. I'm not sure I can find the street again; I left in a daze, and it was a queer little street, ugly as sin, and only a block long. I turned down it to get to the beach.

Part way along this block of very small houses with one-car garages, all old and seedy, I noticed that one had a small well-kept flower garden in front, and in the midst of this bright spot was a dirty child about five, tied hand and foot and wound around and around with heavy twine. It gave me a turn. The child lay still, face hidden in the leaves. I was appalled that no one had seen this little person or called the police. She might still be alive. I felt sick as I bent to see her. She was still warm but lay with closed eyes and open mouth. Without thinking, I quickly cut the string with my pocket knife and lifted her. Suddenly she opened her eyes, looking at me with sullen hatred, jerked out of my arms and stood up. She hit me with both fists and kicked my shins. At the same time there was a roar of homemade roller scooters down the hill street and three children, all dirty, stopped.

"Look what you've done," a small boy said, indicating the ruined string. "She's the dead body."

The others stared at me with a suspicion so deep that I felt guilty. Just then a woman appeared, indefinite in the dim room behind the screen door, and the children left without haste.

"Are you my ten o'clock?"

"I beg pardon?"

"My ten o'clock. Don't stand there, please. Come in."

"But—I—"

"Come in." She opened the screen and glanced up and down the street, and appeared to be in a hurry for me to get in out of sight. I went in. "No need to be embarrassed. A movie star, a name that would make your mouth water, was here last evening, and a scientist from the rocket center just left."

I must confess I was puzzled.

"I get all kinds," she assured me. "But I never reveal names."

She said these things in a pleasant voice, smiling and walking ahead of me. She was wearing her hat in the house which seemed odd to me, a small flowery affair perched on a head of naturally curling sandy hair. I remembered reading that fashionable career women wore their hats at their desks, and I was tempted to smile at this caste insignia. She wore her inexpensive clothes with a certain businesslike flair, yet there was something warmly old-fashioned about her and the whole room. A rare fragrance too. She caught me breathing in.

"I'm baking a frozen pumpkin pie. Like pumpkin?"

I was about to thank her and be on my way when she startled me again.

"This must be your first time. You're going to make me late with my eleven o'clock, so we'd better start. What will you have, the regular?"

"The regular what?" I nearly shouted, coming to my senses in the midst of all this nonsense.

"Regular or trance, sir."

I stared at her.

"Because we're so late, I suggest regular."

I still stared.

"Do you want your reading, or not?"

"No, I don't!" I said, "And I don't know how I got into this house, and I am not your ten o'clock. Please excuse me. There is some mistake."

"Certainly, sir, if you feel that way."

I felt rude and sorry for it, and said so.

The telephone rang. I gathered that the ten and the eleven o'clock were friends who wanted to change to another day. The telephone rang again and someone wanted urgently to come by at noon. I watched her. Her small face bones were lost in flesh. She wasn't bad looking at all, and I had the feeling that her friendly expression was not put away with her hat.

She went over to a small dining table and sat down, indicating a chair to me. "I'm getting words, words all around you, books, that's it, and words in your head too. You have a lot of fine thoughts and feelings you never express except to yourself. Reserved. Afraid, maybe. Well, you needn't be." She closed her eyes. "My goodness, but you are coming through to me! That tall, sharp-faced girl with blond hair, long ago, her name begins with R . .. Ruth, no, Ruby. Ruby, isn't it?"

I said nothing, sat down, determined not to give her any clues. I felt so ridiculous that I glanced toward the door and saw with relief that she had closed it.

"Well, it's Ruby, I know that. She made fun of you when you quoted a love poem to her, and you've clammed up ever since."

How could she be reading my mind when I hadn't thought of Ruby for years?

The woman in front of me began to shuffle a deck of cards thick with use. She dealt them out, talking all the time about coming events. The plastic tablecloth was an abomination, and an annoyance to me.

"Those cards," I interrupted her, "they don't know anything about me."

"But *I* do." She smiled sweetly. "They help me concentrate, since you are such a doubter. But don't underestimate the cards themselves." She went on with her revelations.

In spite of myself, I thought what a wholesome-looking woman to be in the sorcery business.

"I see you walking out of the shadow onto a long sunny road. Your footsteps are ahead of you and so are those of another. You step ahead into yours but there is no one beside you to step into the others."

"What does that mean?"

"Behind you they might mean a loss, but ahead of you, someone is about to enter your life."

"Unwelcome," I said. "I like my life the way it is."

"Well, I can't help that. I am only telling you what comes."

She stopped abruptly and put the cards to one side. I watched her face for some mysterious expression but the whole time she might have been a housewife ordering the groceries.

"What is your fee?" I asked, taking out my billfold.

"Three dollars, and five dollars for trance, but nothing to you. You came here, as you would say, by accident. But when things started coming through I couldn't resist telling you."

"I'm afraid I've never set much store by fortune-telling."

"Fortune-telling is an unpleasant phrase," she said, without offense. "Unscientific. I'm sure you've read of Extra Sensory Perception, ESP, and the serious scientific investigations."

"I did read that it was much higher in dogs than in human beings."

She laughed at me gently.

"Where do all you fortune-tellers, excuse me, go to learn such things? Secret schools?"

"I was born with this gift. When I was a child I told what came into my awareness even more clearly than now, but I learned soon to conceal it or be laughed at. Just as you," she added slyly. "Nine years ago when I was left a widow and had to consider quickly how to earn a living, I remembered this gift and felt guided to use it. Word of mouth brings many people to see me. I am careful just to make a living, not to profit."

She spoke sincerely, I believed her, and under my astonishment at her humility and lack of mystery, I felt admiration and apology.

"I must have my lunch now and rest a little before my twelve o'clock."

Again I admired her, admired the straightforward way she put me out. I insisted on paying but she absolutely refused.

I left in a state of bewilderment, failed to notice the name of the street or the cross street, walking miles going over all she had told me of my past, my character and the hints at my future. The whole thing was incredible, and I was embarrassed to admit that I could find no reason to doubt her.

It is the ninth day of my vacation. It isn't entirely wasted as I have combined my love of walking with my search for that little street where the fortune-teller lives, and while it seems to me that I have walked in all the streets of all the beach towns, I have not found that one. At times, I believe that I was never there, that the whole thing is a fantasy brought on by so much reading. Then, I remember those footprints.

My reading has suffered. Many nights I came on the bus to walk by the ocean. When I did go to the library, I read from respectable books and magazines on various psychic phenomena, and am almost ashamed to say that my views have altered somewhat. It is still a skittish subject—unreliables in this field as in all others.

My object is to call upon that woman again, be able to converse upon the scientific aspects of her profession, just to show her a respect that I fear was rather lacking before. Then, perhaps without humiliating myself, to ask for a reading; she may once more find me "coming through" and be able to tell me about the person who will sooner or later walk in those footsteps beside me. This time, of course, I will insist upon paying her fee.

I can discuss these footprints with no one, no one, for fear of being thought deranged, a judgment I have already passed upon myself. Nevertheless, it is no joke to have such a nebulous idea planted in one's mind where it lies in wait, and to have lost the only person who can perhaps release me.

For nine days I have been plagued by an apparition who walks across my thoughts. I try to imagine *her*, to bring her to life so that I can cast her out. Yes, cast her out. Before I became obsessed in this hopeless and idiotic way, my life was fine, lonely, it's true, but I wasn't complaining. I kept busy. No use to linger on the painful fact that in all this huge city I have made no real friend. Acquaintances, yes. And we have some good discussions at the post office. The Mozart fellow and the Wagner man were going hammer and tongs when I left. I learn a lot that way. But, how can I cast her out? Is it possible? She has become a part of my life. I cannot take a step without thinking of her.

Last night when I arrived home, the apartment looked barely large enough for me. But this was going too far, and I said as much to the spirit of her who haunts me. This place has years of my own stamp, although someone else might enter and imagine that no one lives here; that is, unless he or she *(she?)* looked into my bedroom and saw all the library books and the paperbacks piled up beside my bed. What a perfect retreat for the bachelor that I am!

I am making progress. I took a vow to waste no more time in search of the fortune-teller's house, to get hold of myself and resume my life. It is impossible to go back to where I was, but I can put this adventure in parentheses, and go on from there.

So I thought, but now, I am also growing superstitious. A luxury in this enlightened age. From now on, I shall keep all boasts of progress to myself, give them no chance to turn on me. For, here I am at the ocean again, and I am walking in an ugly beach town. Many of the others were pretty, so—yes, I am in the vicinity at last. How could I ever not have found it before? There is that abandoned King Tutankhamen building which aroused memories of my youth, that foolish period in the twenties when the girls tried to look like Egyptian beauties, and even their dresses were printed with the old fourteenth-century Pharaoh's tomb and its treasures. But I am not one for nostalgia. Very soon now I shall find her street, the fortune-teller's, and I shall waste no time; I shall ask her to exorcise this phantom.

"Look out!"

Such a roar. Off the sidewalk just in time. The same dirty children: two of them pulling a toy wagon, and in it a sailor's duffle bag and in the duffle bag the same little girl, the dead body. Her head is out, the bag drawn at her throat, and her face once again obligingly simulates death. What, I wonder, will happen to that child when she grows up?

Well, here is the miniature house with the miniature garden. I must make a mental note of how I got here. King Tut will do the rest.

Interesting. No answer to the bell. Once more. Patience now. Still, no answer. Beside the door is a little wooden box with the words: *Leave a Message.* How would I identify myself? I gave no name, did not ask hers. Anyway, why should I leave a message at all? But, how can a woman like this simply lock the door and go out when people high and low are calling on urgent matters, none more urgent than mine? I must see her, I simply *must.* She got me into this; she will have to get me out. In a few days I go back to work. How can I keep my mind on government business, money orders, and registered letters when at any moment a strange woman's steps will join mine, and the whole snug pattern of my life will be undone? Never again to go nightly, if I wish, to the public library; never again to read silently in bed; never again to walk miles and miles, in a country where no one walks; never again to come home to an empty house, to a can of fine sardines with slices of onion. A tomato. An apple. Later, my pipe. Alone with the many thoughts that leave no room for more. No. Instead a warm dinner, talk, the clatter of dishes, talk, TV no doubt, books unread, life flying by.

Another ring. No answer. Why is the blind down? Moved. Gone. Well, this is the end. I am lost. I have always been a calm man. Once my thoughts were orderly. Lately, they rush and tumble. Well, nothing for it but to go my way.

What, may I ask Fate (I am now ruled by Fate; how else explain the footprints?), what *is* my way? Before Fate can reply and cause more damage, I answer myself: my way is the library and there I am going. I will find clarity there. No time to ride into the city. I'll inquire for the local library. No, I must go to my own. I want to read more from a book by the English essayist Lucas, *The Search for Good Sense.* It turned out to be over my head, but the title promises. I have never used this word in my life, but I use it now: I am *desperate.*

Good to be back in the library, like coming home. Found my book. Oh, this respectful quiet. Here's a good chair by the window, natural light streaming in. If I can have an hour or two of peaceful reading, I can get control of myself, accept the cruel fact that that fortune-teller has moved, disappeared, vanished. So be it. Here's

Lucas to give me a hand. This doesn't apply to my problem, but just as well, gets my mind off myself.

Odd, that woman's back looks familiar. My attention was not in the habit of jumping about like this before. I wish she would turn her head. No one from the post office. I'll just walk by the stacks and glance at her. Hm-m-m. Reading one book, another unopened. *The Romance of the Mails.* It's she, all right, the fortune-teller. So, that's it! Footprints, indeed. She knew all about me with her ESP, a bachelor, good job, savings, government pension when I'm retired; she planted those footsteps in my mind, and she knew I'd come back. Probably practices Black Magic, too, and could will me back or send herself in some weird or enchanting form to influence me. This is, of course, now I see it, the reason she wears these plain, nice, housewifely clothes. Well, Madame Psychic, you will never see me again. I see my own footprints straight ahead, *alone.*

It is possible, though, that she is a simple good woman, with a strange gift, and that she did see those footsteps? No, *The Romance of the Mails* proves what she is up to.

"I beg your pardon." She is speaking to me very low and rather sternly at that. Well, no wonder, I am just standing here staring at her books. "Oh, aren't you. . . ? Well, how nice, how surprising." She indicates the book on the mails. "Have you seen this? I had to come in to the main library to look up some old books, and just happened on this."

Just happened. "Very nice to see you. I won't interrupt you."

"Thank you," she says, "I do have to finish."

Now, what to make of that? Well, back to *Good Sense.* A sly one, clever too. And why not, since she can read my mind? At least, such a woman doesn't have to be told when she isn't wanted. I'll have to read another day; I can't concentrate.

Out in the sane fresh air again. A free man, cured of my aberration. I'll sit here in the sunshine and enjoy my sanity.

Is that she again? I've been here longer than I thought. I'm bound to speak to her. After all, she is no ogre and neither am I.

"Just loafing today." I laugh like a free and happy man.

"Have you been to the beach lately? The weather is just heavenly."

"No. I've been cooped up in this library, having a fine vacation reading all I want for a change."

"Oh." Her voice is sympathetic. "On your vacation, you should get some sun. I get out every day for a short walk. But this is the free day I give myself, and I'm eager to get home." She is walking away. "It's nice to see you again."

Women! I wonder if I am mistaken about her? If I am, then the footprints are real, and I need her help. Everything is starting up again! Will I ever get out of this trap?

"Is it asking too much. . . ?" I begin walking fast after her.

"Oh, would you like a ride to the beach? I'll drop you anyplace you say."

"Thanks, but what I really want..." (how embarrassing) "...is to ask if you could possibly give me a reading this afternoon?"

"Oh, dear, is it that urgent? Would tomorrow do?" Her expression is kind, concerned even.

I feel bold, and, yes, desperate. "It is urgent."

"Oh, dear." She is hesitating. "I do want my *long* walk today. You see, today and Sunday I take very long walks." She is considering. "This suggestion is rather unorthodox, but if you care to walk part way with me, I'll see what comes through."

I thank her too fervently, but it is a relief.

She is a good driver, serene in heavy traffic. By taking the freeway as far as it goes, we are at her place in less than an hour. She hasn't said a word. Getting her psyche together probably. I am trying to keep my mind blank. Impossible.

I wait while she changes to casual clothes and sneakers. As soon as we are on the beach she takes off the sneakers and walks barefoot, and suggests I do the same. There is something intimate about this, but she is so impersonal that I feel unaccompanied. Walking is easier on the damp sand and now and then the tide rolls in deliciously over our feet.

"If we have any luck out here and anything of help comes through, you are at liberty to go back whenever you like. I don't want to impose several miles on you."

"Impose? I'm a great walker myself."

"Not really?"

"I am. Walking and reading are my great pleasures."

"Very rare." She says this with true appreciation.

"You don't need your playing cards?"

She laughs. "At this time of day when the people have gone, there is nothing better for me than the ocean and the beautiful sky." She takes a deep breath. "And my feet in the wet sand."

It is only now, this very instant, that I see them! *Them!* I can hardly believe my senses. I have a queer prickly feeling—awareness of all my pores, of the hairs rising in primitive terror. I must look back at once, but I cannot, I cannot turn my head. My gaze is fastened on the scene before us. I feel cold, an unearthly cold.

"Look!" My voice sounds like a croak. "Look!"

She looks at me strangely.

"No, not at me! Look there, ahead of us!"

"Why, I don't see anything unusual."

"The footprints! They are there, and we haven't even walked there yet. Isn't *that* unusual?"

She is smiling. All the simplicity is gone. That smile is so frightening in its utter occult sweetness that my body responds with the strength to turn and look back. What I see now is even more appalling. There are no footprints behind us! I feel chilled to the bone. I am in the presence of something obscure and unknowable. And I am trapped. By her. But I will not be. I will run, run. I cannot move. My feet are fast in the sand, with the steps before us that we have not taken, and none behind us where we have walked.

I have this mad thought: here is my Destiny, face to face. There is no use to resist. It was destiny that caused me to pass her house that day, and she knew it; destiny today at the library; destiny now. There is no free will. How can I deny this proof? There is no way out. I must submit, but I shall try to do so with dignity. I want to fall on the sand and weep.

"Do you feel better?"

"Thank you, I'll manage now."

"Was it this made you ask for the reading today?"

"Yes." My voice is barely audible. I am a modern man, scientifically oriented, and I have just been through the experience of a lifetime. Bewitched. I want to be quiet, just to walk, and not to look at the sand again.

"Try to relax," she is saying.

"It takes time." She should know that without ESP.

We walk for a long while in silence. Since those cursed footprints "came through," there is no need to talk. But I am not a devious man, I don't beat about the bush. Already I am wondering whether or not we should give up both our places and find a new house or apartment; or perhaps she should move into mine. Give up fortune-telling altogether. The income would be nice, but—well, we might drop the cards and use only the scientific approach.

"How would you feel about giving up your work?"

"Why should I?" she replies. "I'm twenty years away from the pension, and even then, I'll keep on because it is my purpose in life, God-given, the way given me to help others."

Have to go easy on that for a time. I can see she wants her own money; and how many people understand their purpose?

"Have you lived at the beach long?"

"Years, and I'd never live anyplace else. Don't praise the city to me."

Since she knows my fate is sealed, so to speak, she is not giving in on any score. This will be a long way from my work, and I cannot help thinking with love of my little private apartment. I'll bide my time. Things change.

"Are you tired?" she asks kindly.

"No. Remember, I love to walk."

"Well," she laughs, "we have that in common."

I feel better. I may as well accept the inevitable. "What, may I ask, are your opinions on marriage?"

"My goodness, you are curious. But an exchange of views is the best way to get acquainted."

"Very necessary."

"Personally, I don't care to go through that ceremony again. But each to his own desire."

This is really shocking. A woman of her age, too. Not at all bohemian in appearance. First one I've ever met. "You will pardon me, but I thought of you, that is, I respected you as a more traditional woman. What do you recommend in the place of marriage?"

"Nothing in the place of marriage. Marriage is fine. But for me, I recommend living alone just as I am. I love my work, my tiny house, my freedom."

This woman is perverse, as I've read women are. After leading me, forcing me really, into this fated position, she wants me to go through the game of proposals and refusals and more proposals.

"Don't you think we should turn back?" she asks.

Oh, that I could! But what is the use? When I recall those footprints for even a moment, I get the same strange feeling that this woman who is to be my wife is, in all probability, a witch, an enchantress, though she appears neither.

We turn back, walk a short distance when she suddenly stops. The sun is down now, and breathtaking clarity is in the air, making everything brilliant. The reflected last light has turned the water amethyst. We watch the color go and the water become gray, heavy, ominous, its powerful tide pounding farther up the beach.

She is standing in the deep water. "You are coming through to me now," she says in a contradictory way, and begins to laugh and laugh. She runs up the beach and drops onto the cold dry sand, looking at me, pointing even, and laughing.

"The footprints!" She screams her words in this fit of laughter. "I *thought* you were talking awfully queer." She gets up and runs about, bending over, bobbing up, laughing without control. "You were even proposing to me! Trapped by Fate," she mocks. "Oh, you were funny. Please forgive me, I can't stop this crazy laughing." Her words tumble about so that I can hardly understand them. "I forgot all about those footprints last week; I see so many people. Then, you were shocked because you thought I didn't believe in marriage. Oh, you poor good man. Is it possible?" She stops to get her breath and goes on. "I don't want to marry anyone. I like my state, now that I've got used to it. I am 'set in my ways' and so are you. You don't really want to marry anyone, either, do you?"

"Then, what *about* those footprints?" I demand.

"I shouldn't have done it; I really don't do such things, but I *saw* you alone reading, reading, reading; and I thought you seemed rather lonely that day. Sometimes a person is set free to hope, or act by a suggestion, and that leads to a less lonely future, or..."

"I'm not lonely," I say, sorry at once that my tone is defensive.

"Then, I made a mistake."

I feel rather angry. All that laughing and deception, and offensive pity. "Then, what about the real footprints? The ones here today in the sand?"

"I've seen them many times. Someone has walked along and left a trail of prints. You weren't noticing before, but you did notice while they were still fresh ahead, and after they had been washed over or saturated behind you. They would not have seemed mysterious at all if you hadn't been in such a state, and I'm terribly sorry. Really, I am. The rest of the reading was true, wasn't it?"

"Yes, that was the trouble."

"May I invite you in for a cup of tea when we get back?"

"Thank you."

"I'd even ask you for dinner, but this night out of all the others, I just open a can of tuna and make a salad from my garden." She pauses. "I hope you'll forgive me about the footprints."

I suppose I may as well forgive her, now that I'm free. And I actually enjoyed all that laughter. She is quite a woman.

"As you haven't planned dinner, perhaps you'd join me." I am inviting her mostly to show that I forgive her.

"I'd love to," she says.

I feel like a new man. I don't believe a word she said explaining away those footprints. They were real—both times. She's just embarrassed to be caught in her own destiny business. I'll have to go slow.

The Vine by Root
Embraced

Nurse Ko Mai Ying lived in the small happy household of her First Uncle Ko See Ming and his two servants and their child. Her parents had died of the plague in the late Twenties when she was fifteen, and the six years with her uncle had brought her closer to him than she had felt to her busy, fashionable parents. Ko See Ming was busy too, but not fashionably so; he was a scholar busy with his books and his students, many of whom imperiled themselves in actions for reforms. Ko See Ming worried about them and cautioned them, but he too was a man of ideals. He permitted Mai Ying to attend the university and to study nursing, as she wished. And now, she had been more than a year at the hospital.

"Well," he asked her on one of her days off, "what has happened to all this talk of your wanting to study medicine in the United States?"

"I want to," she said blushing, "but I feel sad to leave the hospital." There was one thought she would not confide to her uncle. He had never married, appeared always reluctant to discuss his youth, and yet he was too wise to have lived only within the covers of his books.

"You do not look like a nurse or a doctor, anyway," he said, teasing her, "more like a flower."

"What, Ming-Sook, does a nurse or a doctor look like?" she flared. "And what flower?"

"O, not a jasmine or a pear blossom, but a daisy perhaps."

"Good," she said, believing him.

"A pretty daisy with attentive black eyes, not vain like the jasmine, doused in perfume, but tender just the same, and innocent."

"O, Ming-Sook!" she laughed, and blushed again, wishing that Dr. Chung would think of her as a daisy.

"I understood," her uncle said, "that nurses soon got over blushing."

"My work is not all of me! Should I change altogether?"

"No, no. But, tell me, who is this young man, the thought of whom makes you blush?"

"There is none," she said sternly. "The blood flies to my face at too many things. It is embarrassing."

"You are a strong girl," he said, "but sensitive too. No need to be embarrassed. Besides, I hear you are a good nurse."

Mai Ying was a good nurse; although new in experience, no one need question her serious intention and her desire to help people in their suffering. Because of this she felt subtly related to Dr. Chung Wai Tong. Dr. Chung was thirty, an age, in his country, when he should have been married and the father of children. Because he was so preoccupied with his work, because his reputation in the hospital was respected and secure, no one made jokes to hurry him, no one, that is, except the worn old men. Even they were cautious before his stern face and dedicated ways.

The nurses were afraid of him, but only because they suspected he could divine their inadequacies, and more so, because of his purity. Their harmless flirtations took on an aspect of evil in their own eyes if Dr. Chung's clever eyes saw them. It seemed to them that he needed no respite from the hard, tiring work; but as much as they admired him they could not wholly imitate him.

Mai Ying was not afraid of him in any way. Even his purity did not frighten her, but rather attracted her; she was more afraid of the worldly men and their bright talk and bold eyes. When the other nurses spoke of Dr. Chung's quietness, she only smiled to herself because to her his smooth, withdrawn face was not quiet at all but suggestive of emotions which she could not read, a turmoil under the surface which fascinated her curiosity. She indulged in romantic thoughts about Dr. Chung, which was against the rules, but who could govern such irrepressible mysteries?

She expressed her desires in the quality of her assistance to him, working so untiringly that he at last appeared to notice that she was devoted to him as well as to her work. This was very embarrassing to her although she had dreamed a thousand times of such recognition and its blissful results. Each night before she went to sleep she tirelessly sent her thoughts through the same fantasy: she would go to the United States to study, Dr. Chung would go for special study; they would return and work together, two doctors, in a hospital with the most modern equipment and the most progressive treatment. Later, she would take time out for two children, but she would always practice beside her husband, giving the three of them her abundance of love.

In a moment's rest from duty, she secretly watched his face for a sign, and was sure that she saw the change she felt in her own: an articulate warm glow filling the eyes, so that they must avoid direct looks; a softness come to the tense mouth; his whole face alive with communication, held back.

Before he had spoken to her, she was summoned by her uncle and told that Dr. Chung had asked for permission to marry her. Since Uncle Ming was a remarkably modern man, he withheld his willing permission until he knew her wishes. She was so overcome by this answer to all her yearning that she nearly fainted.

"For such a little one," Uncle Ming said, "such large feelings!"

She smiled at his goodness.

"You treat me as a son," she said happily.

"As a daughter! As a daughter should be treated."

There could be no objection. Dr. Chung came of a good family. "A family with money," her uncle said, "but don't let this be important to you. It is important only to the outward eye trained in search of its customary value." Wai Tong was the only son and therefore given every opportunity. His four sisters, all older, were married and now attached to their husband's families. His father had died when he was a child. After his sisters married he and his mother lived on in the large old family house, alone except for the servants and the visiting relatives. Wai Tong had never been away from home, since the university and this hospital were in his own city.

They were engaged and Mai Ying moved through the days as in a silky dream. But there was one disappointment. Her work that she loved and for which she had prepared in desire to help the sick was suddenly as nothing. Dr. Chung did not request her resignation; he assumed it. Discussion had the air of superfluity. He was a man of tradition. In love, she had neglected to notice that, and there had been little conversation between them. Mai Ying became troubled by a sense of waste and uselessness. She had no taste for the fruitless lives of women who strenuously pursued their own pleasure. She had been surrounded by that dead sea of restive leisure all her life and she yearned toward the fertile landscape. How could she go calling endlessly, receive guests endlessly, sleep late from night parties, play bridge and mahjong, go to the dog races, the horse races, the bay shore, the mountains, shopping for pleasure instead of necessity? Would she not remember the people in their narrow beds wanting a drink, wanting relief from pain, wanting death, wanting to be well again? These things she said only to herself, quietly in her mind, because—was it not a fact that she wanted to be married? Wasn't it a miracle that she was marrying a man she loved? Through love she would lead him to understand her desires.

They were married and she moved into his mother's house. Madame Chung, a small, heavy-faced woman of uncertain age, accepted her with courtesy but no warmth. Her eyes shone only for her son. In his presence her morose face became animated with youth; her voice rose lightly; she chaffed him for his silence. Mai Ying at once felt herself an intruder but she believed the old woman in some way glad. She gave her the attention she had so recently given others, quietly, modestly, waiting for the mother's affection to grow.

Relatives came and went, the smothering, numberless aunts, uncles, cousins. There were large chattering dinners at which the laughter and hardly concealed animosities fastened themselves to her clean and tender mind in whirling, mis-mated patterns. Mai Ying was soon aware that there was little affection within this family but instead a determined collusion that wore the face of loyalty. How often she longed for the company of Uncle Ming even in the new weeks of her marriage! Together they always spoke of his ideas that were warm with sympathy and kindness, of her work, of the future of their country. Often they had been joined by professors from the university and by her student friends. Their speech was not masked as that of the Chungs, but wore its true face. They talked simply or importantly, they made plans, they were serious, they laughed, they drank tea, and Mai Ying had gone to bed with her whole being aglow like a lamp in the dark lighting a path.

Where in this house of dead talk and corroded spirits was a light on any path? Her thoughts of the future burrowed in a dark tunnel. She heard the heavy door at its end slammed to with muffled sound as if by a slow damp wind. It was her duty to stay within this family whose wealth bought them no stores in the public market of the heart.

Her husband was the only image of love and she waited for him each night with trembling expectancy which she had learned within the first days of her marriage to conceal before his mother. Wai Tong was not talkative and often ate his meals in weary silence, but when he entered the door she noticed a subtle glow under his pale skin, and his eyes though shielded revealed a message.

At night in their room he was withdrawn and shy and because of her own intimate shyness, they could not approach the full expression of their love. Each day she thought of little ways to cross this cool stream of virginity between them, and each night she failed.

Her amah watched her with a patient, closed face, but if they were in the room together the old woman's face creased into wrinkles of humor and mischief. She kept her voice low, telling her the tale of her marriage night. And a good thing, she said, there was no amah in the household of her husband's family to check the marriage bed and report to his parents; the husband of her lady had initiated her against her will.

Mai Ying blushed in shame and confusion at the everyday words splashed on the tender poem of her desires.

"I am old," her amah said. "In the end we are all alike except for station and that is natural."

Mai Ying opened her lips to object but closed them quickly. The old woman's loyalty lay with Madame Chung.

"In a little while your blood will stay where it is and not fly into your face at the mention of a man and a woman. That too is natural." The furrows of her face tracked merrily upward towards her eyes like the imprint of a hen's feet in the soft earth. "Besides," and now her mouth turned down like the curve of a rooster's tail, "it is only a burden when a woman is tired, and when is she not? A woman like me. For that time with a woman a man has no flowers or bird songs; he puts them only in the poems."

"Perhaps not all men," Mai Ying ventured, "and it is good to have poems."

"Poems!" the old woman said bitterly. "When will the great he-male of this earth act as he speaks?"

"He will!"

"He? Cher da pow! He rolls out the big guns!"

"Not all, amah. Some both speak and do. Some have no voice. Have you?"

"Hah! What a voice I have! It can be still as a mountain, or coo like a nesting bird or roar like a beast. Do you think even a whisper could reach through the thick walls of this house?"

"This house is old, amah, it is falling down."

The old woman was confused, then she said in a low, sly voice, "There is rot in this house but not in the walls."

The girl was silent.

The amah said playfully, "So? You are going to be a man?"

"I never said that. I want to be a woman. A whole woman, free to help."

"Help what?"

"History."

"Eh?"

"Ourselves."

"Such wild talk! Student talk! You are young and will come to your senses."

"No! No!"

"Well, don't worry now. In secret we are as good as the men. As for help, haven't we always worked ourselves into the grave? If you mean me to read a book or write one or make a public speech and spectacle of myself, then, I cannot."

"O, there are many things we could do!"

"The best is to seduce your husband as soon as possible. It may settle many things."

That night Mai Ying spoke to her husband about returning to the hospital. He put on an air of aged patience and he appeared to be delighted with her.

"You are like a child," he said. "How do you forget so soon that I should lose face?"

"O, face!" she said impatiently.

"You *are* a child, but you will learn its importance."

"And its inflexible strength!" she said. It had the grip of a dead man's teeth on all their lives but she dared say no more.

"It is unfortunate for women to be educated," he said coldly. "Their minds fly off toward every new idea and they have no respect for the things we have lived by for centuries."

"I have respect for the good in our tradition; I have none for the false."

"Go to bed!" he commanded.

She went softly to bed and after a while she spoke gently into the stiff silence that filled the room and pressed against their breath. "I was not a child in the hospital."

He took her into his arms, but she could only weep and he tried to console her, speaking tenderly, almost with love. To her ears his words sang against the silence like little bells. In the first of her sleep she heard the cautious slup of small slippers beyond the door. Amah, she thought drowsily, but she was too much wounded and in love to be angry.

"Little wife," the small bells rang far away, "do not go to sleep."

But the bells rang like a whimper, louder and louder, and they were not now her husband's voice but a voice in another room, someone in pain. She sat up in her bed, thinking she was on duty, thinking that someone needed her.

"What is it?"

"Mother!" he said. He leapt from the bed.

"She is ill. Go quickly."

They hurried together down the hall and entered her room without knocking. The old woman sat stricken in her bed moaning and crying.

"Where is the pain?" Mai Ying asked kindly. The mother waved her aside and spoke sharply to her son.

"She does not want anyone to see her when she is ill," he said simply. "Go back to sleep. I will take care of her. She is used to me."

He did not return all that night, and for three days the mother lay in her bed, seeing no one but her amah all day, demanding her son's presence all night. On the fourth day she appeared well and sat in the garden. In the afternoon she sent the amah with a message that she wished to be amused and Mai Ying joined her for a game of cards. Time after time the mother won and finally, clapping her cards upon the table triumphantly, she declared, "You are no competition for me! You have youth but I have experience. Tell me, now, which is best?"

Mai Ying's thoughts, that had taken refuge in the green dusk of the magnolia tree because she felt the other woman pierce her tenderness, clung briefly to its white flower. A magnolia tree is always planted in a rich man's garden, she mused.

Madame Chung waited. She grabbed at a baby spider letting itself down from the tree; catching its life line she blew the insect to and fro with her heavy breath. The little creature appeared to climb the air, retreating, but going toward her hand where the thread was held. She pulled, trying to break it, and, failing, let go. The spider fled with all the fury of its instinct and swung free.

"Which?" she said, bored.

"Experience," the girl said, without knowing, but she saw by the woman's lively demanding eyes that she expected this answer.

"So." Madame Chung pursed her lips with satisfaction. "Youth wears away, experience grows. I am no longer young, but I shall never be old."

Mai Ying wished to be excused but she dare not leave until her husband's mother released her. There was a long silence in which the woman sat ticking an earring back and forth with a thick forefinger. She seemed highly pleased with her victory at cards.

At last she ordered tea and while they waited she studied the girl minutely.

"Daughter?" she said in a tone of delicate mockery. This was the first time she had used this name, and Mai Ying felt frightened that she was about to command her to some impossibility.

"Yes, mother."

"Are you a proper wife for my son?"

The girl started.

"Your amah has brought me no evidence from your marriage bed. Have you had lovers?"

"No! O, no!" She began to tremble.

"You are a modern girl and your ideas are not mine. You have worked, and it was not necessary. You have been free with yourself."

"But, I have not!"

"Then?"

"Please, I cannot speak of. . . !" She rose and would have left the garden.

"The tea is here. We will play another game of cards. You must improve yourself. You must learn how to speak to your elders."

In the evening Wai Tong's barely concealed eagerness to be with his wife withdrew when Madame Chung revealed that she had been offended. They retired early. Mai Ying had been drained by the mother of that day's spirit and strength; she felt weak in her loneliness and she asked a simple question seeking comfort.

"Do you love me?"

The doctor took off his glasses, placed them carefully on top of the old teak-wood chest with his ring and his watch. He appeared naked to her as if he had just taken off his clothes in public. He slipped the knot of his western necktie.

"Love," he said slowly, "is an invention of women. I do not believe in it."

"Then, what have we?" she asked, frightened.

"Marriage."

She turned on her pillow, unable to absorb any new sensation. She felt exhausted, her mind was spinning slowly into the dark pit of escaping sleep. Her love ached in her thoughts like a throbbing pain.

In the clear, hopeful morning she asked herself why she loved this man, and there was no answer anywhere save love. Her intelligence might enhance it, but it had no power to diminish it. This was new knowledge, as was the discovery that by love her pride was assailed, cut down to its roots like a plant in the strenuous season. Only another climate would urge its new leaves into the dangerous world of sun and storm.

She went to see her First Uncle. He was in another province but would soon return. The sight of his door gave her courage; she was surprised to feel by renewal that she had been lost to herself these long weeks. His birds in their cages had been brought out to sun and she decided to take one pair back with her. As she walked along the street her hand fitted warmly over the worn wooden handle shaped by her uncle's hand, for he often took his birds walking.

Her First Uncle was like a strong fresh wind blowing steadily. A reminder of him was needed in the dark house to which she must return, and where she was now under the command of her husband's mother.

That night, as every night, there were the amah's secretive slippers outside her door, slupping away in disappointment. That night they were awakened by the mother's cries of anguish, and again Wai Tong rushed to her in alarm. Mai Ying remained in her bed, waiting, longing to be of help in illness, even though she had abandoned the hope that the mother would come to love her. The moaning died away, the night quieted, and later, much later, the doctor returned to his bed and fell heavily asleep. Mai Ying lay awake desolated by his presence, by the warmth of his body and the delicate odor of musk brought back from his mother's rooms. Perhaps this devouring mother would die some night in her illness. She could not deny the wish and yet she felt ashamed, and afraid of the guilt which clung to her mind. The morning would dissipate these dark thoughts and she would renew her efforts of affection to the mother. It was true, and no blame should be made, that one could bear his pain in silence and another could not.

In the morning Madame Chung kept to her rooms, but in the afternoon Mai Ying glimpsed her dressed well, wearing her best jade in her ears, and on her hands, stepping soft-slippered into the rickshaw, commanding the puller and going off toward the city. Mai Ying sat in the garden and read, urging her mind to reach for a larger pattern than was encircling her within this house.

How happy she was when the old woman did not return for dinner and she and her husband sat at the large table alone. Then he appeared the young man in the hospital whose eyes betrayed an emotion her tender probing since had been helpless to release.

"The lotus is blooming on the pond," she said with delicate eagerness. Then, fearing her boldness with him, "Today I read in the garden." She would not tell him she had read a serious book; that would only disturb this rare moment.

"The scented-nights are in blossom, too," he said smiling at her, and she felt this was a gesture of love. This beautiful white flower, open only at night, was a flower of lovers.

The garden was cool and fragrant with the moist quiet leaves and the fertile earth and the enchanting perfume of scented-nights gleaming like small timid moons in the dark. She spoke of her birds, and he was silent for a moment.

"Are you lonely?" he asked.

"Not with you. And in the day I wait for you." She longed to say to him that she wished to be busy, and not at his mother's command, but that would only make him irritable.

"You are a good wife," he said gently. "We shall spend our lives together."

She could not speak. Her hopes unfolded like a stricken bud reviving. In time she would persuade him to understand her need to be useful.

They heard the running feet of the rickshaw boy and the crunch of wheels in the lane. She could sense her husband's withdrawal with no word spoken. Mai Ying wanted to go to her room to avoid seeing the mother, to pretend sleep, but that would be a discourtesy. Instead she called for tea to be made and soon they sat at the table listening to Madame Chung's recital of the day. Her small eyes glittered and her energy filled the room with restless demands upon their attention. Mai Ying saw how the mother drew him out of his silence; he spoke little but his face waited for her every inconsequential word; they laughed together so quickly that she must hurry to become a part.

Abruptly the mother rose and said goodnight.

"How I shall sleep!" she said loudly. "I am worn out with such a day!" She walked toward her rooms, tottering a little, not with age, but from the high heels of new western slippers she had never before worn.

"My mother is like a young girl!" the son said delightedly and the mother looked back at him and laughed, a small low wicked laugh of pleasure. Mai Ying felt a shock of knowledge pass through her mind, too mercurial for her to catch and hold. She too rose abruptly and went to her room.

Long after midnight the mother's low whine came to them along the silent hall clawing like a rain-wet cat at the door of their consciousness. Wai Tong sat up in bed, rubbing his face, saying wearily, almost with anger, "Mah, Mah!"

Mai Ying sat up too. "Your mother is not ill!"

"Hush!" he said. "She has attacks. She overdid herself today."

"You are a doctor. Why don't you cure her?"

"My mother's illness I cannot cure," he said tiredly, "but I must do what I can. Go to sleep. When she is asleep I will come back."

The mother's voice rose and the cries became words: "I cannot endure this! I cannot endure this!"

Wai Tong rushed from the room.

Mai Ying lay in her joyless bed wondering why the amah never answered these night cries. It came to her also that the soft steps of the cautious slippers that crept nightly along the passage and waited like ears under their door were those of the mother. Trembling, she rose in silence and went on bare feet along the hall which was now like a narrow unlighted street of hostile doors. Her heart thundered into the stillness. Her body was cold with fear. She felt her way counting the doors with her touch. And then she heard—that which her ears denied and her mind refused and her heart repulsed. And over it, like mold on a leaf, the gluttonous monotone of the old woman. The girl sank down sickly in the dark, alone and lost in a pathless jungle, where birds screamed and beasts sprang and leaves moved, growing before her eyes; where fallen fruit decayed in an hour and sultry vines abandoned their roots and embraced a tree.

Where music drifted, eons old, from a faraway stream of clear, clean water, casting a spell, making a poem in the jungle. The dance. The joyous elements of dance forever broken in discord and in ruin, forever stolen and forever stained.

"I heard," she said humbly, and her voice in the darkness was a woman's voice she had not known before.

He was settling himself carefully, quietly into bed. He sighed, inviting sleep.

"I listened." Her voice was low; she wondered if he could hear. She did not care but the words ticked in her mind like the seconds of time which pass unaided. They came to her lips and she heard them from another place take the shape of sound and explode in fragments falling dully on the air. "I heard."

He sighed.

"I will go away," she said.

He touched her hair. She moved her head away.

"I will go to another hospital."

"You are my wife."

"*I* am not your wife."

Silence.

"Did you marry me to save your face?"

"Please let us go to sleep," he said desperately.

"Did you?"

He swung out of bed and paced about in the dark.

No more words came to her lips. Her mind was still. A dazzling white space blinded her thoughts as the eyes are blinded by gazing directly into the sun.

"You had better go to sleep," she said.

He fell down on his knees by the bed and wept a long while. She became aware that she was searching feebly about in herself, as in an old trunk belonging to another time of her life, for pity. The pity she found would not fit this new experience. Everything in the trunk looked strangely out of date. She seized love for a moment and drew it on her mind like a glove, and all the seams gave way but her mind remained pinched into its lovely cruel shape.

He was mumbling in his tears. He was crying for himself, not for her.

"My father—" he was saying, "—died when I was five. My mother took me into her bed—" He sobbed without control.

"We—she will never give me up, never, and—I cannot leave her. I—I tried. She will not let me go." He was silent for a time, not weeping. "Mai Ying?"

"Yes."

"You love me but I cannot love. It is too late. You are young and your nearness tempted me. I must have a wife. I will be kind to you."

"Try to go to sleep," she said and it seemed to her that he was a stranger in a narrow bed calling the nurse out of his nightmare.

He got into bed obediently and lay sobbing in the dark, less and less, and after a while he fell asleep. She lay awake staring into the fading night, but when he rose to leave for the hospital, she pretended sleep.

When she heard the rickshaw pull away, she dressed and went into the garden, carrying the bird cage along the paths in the thin morning sun, gathering comfort from the two little creatures that depended upon her. She felt emptied of all emotion save a cold desire to speak to the mother, to finish with her obedience, to flee this house.

The mother always slept late, but the girl waited with unnatural patience, drinking tea, watching the birds. She felt like a mute spectator of all that would soon take place. When the amah told her that Madame Chung had finished her *jochan,* Mai Ying went in and sat at the table, looking scornfully at the old woman. Madame Chung poured a cup of tea and set it before the girl. Her face was eased; she gave Mai Ying a little smile of greeting. A bit of *congee* remained in her bowl and she dipped the china spoon twice to get it all. Then she sat peacefully chewing a cake and drinking tea.

"Cha," she said, indicating the girl's tea with a finger tipped by a long painted nail.

The girl did not touch the tea. She felt alive only as a machine is alive by a power outside its own locked mechanism.

"Last night," she said. Her body trembled but her voice was dead and cold. She felt weary, as if she might have to rest before going on. A subtle identification had taken place; she was her husband Wai Tong whom she loved; she was a young animal lying wounded in sight of a moonlit clearing, and the jaws slavering in the dark were the old woman's lust.

"I listened!" Her voice raised like a cry for help.

The mother's face was smooth like a rock. Her hair strained the skin of her forehead, pulling the high-penciled brows upward away from the fleshy nose. Her mouth, long set for dominance, held like two leather straps ready to lash. Her eyelids were down like small-fringed curtains on the face of a bawdy house.

"You heard nothing."

"I heard."

"You imagine."

"Give him up." She waited. "Or I shall—"

The mother's lower lip flapped uncontrollably for a moment, then her large upper teeth pinioned it angrily. The girl looked at her teeth, one missing, and the others mended with yellow gold. She saw for the first time that without gaiety Madame Chung was ugly.

"No," said Madame Chung quietly, and she smiled as when she had won at cards. "You will live here with me and my son. You may have separate rooms."

"O, I cannot!" Mai Ying said desperately. "I am dutifully asking your permission, but I shall leave without it!"

"You are a member of this family now," Madame Chung said slowly. "You will not soil our face."

"I am not the only one who knows," the girl said, remembering the amah, remembering the relatives. "Others will know without my telling."

"Precisely," Madame Chung said boldly. "It is your duty to save our face by destroying this ugly rumor."

"Then you must *lose* face!"

Madame Chung clapped her hand over her own mouth in a gesture of fearful surprise. Mai Ying stood up, leaning on the table for support.

The mother jumped to her feet at this impertinence and all the fury she had been concealing exploded in a loud howling scream of jealousy.

"Geen yan!" she shouted. "Dirty vamp!" A large vein swelled on one side of her forehead. "You sing-song girl! You—you broken package!" Her hands clawed the air in rage and appetite for the young girl's face.

Mai Ying picked up the cage with the two silent huddled birds, and walked out through the scented garden, out the heavy gate, and without memory of the lane and after that the turning streets, the time, the weariness, she came to her uncle's house.

He was alone, mending the tiny bamboo house of a pet cricket for the child of his two servants. When he saw her he was surprised and happy but his face changed with concern. She stood holding the birdcage tightly, and he gently unclasped her hand. This gesture released the tension of silence, but her speech came stiffly as it had since last night.

"Ming-Sook, do not make me go back!"

"Make? When have we dealt in such ways here?"

She tried to remember the ways of her uncle's house.

"Sit down, child, shouldn't we talk it over first? You are a very independent young woman. Perhaps—" he smiled.

She could not smile in return, but she sat down, remote and falsely calm, facing away from him into the courtyard. Her voice as if disembodied recited her news.

The old professor lifted a tiny porcelain figure from its wooden base and studied it while he gathered his thoughts spilled like grain from an overturned cart.

The child came in with his cricket in the open cup of his hand. The old man sent him away, promising the mended house by evening. "Let your cricket go about as he pleases a bit. He will like you better." The child stared at the distraught girl until she spoke to him. He giggled and ran out.

"I feel destroyed, Uncle Ming. I am walls and windows and no rooms inside. And it will never change. I know."

"Everything changes."

She looked at him curiously.

"Work," he said cautiously. "Work is like the surface stitching of a deep wound. It holds the severed parts together while the wound heals from within. It is not the whole cure. No one must be so careless as to think that. We only assist nature."

She was silent.

"Mai Ying, you have not forgotten all the people who can afford no other cures than nature?"

"At this moment," she said, ashamed, "it seems that I have. When I find myself—"

He nodded at this slip of hope.

She thought, I must learn to sleep and to be awake with this person that I am now. Already I cannot remember any other self.

"We go through life shedding our selves, growing new ones."

"Have you?"

"Many times. I have lost and I have found; it is not all destruction."

It seemed to her that these sensible truths meant nothing and yet her reasoning mind urged her with the faint voice of one buried in the debris of a ruined house, to listen.

"A divorce, too, is necessary."

"O, Ming-Sook," she said sadly. "You are not afraid of anything!"

"Many things."

"Of losing face?"

"No. I am afraid of dead ideas. They are as dangerous as a corpse in the street spreading corruption. In such an old moldy pocket of our life you forgot the clean air and the sun." He stood by the window in the flecks of light and shadow cast by a persimmon tree, and sorted the ideas that came to his seasoned mind. "My friends, the students, still come here," he said proudly. "They are like the climate of clean air and sun. They ask of you. They would like to have you with them." He smoothed her black hair. "Not at once, of course."

Her thoughts felt like a wounded, unbandaged hand over the terrible hours. "Perhaps by Moon Festival."

"There's time enough," he said, "always time."

Her tears began.

Uncle Ming led her to the couch in the sun-filled corner of the room, "Lie here, close by," he said. "I must finish mending this home for the cricket, or I shall lose face with the small boy."

Matriarch of the Court

———⟶———

M r. Carlotti was always saying that everyone and everything should have a mate. Because of his concern for
the nature of things, he was determined to uproot the
ancient date palm and plant in its place a female walnut tree. The
male was standing less than fifteen feet away in the same patch of
earth surrounded by the small bungalows of Roma Courts.

Lately this long-postponed labor of sentiment had been has-
tened into action by less romantic reasons, and the men from the
tree company had arrived and were consulting with Mr. Carlotti
about the overhead wires and the direction in which the palm
must fall. Because of a clothesline and an old storage shed to the
back, and the closeness of the bungalows, the only open space left
was toward the walnut tree. This news justified a change of plans,
and the men withdrew to the street where they leaned against the
fenders of the truck and talked over ways to protect the walnut.

The tenants of the inner court were in a turmoil of curiosity,
resentment, or pleasure. The spectacle of building or destruction
that fascinates everyone was already engaging their hungry attention. They waited behind window screens or drifted into the yard,
exchanging views.

The tenants of the inner court were women, unmarried or
widowed, and they had occupied the same tiny apartments for
years at rents which came within their pensions or shrunken

wages. The places were rundown, but not shabby because of the concealing vines and flowers—which appeared to be in league with Mr. Carlotti's frequently announced inability to buy paint. Cockroaches held nightly rendezvous in the kitchen sinks and cooking utensils, and could not be cleared out because of the rotting foundations. The plumbing was rather uncertain, especially when the roots of the date palm got into the sewer. This was Mr. Carlotti's more practical complaint against the old tree, but not the one which precipitated its demise.

The date palm was of no interest to the tenants of the outer court. Because of the garages, the court was large and paved. It was even rather imposing. Mr. Carlotti had lined the drive with roses and honeysuckle and jasmine. And he had furnished the spacious cul-de-sac with copies of old Roman statuary, around which cars were obliged to maneuver skillfully. In the autumn, Mr. Carlotti, who had been a barber in his youth, denuded the whole court with his overzealous pruning, shearing all plants to the ground. This was autumn and the women of the inner court trembled for their favorite flowers, which they had surreptitiously watered and plucked all summer. They trembled still more for fear that Mr. Carlotti would take it into his head to improve his property and raise the rents.

After the war he had modernized the outer apartments and rented them to new couples, but the inner court, more hidden, and separated from the drive, was as old and worn as ever and they wished only for it to remain so.

In this small place was the garden—the patch of earth with the two trees and a scattering of flowers and grass. It was claimed with rather fierce passion by Miss Isabel Adair, who occupied the only separate house, more run down than the rest. Although the others had a few feet of earth around their doors where they tended their private flowers, no one dared tend or pluck a flower from the larger garden in front of Miss Adair's porch. She occasionally neglected the garden, but never the potted plants and the little flowers that grew close to the edges of her porch. She spoke to them as to her cat in a carrying, professional voice and she stood on the walk in a queenly way in her faded cottons and sagging sweater, gazing with profound affection upon the date palm. When any of the women dared complain that it shut out the light and caused them to burn electricity in the daytime, she declaimed, "It's as rooted here as I am!" in a voice which retained some of its beauty and all of its power, and which was known at times to intimidate the landlord.

Now, while the men were conferring in the street, Miss Adair held her audience: Miss Fern Pintz, who appeared no more than a head as she pressed her face against her kitchen window screen; Mrs. Hart; and several others who listened through partly opened doors.

"I've been here longer than any of you," she said. "Why, when I first came out of stock and moved here to be close to the studio—the old Famous Players Lasky—that tree was here, old then. I had never seen a palm and I thought it was a luxury. I couldn't see anything but that tree—a palm tree in my garden! I was young, mind you, and—" she laughed, "so was this court. It was absolutely adorable then!"

"What's wrong with it now?" Mrs. Hart said in an unusually loud voice, mindful of Mr. Carlotti, who was a sweet and gentle man who never went banging about the place. "It wouldn't be home with the least change. These modern places are as cold as Fern's heart." She giggled, pretending not to see Miss Pintz, whose appreciative laugh came out of the darkness of her window.

"Well, I wish mine had been colder," Miss Adair said casually.

"Isabel, you're the limit!"

"Better to wear out than rust out!" Miss Adair called. Accurately wounded, Miss Pintz disappeared into the gloom of the bungalow, repaid for the latest intelligence she had borne through the inner court about Miss Adair's past: an invention that Miss Adair had never been more than a "dress extra" in films. Actually she had spoken brief lines. There was quite a difference.

Mrs. Hart came to life. "Well, you can't say that about me. I'm a widow, and my husband worshiped the ground I walked on. Many a time he—"

"Such husbands die young." Miss Adair turned toward her porch. "Wouldn't you think these darling little pansies could speak? Look here, Vanessa!" Mrs. Hart gazed obediently. There was no use denying it; Miss Adair was the matriarch of the court. "Hello, you cunning little things. Speak to Mama!"

"They *are* sweet," Mrs. Hart said softly.

"If I make this place look any prettier, Julius Caesar will raise the rent," Miss Adair said. "Then I'd have to go back to the fountain pen factory, assembling those darn little things that nearly drove me mad."

Mrs. Hart laughed with Miss Adair, but she remembered that Miss Adair's age was against her. Not only that; she suddenly remembered the palm tree, and a neighborly tenderness rose in her for Miss Adair. Didn't she recognize what Mr. Carlotti was doing? Or did she? This was the second step. The first was last week when Mr. Carlotti repaired the broken bricks in the foundation of her porch and dared to trim her little flowers. To touch her flowers was as brazen as anything.

Mr. Carlotti and the three workmen came into the court. The women retired into their separate preserves. Miss Adair played her old piano loudly, as if in final protest.

"Well, it's gonna tear some branches off that walnut, that's for sure," one of the men said with authority.

"Be as easy as you can," Mr. Carlotti begged. "And get all the roots. I want to put a mate in this hole."

"A what?"

"A female walnut."

"Oh, sure. You ought to had us bring it, plant it now."

"I've picked out a special tree and she's waiting."

"A nice little virgin, no doubt," another of the men said.

"Young and strong, well-branched," Mr. Carlotti said disapprovingly.

"First thing you know, you'll have a lot of little walnut trees runnin' around underfoot, and it ain't every tree that can support a family these days with fertilizer goin' higher and higher."

Mr. Carlotti laughed and pushed his hat back. "Well, men, watch out for the telephone wires overhead, get all the roots, but don't break the sewer pipes. Be careful of my walnut tree here. I've got some pruning to do. I'll be in the driveway."

The men efficiently went to work. They sweated and swore, and trampled all the small plants into the earth. Their business was trees. The blue jays living in the walnut tree squawked at them and flew menacingly over their heads.

As the men hacked at the lower palm fronds the court clouded with old dust.

Miss Adair burst out of her little house and said in a tearful voice, "I never thought I'd live to see the day this magnificent tree would be murdered!"

"Maybe you won't, lady. This here palm's a tough baby."

"Well, thank God for that!" Miss Adair breathed.

A falling frond struck the new hibiscus. She winced. Another crashed down upon the woody cyclamen.

"I hope you can save *that* plant. That is my child! I planted it seventeen years ago!"

Without glancing away from his work, the man who felt himself addressed said, "Seventeen years?"

"Yes. I've lived here far longer than that."

"When this tree's out of here, you're gonna start gettin' some sun."

Miss Adair went quickly into the house and closed the door. The husky sound of her sobbing drifted out the window.

"That old dame's been pretty good lookin' in her time," one of the men said kindly. "Notice the way she throws her voice around? Probably been somethin' once."

"Hollywood's full of 'em. They all been stars. The sky ain't big enough to hold 'em."

"She never said she was no star."

Miss Pintz passed by going to the incinerator with a few papers.

"One good thing about guys like you and me. We're workin' stiffs, and we damn well know it. When we get old, no monkey business to look back on—just hard work."

"If you ask me, I'd as soon look back on a little less of it. I ain't got time to improve myself."

They laughed.

"Tearin' up and replantin' the best damn trees in the world. You're improvin' the face of the earth."

They worked for a long time without talking. The sobbing in the house stopped. Miss Adair's aimless footsteps sounded and then an abrupt rip of notes as she slashed along the piano keys with one hand.

"The fellow who owns this place was sayin' when he gets that new tree in and the dust settles, he's gonna paint this old gal's house and fix it up. Maybe that'll cheer her up some."

A heavy sigh was projected into the court. A long and fairly interesting conversation between Miss Adair and her cat followed. After that she played pensively and roughly at once as if she were having an argument with herself on the piano.

Mrs. Hart opened her door slightly. She spoke aloud to herself as was her custom, shaking her head slowly over the repairs she was making in her winter coat.

"Poor Isabel. She'll be lost without that old wreck of a piano, and they'll never permit her to keep it in a furnished room. And no garden, too."

One of the men said, "Nature's a funny thing, ain't it?"

Mrs. Hart said, "As intelligent as she is, I wonder she hasn't caught on to the meaning of Mr. Carlotti's uprooting that old date palm. I always think of it as a female what with all Mr. Carlotti's talk. Maybe it is. Every year she produces some skinny bunches of sterile dates. Poor old thing needs a mate, too." Mrs. Hart sighed audibly.

A violent crash, terrible and slow, punctuated with cracking and straining, sent a rush of air and dust against the windows of the inner court. A low, carrying moan of realization came from

Miss Adair's bungalow. The old tree crushed the tender plants beneath it and scratched the young walnut, tearing away a few branches but doing no serious harm. It lay in the small garden like a great primordial beast brought down, its scaled hide without the movement of breath, its feet separated from earth, its security in the pattern of things undone at last.

Mr. Carlotti came running, and all but one door opened. Everyone gazed upon the tree, its torn-out roots, and the great hole left in the inner court.

"Now, the next problem is," said Mr. Carlotti in his gentle voice, "the easiest way to get this old matriarch out of here without tearing up the whole court. The little garden is already ruined."

The door of the ominously silent bungalow opened wide and Miss Isabel Adair walked in her queenly way to the edge of the porch. Her hair was combed and her face was freshly and carefully made up, especially around the swollen eyelids. She straightened her sweater and gave Mr. Carlotti a full blast of her personality, a peculiar unblended mixture of independence and charming co-quetry. She revealed her own good teeth in a smile for everyone.

"Don't worry about this gallant old palm tree, Mr. Carlotti. When she leaves this court, it will be with colors flying, even if she ends up in the junk heap." She glanced at the uprooted tree and quickly away, to the listening faces. Then she drew a small feather duster from her pocket and turned her back to them all, flicking the delicate feathers over the green leaves and flowers that grew in a border along her porch. The dust rose and Mr. Carlotti sneezed. She stooped and blew her breath into the articulate faces of the pansies.

"My babies!" Miss Adair's proud whisper, faltering only a little, carried to everyone in the silence.

William Shakespeare

The boy sat quietly at the long kitchen table on the far side with his back to the high, old-fashioned cupboard. Here he was out of the way of his mother who worked between the big hot range and the table. She was making pies. The kitchen was pleasantly warm and smelled of fruit and crust. Winter frost ornamented the windows. Cleanliness and order lay on the room like a carved pattern. The boy wrote slowly on an oblong of cardboard cut from a box lid. Others, used and unused, lay on the table in separate piles. He wrote laboriously, the words making the long journey from his mind to his lips to his pencil as if in constant peril of being lost. The letters were huge and al-most perfectly shaped. As he moved, the strong muscles of his shoulders and his arms strained at the worn cloth of his coat.

His mother was like a dainty sparrow in her long, dark cotton dress, with her black hair coiled high, pulling her humorous eyes up at the corners. She smiled at him once, showing her own good teeth and closing her eyes in a little wink. He looked at her wonderingly, his thoughts on the words he was about to put down, then he smiled sweetly, and his grave eyes in a face so like her own emitted a spark of sly humor.

She did not speak to him or disturb him in any way. He was the oldest son, nearly twenty, and after working hard in the summer fields all day, or long at the winter chores, he had earned this quietest hour to himself. She was not disinterested in what he was doing, but she had no curiosity about it, rather a respect for his privacy. The two younger boys, near his age, but neither handsome nor strong as was Spencer, would be coming in to supper soon, washing up, talking to their father, and Spencer would put away his cardboards and sit at the table watching, taking no part.

Their steps crunched now across the frozen yard, and Virgil came in ahead of his father, which was unusual, and Purvis held the storm door back for him.

His father was carrying a lump of blanket in his arms. He came near the heat of the stove and turned back a tip of the cloth, exposing the damp head of a newborn lamb. Feeling the warmth, the animal instinctively nuzzled forward but not finding the sustaining softness of its mother's belly, the head sank uncertainly onto the rough blanket.

"I declare, Earl!" the woman said.

"It's a lamb in the dead of winter, Girl!" the old man said. "Born outa season. That buck got ahead of hisself. So did the ewe, I reckon. Couldn't wait to lamb in the spring."

The woman made hurried preparations to care for the lamb.

"The ewe mightn't live," he said. "I been pettin' her; about all I can do now. We'll go out again after supper."

Spencer came over and looked at the lamb and took it in his arms.

"Lay it on the oven door," his mother said. She made a thick pad beneath the lamb. Then she handed Spencer a nippled bottle of milk and when the lamb responded to the warmth, the boy pressed the nipple tenderly against the seeking mouth. He remained seriously at this task until he was called.

He hurried to wash and sit down when he saw his writing still on the table. Virgil was sitting next to him but he hardly glanced at it. He was hungry, waiting impatiently for grace to be said. Spencer snatched the sheets up and rushed to his room, which was the only bedroom opening onto the kitchen. When he returned his face was stolid, ready for grace.

The talk was sketchy, of the lamb, the stock, the weather, and the winter wheat growing now under the snow. They ate with hunger and relish and sometimes did not speak at all. There was a shy affection between the old man and his wife, which after all the years still took a form of quiet flirtation. Virgil insinuated to Purvis that he knew a good deal about him and the Watson girl. Purvis merely grinned. Spencer ate silently as if the table were divided. There was no unfriendliness. The food came his way, he helped himself, and passed it on. No one directed any of the conversation to him. He took no notice as if this were the customary manner. Only once when his father spoke to him, using his name, Spencer smiled deprecatingly at his mother, but she too ignored him, since his father was speaking to her. The boy's lips moved softly, forming the whispered word, but no one heard.

The lamb struggled in his blanket, fell off the oven door, freed himself and tottered across the floor. His oily coat sent a pungent odor through the warm, fruity air.

After the meal the old man fixed a box which would enclose the lamb's uncertain strength. Then he turned on the radio and in the midst of the sound he read his farm paper. He listened as well, for now and then he turned away from his reading when the voice demanded more than half his attention. Soon he beckoned Purvis and the two went to attend the ewe.

Spencer resumed his writing on the cardboard, and kept on long after the others had gone into their cold rooms to bed. When the fire had died, he made a cautious trip to his own room and returned with a magazine and two heavy dumbbells. He stealthily fastened the outer door back, letting in the zero wind. He removed his clothing and opened the magazine to an advertisement of a muscular man wearing a leopard skin. He looked with wonder and approbation at the exotic hide and the extended muscles. Then he lifted the weights over his head until his strong arms tensed and the muscles quivered. He lowered and raised them, breathing in the cold fresh air, until the proper time had passed. After closing the door, he secreted his possessions in his room and got into bed.

In the morning he ate his breakfast humbly with the others as he had done all the years since he had discovered their indifferent contempt for him. The ewe had died in the night and he was given the job of skinning and burying. After the midday meal there was little for him to do and he remained indoors silently preoccupied with his writing. Once his mother interrupted him to give him a hot buttered bun. He liked these manifestations of her affection for him. He had slyly noticed that when they were alone together his mother behaved in a way she neglected when the others were present. He accepted this as he accepted their strange attitude, but he did not forgive her.

One day in the early spring when he was feeling restless because he had completed the manuscript which had occupied him for several years, something unusual happened. He had just cut new cardboards from all the boxes he could find and new sheets from paper bags and sat down at the table to begin a new piece of work. His mother was pleased because she did not like to see him mooning about when his farm work was finished. He had wanted to go to town to buy a new magazine and she did not wish him to go. Although the town lay twelve miles away, she had to watch him or he would walk. It was easy to see him on the flat plains; she would have only to call and he would return.

He had just settled himself at the table when his father flung the kitchen door open, laughing and talking, and admitted a young woman. Spencer looked at her in amazement as if he had never before seen a stranger. He knew at once that she was from the town.

"Girl," the old man said, "this is someone from the newspaper. Miss Campion. We been looking at the stand of wheat. She's writing about the wheat."

The woman went forward with her hands folded easily over her stomach and gave the girl a shy, smiling nod.

Spencer watched the friendly way the girl greeted his mother, and could hardly believe that anyone would smile like that at someone unknown.

"Make yourself to home!" the old man said. "Girl, have you something to eat?"

The mother was already setting out a pie. Spencer rose without being asked and brought the pitcher of milk. The girl looked at him expectantly.

"Oh, that's Spencer," the mother said.

Spencer acknowledged her with a gentle smile, a rare secret smile of awareness.

The girl gave him a wonderful smile in return—of recognition.

"Hello, Spencer," she said, and her voice was different than it had been the moment before. Her eyes came slowly away from his suddenly beautiful face.

"No," he said quietly, to her. "I am William. William Shakespeare."

The girl blushed, ever so slightly.

"Don't pay any mind to Spence," the old man said kindly. "He ain't quite bright."

The girl looked right at Spencer now, whose eyes waited for her words.

"Hello, William," she said, very low.

An ecstatic radiance came into his face. He sighed. Thin cunning slid over his strong cheekbones and down the corners of his triumphant mouth. Then he smiled with disarming innocence.

"See, Mama? *She* knows me."

His mother nodded at him as if she understood. "Pour the milk, Son."

He obeyed her. The father winked at the visitor but there was nothing malicious in his expression.

They sat at the table together, but Spencer said no more. His big hands idled with the pencil as he watched the girl.

"Would you like to see the new lamb?" the old man asked her.

"Oh, yes!" she said, and when she had thanked the mother, the two went out toward the barns.

Spencer went into his room and closed the door.

As he hurried, he watched from the window his father walking with the girl from the barns to the car. Just as she pressed her foot on the starter, Spencer ran into the yard. He carried a large package about six inches thick, wrapped in newspaper and tied with heavy string. As he thrust the package into the car, his face contorted with silent pleading.

"Spencer! Take that junk back. You ought to be ashamed, taking advantage of company!" The old man pulled the bundle from the seat and Spencer grabbed it and pressed it this time into the girl's hands. His face now had a stolid, arrogant, stubborn expression against his father. He held his hands on the package and looked at the girl with humility.

"Please," he begged. "Send it away! I don't know how. I can't go to town."

The girl seemed uncertain only a moment, then she placed her hands beside his.

The boy stood close, guarding his treasure. Her eyes looked deeply into his, as if searching for something far back.

"Please," he said very low. "I know who I am. They won't believe me. But you know, too. Help me, be my friend!"

At this last naked appeal, the girl's eyes moistened. The old man looked at her apologetically. The large strong boy stood between them.

"I'll try," she said, looking at him directly. "Listen! Writers have to try a long time. If it isn't quite right yet, I'll send it back. You might have to change it some."

Spencer nodded and stepped back, releasing his grip. His face appeared stunned. He turned and ran toward the house.

The old man clucked with exasperation.

"I don't mind, honestly, I don't," the girl said.

"Don't bother with it. Don't even send it back."

"Oh, yes, he'll remember."

"Maybe, but he'll have a roomful by then. We can't keep any paper or cardboard. He writes on everything. I swear, I don't know where he got hold of the name William Shakespeare. Some teacher, I suppose. They mostly room here."

"It's strange," she said, as if to herself, "I didn't know. He's so—" Her voice trailed off in disappointment.

"He's a fine looking boy, all right," the old man said knowingly. He waved her out of the yard.

After the visit of the girl, a subtle change came over Spencer. His mother noticed it first, then as it grew from day to day and week to week, the others saw it too. He worked less in the fields and wrote more, and when there were no more boxes or sacks, he demanded pay to go to town and buy paper. This was refused as wasteful, and he walked to a neighbor's and brought back an armful of materials. He demanded to be addressed as William. He lost his air of humility, and took to exercising both morning and night with the dumbbells. He spoke to his mother of hunting a coyote in or-der to get a skin of some kind to wear at these times. She humored him or ordered him about. He adored and obeyed her, and even spoke of buying her a new dress when he sold his book. Some days, it was a new comb.

All spring the wind was high and it came like an endless, penetrable wall of powdery dust. On the rare days when the wind was low, the dust came in a silky, smothering mass, and when it did not cease, sheep and cattle strangled. The crops bowed down. School children were lost, and the searchers held to a long rope so as not to be lost with them. Dogs slept indoors. People went about their work wearing cheese-cloth masks.

In the Blair house, as in others, dust settled in the food, in the beds, on the furniture, and stayed like fur in the mouth and nostrils. Canvas was nailed over the windows and fresh clean air was a remembered delight. The mother wiped the dust from the kitchen table a hundred times a day. She watched Spencer, who seldom went out except to the barns, sitting at the table day after day writing on the scraps of paper that remained. The dust had dulled his hair and clung like gossamer to his long eyelashes. He wore his mask only when he exercised with the dumbbells. Although he had become arrogant with the others, he remained gentle and tractable with her. Always now, she addressed him as William, so there was no point of dissension between them.

He went every morning to the road for the mail, and took pleasure in bringing his mother a letter or a paper, since the mail in these days when they lived in an enclosure of wind and dust was more important than it had ever been. On the morning his manuscript was found leaning against the post, the day was what they called a Black One, and Spencer had carried an end of the rope attached to the door so as not to lose his way and wander about in the yard longer than was necessary.

He brought the big package in and placed it on the kitchen table and looked at his mother with a mournful face. She had accepted it simply as an expected event; and her only surprise being to see the manuscript at all, her face gave him no answer of shared grief. It was hard to find words for a disappointment that was strange to her.

He drew a finger across the address and read aloud bitterly, "Mr. Spencer Blair," as if this name were an enduring sorrow beside the momentary distress of the refused book.

"Now, Spencer." His mother spoke soothingly.

He looked at her with horror, his face contorting as if the emotion were extremely painful to him.

She had no idea he would feel so stricken.

"Let's untie it," she said cheerfully. "Maybe there's a letter."

He continued to stare at her, and when she had opened the package and found no letter, he did not seem to mind. He sat down at his place as if he were weary, with all feeling gone. He watched her bleakly.

II

The mother lifted the cardboards one by one, studying them curiously. A strange coolness in her lifted the fine hairs along her arms, followed by a deep, warm yearning to help her son, to protect him. She was looking openly into a space of his mind where no one could be admitted, and all she could think of to give him was her pitiful kindness.

She hesitated over one beautifully symmetrical portion and forced her mind to repeat what she saw. Words, hundreds, thousands of them, and they were all unrelated, lost, strangely dropped together out of his eager, blasted mind. The ruined, meaningless thoughts with no beginning or end, words that he could not consciously know, and altogether they made no sense. Not one sure, clear thing came through, only chaos. She went on lifting the heavy sheets, and there on the final page, in large, innocent letters he had set down for all the world to know and to repudiate the doubt at home where he needed a believer, a friend with faith—Written by William Shakespeare.

She had not known this son, and now she looked at him with troubled awe. His face was closed and grave.

Perhaps she could release him. She felt guilty that she had not concerned herself before. He always obeyed her.

"Spencer," she said gently, as if waking him. His mouth trembled slightly. "Spencer, you must not do this any more. Do you hear?"

She waited in the hollow stillness so long that she began to hear the little sounds that deepened the stillness, their breath, and the fine grains of dust softly pelting the walls of the house.

"You can do something else, Spencer."

His head sank a little as if he were hiding.

"How would you like to have a guitar or a fiddle?"

He sighed.

"Spencer!"

He sprang up wildly, holding his strong-muscled arms out tensely, fists clenched. The veins in his forehead distended. His dark eyes were fierce and despairing. Tears ran down his face, making small paths in the dust.

To her, he had always been docile, pliant. Suddenly she thought of the leopard skin, and shrank back, then she recovered herself and smiled at him the sly smile that was his too, thinking how foolish she was, how foolish she had been. She gathered the manuscript up and held it out to him.

"Son, why don't you write something else, and sign it Spencer Blair?"

He howled, a great wounded howl, and sprang out the door. The black dust poured in and muffled the sound of his madness.

Forgetting the mask, she turned her apron over her head and went after him, calling his name, following his slashing wordless cries. It was impossible to see far. Objects very near were furry and came up quickly out of the sifting dark. She covered her mouth and nose and sheltered her eyes, and ran desperately, sometimes feeling ahead with one hand. Then she lost him. There were no sounds, not even his footsteps. She stood still and called his name, the long rising and falling way she had called him as a child. She listened. There was only the softly falling dust as stealthy and smooth as a cat's paw. He had fallen. She began to walk slowly, to search for him.

As she moved she heard something as delicate as breath behind her, and she whirled about, but it was only the silky wind. She went on cautiously, fearing to strike him with her foot.

"Spencer," she called tenderly. "Spencer, it's Mama."

The hard driven weight of the axe plunged against her shoulder and sent her sprawling on the ground. She lay there stunned. An instinct sprang alert: she was hearing his silence, sensing his presence, his enormous strength. She felt herself rising and flying forward like a bird, like the meadowlark from the grass. She heard the crunch of the axe split the earth behind her.

She heard his voice reaching for her through the secret lethal wind.

"William!" he shouted. "William! William!" in loud and final and sorrowful assertion.

The Tea Party

Holly stood alert, secretive, one hand on the faded drape that made a boundary between the living room and her bedroom. The door leading to the two other rooms was closed.

Her father's chair scraped tersely on the kitchen floor; he had finished his lunch. Every noon he came home along the small-town streets from the tin shop where he worked, and it satisfied him to exchange a few words with her before he went back. Not today, she wished, please not today. She could not face the concern and disappointment in his searching eyes.

"I ought to look in on Holly," he said to her mother.

"She won't welcome it today. Today it's been a year exactly."

"All the more reason," he said. "She ought to get out of the house. Out in the world. All year living like a hermit. It's a commonplace ailment," he sighed hugely. "Except when it happens to us. That's just it."

"Her heart is really broken," her mother said.

Oh! Holly thought, I can't endure that silly phrase. If it's true, it's my secret, mine only.

"And in such a little town, it's hard," her mother kept on. "Everybody knows everything."

"Well," her father said, "that young fellow turned out not good enough for our Holly. But she's so shy it's a wonder she ever got *him.*"

"Sh-h-h—"

Holly waited. That was what her father said: it was a wonder! The rubber-edged screen door fell to with a controlled thud like the sound of her father's thoughts. She swayed in a moment of release from his affection and criticism.

The house was silent, but Holly resumed her listening posture.

"La, la, la, la, lonesome and blue . . ." her mother sang. Holly trembled. When was her mother coming in? She would open the door in a moment, after discouraging the father, and with her gentle determination, say, "Holly, why don't you walk downtown? Maybe a limeade in the drugstore where all the students hang out. See your old friends, a nice girl like you."

When her mother did not come, she stood at the only window in the living room and looked at the old house next door. Part of the wall had been painted once and the rest left to sand and wind. Mrs. Polk was sweeping the front walk. Her lips moved delicately. Aspen leaves flew off to each side in excited flurries as if they were the very words Mrs. Polk was addressing to the walk.

Holly watched Mrs. Polk with distaste and an admiration of sorts. She kept to herself. She wore old evening dresses for house-work. Today a coarse sweater hung over her soiled, beaded sack of a dress, fashionable in the twenties, its hemline fringe bobbling against her thin legs, fattened by wrinkled stockings. Mrs. Polk's youth must have been filled with evening dresses, but after that, who knows when or why, time, for her, had stopped.

Holly's mother came suddenly into the dim room and seeing her standing by the window, glanced out.

"That stuck-up old woman," she said, without a grain of hostility.

Holly smiled. Her mouth felt stiff; it would never again give into a wide free expression. Her mother, surprised, smiled warmly in return. Her eyes lighted with expectation.

Holly turned away looking for Mrs. Polk, but she had gone and the wind was blowing leaves down onto the walk.

"It's a nice autumn day," her mother said. "Aren't you going outside at all?"

"As if I ever do," Holly said with all the sarcasm she dared.

"Why not?"

"Why?"

"You want someone to fly in the window, Holly?"

"No. *You* do."

This startled the grief hiding in the blandness of her mother's face.

"You're young; it isn't natural, never going out."

"I suppose it's natural," Holly rushed, "—to go out, meet a boy, and—" she swallowed the choking lump, "—get married."

"You'll fall in love again, Holly. That was only the first time."

"I'm planning my own future, *alone!*" She said this coldly in order to steady her voice.

"The future never comes, Holly. It's here, now, every day."

This plain logic infuriated Holly.

"And you're missing it!" her mother cried, opening the door of the heater blindly. She peered into it as if she had opened a door to the baffling problem of her daughter and was trying to see how she was made, the shape and set of her apartness, all puzzling and strange. "You need a fire here in the living room if you're not going out in the sun," she said in a toneless voice.

"We should save the coal for winter."

"Winter may never come."

When Holly brought the coal, her mother said placatingly, "The kitchen looks real nice the way you scoured it yesterday. You're a real homemaker, Holly. Even your dad noticed, and he's usually too tired to see anything, including me."

The thought of her mother as a woman being lonely in a way even remotely similar to herself was utterly offensive and unbelievable. She sighed loudly, a hint for her mother to leave her alone.

Her mother lingered and Holly had a moment of shame. She struck a match to the paper and kindling and watched the flames grow in the bowl of the heater.

"Holly," her mother said quietly, "would you like to walk down to the station again this evening and watch the streamliner go through? It'll be dark then."

Again! What a despicable hint!

"The agent's wife told me you were down to the station one night asking about fares and places."

"I was not! She doesn't even know me. It was somebody else!" There was no privacy anywhere.

"I thought so too, honey." Her mother went into the kitchen.

Holly closed the door firmly. She stood there thinking of doors, doors with keys, and a large serious room with a massive door and no knob on the outside. The room she was imagining was so familiar that she knew everything about it, its cleanliness, its newness, its air of mornings and evenings, its spring, summer and winter moods, its generous, unquestioning consideration, and its claim upon her. She had furnished it with the love she had once bestowed upon *him* until that terrible night. He had let her wait, dressed for the autumn dance, shy in her first formal; wait in humiliation before her mother and father; wait with no word, leaving her stunned and incredulous to this day. And he had gone to the dance with someone else when everyone was expecting her. Before that night, that whole year of days and evenings, there had been no sign of what was to happen. Her father had said this was not unusual in one so young. If *he* had only hinted once, even the day before, that he had changed, she could have pretended and concealed. But he hadn't had the courage. He had deceived her by being someone less than she thought. How could she ever fearlessly believe in anyone else?

It wasn't that they had planned to be married. They had made little jokes, and others had taken them for granted as *two*, and they had spoken of love intensely. Or, he had. She was awkward with such words, and shy, but she had revealed herself in her own ways.

He had known. And she could not control the unplanned plans that had taken possession of her thoughts.

Afterward, although he was the apparent defaulter, she had been plagued with questions: What was wrong with her? Where had she failed?

Then it was that she had designed the imaginary room, with the windows that would not open, from which she could observe the life outside and still be safe.

She heard the long rhythms of her mother ironing clothes, and at last she felt alone.

She tiptoed into the bedroom and stood before the doorless closet. The catalogue and samples and notebooks could hardly be seen at the back of the high shelf because she had arranged before them her father's good hat and his Sunday shoes. She selected and brought down only a few of the books, placing them on an old three-legged stool near the chair and the stove. She took a little flat key from inside her slipper and opened a locked diary. The years had been changed to future dates. No present events were entered. She read an entry four years ahead and closed her eyes. She saw herself by a small lake among new friends, and they were all laughing at exchanged nonsense. She dove into the water and others followed, but she swam ahead laughing, daring anyone to catch her.

She opened her eyes and turned to an earlier page headed Expenses, and from a piece of paper also hidden in her slipper, she copied the railroad fares to three university towns half a continent away, and a girls' college—her preference over all. Then she figured and entered the cost of books, clothes and even *entertainment,* a nebulous, almost eerie suggestion that made the little hairs stand up on her pale arms.

On another page she wrote down her career as Astronomer, that being work, she imagined, the most remotely connected with a terrifying, overwhelming world of *twos,* and hardly less closely connected with Earth itself. This gave her an odd satisfaction. A sinister draft of cold stratospheric wind blew across her back.

With a secret word, she opened the knobless door of her private room and went in.

There was a pecking on the frosted glass of the living room door. Holly looked around stealthily. Mrs. Polk's nineteen-twenties outline made a dim shadow. When there was no response, she left.

Holly stood up and turned her back to the warm heater, closing the diary. She opened a large notebook marked Furniture, Silverware, Glassware, China. It was filled with lists and floor plans and photographs of table settings. There were swatches of cotton and brocade upholstery, pictures of furniture styles and her own table of color schemes. These she simply looked at in bitterness. Then she forced her attention back to the diary and began to write.

Heavy footsteps on the squeaky decaying boards of the porch roused her to panic. She gathered the books hastily into her arms and started for the bedroom. The intimate sound of the mail being pushed into the tin box reassured her. When the postman was too far away for greetings, she brought the mail in, sailing her mother's letters under the kitchen door and sitting down at once to look through the day's advertisements and two folders she had sent for: *Beauty After Thirty* and *Investments for the Wise Woman*. She silently thanked civilization for the postal service to this remote little town and returned to her dreams.

She had hardly settled into her imaginary room, having just added an antique bench upon which no one would reasonably wish to sit, when a dainty authoritative knock sounded at the back door.

"I'll not come in," she heard Mrs. Polk say cordially. Mrs. Polk of the daytime evening dresses! "I want you to come over to tea. Your daughter too."

Tea! A fearful prospect known only in books!

Her mother was making polite, flustered protestations.

"It's prepared!" Mrs. Polk said, settling all equivocation.

Holly quickly secured her treasures behind the hat and shoes and went to the kitchen feeling tremulous and commanded.

Mrs. Polk was smiling artfully with her thin lips closed, her long parchment face lined with secretive pleasure. A faded velvet wrap was thrown around her bony shoulders, its moth-eaten fur collar held snugly under her chin. Holly saw at once that she had changed to another tubular evening dress.

"Come dear," she said to Holly, and her mother followed.

As they crossed the hard, ugly grassless yard where tiny slivers of broken bottles lay glittering in the sun, the sun pointing so mercilessly at the ugly town that defiled the grandeur of the landscape, Mrs. Polk was saying, "Tea is a lost institution in America. Such a pity, too. It is a part of our cultural heritage. And—" she gave a little neighing laugh and tossed her long sorrel head in a rather sweet young mare-ish way, "—one may say it is a *sign* of culture."

Holly looked down thinking that she might tell her father, who liked tea, that it was a sign of culture, and he would probably say, "The devil it is!"

But the institution of tea, not the drinking of it, appeared to be the meaning of Mrs. Polk's words. The institution was unfamiliar, and Holly felt afraid of this new experience. She glanced at her mother to learn if she were perturbed, but her mother walked doggedly after Mrs. Polk as if this sudden invitation were in the category of all neighborly duties and pleasures, attending broken legs, sickness, funerals and weddings.

"Mind your step."

Gracefully Mrs. Polk led them through the chaos that was her kitchen, a litter of soiled dishes and pans, half-eaten toast, egg shells fallen to the floor and a large mound of coffee grounds in the sink. There was a musty odor that only years could have brought to such ripeness.

An alarm clock turned face downward on a chair ticked away hoarsely.

"It wants to run in that position," Mrs. Polk said as she passed the chair.

Their hostess glided into the dining room and stood aside without a word as they came to a sudden halt before a long oval table covered with a fine lace cloth, set with gleaming, ornate silver and glass and delicate almost transparent china. Tall candles burned in silver candelabra, and place cards with names in spidery script were at every plate.

Holly counted twelve, and, amazed, unable to speak, she glanced down at the dirty rug redesigned by the crumbs of countless meals. She looked quickly back to the table, and there were the things she had dreamed of and never seen before, silver she had ordered on the catalogue blanks that were never mailed, china and glass over which she had long debated and finally chosen, irrevocably committed; the elegant lace, and over it all, the glow of the candles in the dim wintry room. And like her own, the guests were reposing in Mrs. Polk's head. This was of no consequence at all in the rare *presence* of the waiting table; and Mrs. Polk, who was capable of materializing a dream, took on sudden stature in Holly's eyes.

In the thin silence her mother laughed abruptly and said in a cajoling voice, "My, isn't it pretty!"

Mrs. Polk sighed voluptuously. "In those days we cared more for the finer things of life."

"I'm so wound up in everyday work," her mother stated with her peculiar pride and apology canceling each other, "that I've hardly time to look back or ahead."

Holly took a step nearer the table, but as one turns from a dazzling light, she glanced away into a bedroom and was fascinated to see a woman's hat of another era hanging on the supporting frame of a dresser mirror. She knew at once that the hat had been placed there years ago and never removed; it had deteriorated with dust. A breath would scatter it! Under the bed were two high-heeled slippers whitened and warped with the time they had rested there. Old finery and cans of talcum lay on the chairs, and over everything was a coat of ancient dust.

Holly imagined Mrs. Polk young and willowy, perhaps even wearing the dress she had on today, entering the bedroom, kicking off her shoes, and with a wide lamenting gesture, placing the hat, looking at herself in the mirror; and in that moment, closing a door, a massive knobless door. Why?

She looked shyly back to the gleaming table which gave her a luxurious thrill, but she could not forgive Mrs. Polk for the dirt and neglect which was now as astounding as the dinner party.

"In all modesty," Mrs. Polk was saying, "my dinner parties were known even in the state capital. My guests—all that was before the depression—such a shock—and my poor husband—" She let the old velvet wrap slide onto a chair, exposing her greasy silk dress and the long strands of clouded beads. The severe lines of her costume cruelly outlined the stringy pouches of her breasts. "I hope," she said abruptly, "that the leaves have not fallen all over the front walk again. The guests—"

"The wind is blowing," Holly heard her mother say.

"Oh!" Mrs. Polk came back from nowhere. "Now, we'll have our tea!" She arched her neck. Her upper lip drew down, curving her thin nose, giving her face an odd mock assurance.

She left them standing and went into the kitchen, returning at once with a prepared tray which she placed on the chair after pushing her wrap to the floor. She bent to pour the tea into mismatched nicked cups, held the sugar tongs tentatively over the little cubes, and smiled brightly into their faces. She handed them their cups of tea and passed a plate of store cookies.

Holly trembled with excitement and shyness, and the cup sounded against the saucer. She was sure that Mrs. Polk could hear her swallow. Her mother was embarrassed and could only listen to Mrs. Polk relating the distinctions of her invisible guests.

"Mr. Seward was county clerk, and Mr. Glover was head of the Building and Loan. Judge Eldon's wife sat here—"

The tea was lukewarm and bitter from standing. Holly and her mother stared cautiously at their hostess while she gazed upon the table with enviable aplomb.

"Dear, dear!" she exclaimed and rushed into the kitchen again, shoving the mutinous clock to one side, abandoning her cup on the chair seat. She snatched up a gray wet dishrag and hurried back to the table flicking a puffball of dust and sorrel hair that had drifted onto the lace. Then she stood aside holding the dank cloth in readiness.

"It all looks so natural," she said in a pleasantly grieved voice. "Just the way it was."

Natural! Holly thought. A terrible idea came into her mind, a frightening image of the tales old women used to tell of "sitting up with the corpse," of all night laying cold wet cloths on its face and hands. "To keep them from turning dark," said a faraway voice.

Mrs. Polk waved the rag uselessly as if she had no further need for it but could not let it go.

Holly stared in horror at Mrs. Polk, who looked like a mummy. The wasted years lay on the floor with the toast and the egg shells and the ghostly bleached shoes.

Perspiration sprang in Holly's palms. She wanted to escape, to be rid of the teacup, but seeing Mrs. Polk's yellow eyes expectant and secretive upon her, she drank.

"I hope you'll come again," Mrs. Polk said to Holly, dismissing them with ease. She followed them to the back door, poking at her faded hair which would not stay in place, smiling with exquisite reserve.

"Such beautiful things not to be used," Holly's mother said. "It's a shame."

Mrs. Polk appeared puzzled, then she said tiredly, "Such a task to unpack and wash and polish and pack up again!"

"Thank you very much," Holly squeezed from her throat.

At home her mother closed the door with relief and uttered a slow pronouncement, "For the love of Mike!"

Holly went quietly into the other room, closing the door on her mother's awe. She lay on the bed for a long time in utter fatigue, not closing her eyes, her thoughts preoccupied only with the small cracks and lines on the ceiling. Then she got up and took from the closet shelf the Sunday shoes and set them together neatly on the floor. She placed her father's hat on the bed. She gazed at all her catalogues and notebooks and plans. The years of her youth were in them, well concealed.

The journey to the stove was not a long one in space or time, but the anguish of change and the uncertainty of destination made it a sad and fearful expedition to an unknown place.

She opened the heater door and dropped a booklet on the red coals. She sat down to watch, and as the sheets became ash she added more. The fire roared in spite of her care, and once in the space under the door she saw her mother's feet approaching and turn back. Holly sat very still, tightening the muscles of her face, pressing the tears back.

When she had placed the last of the books in the stove, she leaned close and watched. They were heavy, and it took a long time. The little mouths of fire burned and closed, a sigh of ash expired like a breath. Her cheeks were hot and her eyelashes and the fine hairs on her arm were singed, but she felt cold, cold enough to tremble as with a chill.

She looked in at the black and fragile remains, holding their shape as pages still. She blew on them, and they collapsed with an infinitely delicate crash of sound, as if a little van of precious supplies had been wrecked on some far avenue of her mind.

She closed the heater door, and the touch of its warm knob reminded her of that lost other door to the now vacated room.

Rousing herself, Holly went to the window. She thought of the empty shelf in the closet. The scene outside wavered in her unrestrained tears. Her eyes slid fearfully past the half-painted wall of Mrs. Polk's house, beyond to the street with its houses and brown gardens and bare trees.

She hesitated for a long time, then she put on her new sweater that she had been saving and went out for a walk in the clear late afternoon sun.

The Santa Ana

All night the fog rolled up the hills from the sea and filled the garden, and in the morning lay cushioned against the door like an amiable dissolute ghost left over from the night. When Carrie opened the window she could hardly see the little garden table and two old chairs inviting her as they had invited futilely so many sunny mornings.

"It doesn't matter," she said. She spoke to herself and there was nothing strange or embarrassing about it; she felt a certain aware pleasure in her acceptance of this cheerful habit. She had lived alone for six years since the death of her mother, and silence at times was not to be endured. *But I'm not eccentric; just content. I've found my resources. Content,* she thought, but a latent superstition kept her from saying it aloud.

She started the water for tea, warmed the china pot and hesitated before the labeled canisters. "This is my day off," she said, and put in a heaping tablespoonful of black Ceylon so that the tea would be dark and strong with body enough to hold the milk and honey just as she liked it. Her mother had allowed this only on Sundays as a reckless treat. Weekday tea was fragrant and tonic chamomile or a desert-herb mix. On one of the best plates, Carrie arranged a juicy Comice pear, a small papaya, a tangerine and a little cup of sunflower seeds.

Before the kitchen mirror she tied a scarf over her pale heavy hair and glanced at her face. Plain. Plain. But the years had touched it lightly, and health and strength were there.

"Be thankful for that," her mother had told her. "Beauty is simply a burden of temptations." Carrie had sighed then for the privilege of temptations.

"Imagine my ignorance!" she said aloud, feeling stuffed with other women's experience. All day long these women she massaged told her, instead of resting, the most minute details of their lives. Vicariously, she was a many-sided woman of the world.

This made her smile as she carried the tray of fruit and tea into the garden. With her sweater buttoned, she sat at the table eating breakfast, hidden in the amorphous body of the fog.

"I'm in a cloud," she said softly.

Steam rose from the tea into the fog. She ate the fruit with the sensuous delight of a traveler in an exotic land. She drank all the tea, aware of its flavor and warmth, and still she lingered in this private, palpable world. A mockingbird sang a long ripple of notes from the acacia tree and was abruptly silent. Carrie looked at the single cup, conscious of her pleasure, which without any warning at all fled with the thought, laying bare her loneliness. It was a quiescent loneliness, but it came upon her like a new dimension of living as if designed and reserved for this day. An impertinence at her age, she protested, because it was a young emotion, an ache, a hollow place in which her formless thoughts echoed like auto horns in a tunnel, shrill and melancholy at once. She stood up, feeling sad and foolish and chilled to the bone.

An erratic gust of wind shook the jasmine leaves as if with rough intent, and rushed on, pushing the sea air unceremoniously back toward the sea. The wind seemed to come from the same unknown place as her loneliness. She waited. The air grew still. The fog, undone and torn, wavered uncertain. A warm narrow wind raced through the garden bringing a wild fragrance. The fog disappeared. A little whirl of dust flew by. Swiftly the day changed.

Its brilliant air dazzled her eyes. Under a balm of warmth the garden lay deceptive. Like no other morning, this one sang with the pristine mystery of the first morning of time. She felt she could not endure it; it contained a powerful meaning she could not grasp.

When the Santa Ana comes, blowing off the Mojave Desert two hundred miles away, people walking along the city streets are suddenly embraced by a lasso of warm soft wind. The air has a radiant clarity. The atmosphere becomes strange, subtly exciting. People begin to unwind, to gentle, to feel young, to delight in breathing, to be aware of being alive, and sad that they've been dully taking it for granted. The wind enfolds them and kisses them like petals, and they begin to feel in love—in love with being alive; and this is so rare, like a primeval sensation coming up through all the centuries, that they are a little frightened, but the wind soothes them, and a tender wily restlessness sets in. They aren't what they call *themselves* until the wind ceases and they can get back into their protective masquerades. The wind sometimes blows a day and a night. The time is enchanted with an alien beauty. It is as if love had come without a lover.

Reluctantly, Carrie picked up her basket of orderly cleaning tools and went first to the small sanitary rooms divided off for her work. As she polished the glass over her diploma, she read her name there as if she had never seen it before. Carrie Hagen. A stranger, perhaps, if truly known. *Masseuse.* How curious! She studied her hands, whose strength contradicted their frail design. Would they be clumsy tomorrow with the questions of today?

A window blew open and when she moved to close it a mischievous twist of wind jerked it from her fingers and slammed it shut and gently opened it again. The sly foreign air filled the room. She stood in its spell and without knowing why, her throat ached and her eyes burned with tears.

Her mother's words scolded from her youth, "Being busy, Carrie, is the cure for irresponsible emotions." Carrie looked at the clock and turned again to her work, pressing back a passion of loneliness. The whole day's disorganization loomed ahead like an obstacle race. She still missed her mother's sensible guidance, and her clients missed it too. Her mother had welcomed the women as they came and went, exchanging her boasts of health for their migraines and operations, and now and then to comfort them, she complained with lively charm of her very old age. The women came liking Carrie and went away devoted to her mother. It was the same with the only young man she had known. After her mother's death, some of the clients quit coming. When her own grief had subsided into controlled sorrow, Carrie ran a classified ad and her appointment book filled again, its proceeds nibbling at the final bills.

Her mother had once advised her, "When I'm gone, Carrie, and I have to go someday, put 'Mrs.' before your name like a widow. A woman's more protected like that. Remember, dear, a dead husband is more protection than none."

On her last birthday, without having prefixed her name with "Mrs.," Carrie began to feel that she had made a safe landing. She felt snug and secure in her singleness, not even one restless dream of a life other than the one she had.

Today was different, but it was only the Santa Ana wind. She turned from the window and dusted and scrubbed, laid out clean sheets, towels, paper slippers. The slippers, paper shelving, an anatomy chart on the wall were curling with dryness.

When she stopped for lunch and stood at the kitchen door, eating, watching the life in the garden, a flock of migrating birds swooped down into the tree, chattering and eating as if they had no more time than she. One of them flew into the lantana bush, and Carrie got her small, cheap Japanese opera glasses and observed him, a hungry traveler passing through, secure in self-knowledge and certain of his direction. How awesome was his feathered perfection! Again that acute, unbearable awareness of the morning assailed her. She could hardly resist going out into the sheen that quivered over the world of afternoon.

Bewitched, disengaged, she picked up her basket and pulled the vacuum cleaner after her into the living room. The electric wind had dried her hair and strands of it came loose and clung to her cheeks. Her skin felt tight on her body. In spite of these discomforts, her spirits rose with a plan to race through the work and leave before sunset for a drive along the sea.

Just as she was arranging the magazines in an orderly design, the doorbell rang and she answered it with an irritable flare in her eyes, although her cheerful mouth was still tender with thoughts of escape.

The stranger, puzzled for a moment by her singular expression, hesitated in the movement of setting down his case of wares, then with his free hand he removed his hat and said, "Good day, ma'am." A slight accent that she could not identify touched his words.

The rather formal gesture was like a chivalry from another age, so rare were hats in this informal southern climate. A springy bush of red hair appeared to leap from under the hat as if it had reached its limit of confinement. The man's eyes were red-brown, and red-brown freckles spattered his tanned face.

It occurred to Carrie that he was like a harmless, furred creature that one might meet in the woods, and she remained still, respecting his nature, not even returning his polite greeting.

"I wonder, would you be interested in these moth crystals and poison sprays I have here? And powders for roaches and silverfish and ants?" While he sang out these words in a gentle way, he opened the case.

"Oh, come in," she said, disliking the neighbors to see her being talked into purchases at the door.

Surprised, he came in.

"I do need some moth crystals if they're good and if they're fragrant. I don't want things smelling of moth balls."

"No need," he said simply. "A good smell can kill them as easily as a bad one."

"Our deceptive world," she said.

"Science," he explained. "Everything's science now."

He handed her his card and she placed it on the piano, asking him to sit down so that it would be easier to lift the cans and bottles from the case. He sat on the nearest seat, the piano bench, and when she went to get the money for the crystals, she heard him softly play a chord. The piano was in poor tune; she had not played it for years and then not well, but her voice was nice and she had enjoyed singing for her friends until they were married and gradually drifted away from her inconvenient singleness.

When she came back into the room, he withdrew his hands quickly and sat again with his back to the keys.

"Do you play?" she asked.

"Oh, not at all, and not for many a year at that."

A strong gust of warm wind slammed an upstairs window, invaded their presence, and swept on past the house, giving it a rude shake.

Carrie said, "Oh!" Then, "Would you like to play something?"

"Oh, no, ma'am, I wouldn't want to take your time."

"I won't let you," she laughed. "I'll just go on and do my work."

"Are you sure you don't mind, ma'am?"

"Heavens, no." He was obviously harmless, and it would give them both pleasure.

"Well, I only play to make a little sound of something for the song."

"Were you on the stage?"

He laughed. "Far from that! Where I came from as a lad we did a good bit of singing."

She could not bring herself to ask him where that was, thinking she might have been too friendly. To conceal her embarrassment, she hurried into the kitchen and ran the dust mop over the clean linoleum. This pretense embarrassed her even more and she returned to the living room and worked, ignoring him.

He played in a reminiscent, searching way, and then he began to sing in a good voice one lively song after another. At the third one she sat down in a chair and watched his face, which had such a jolly sparkle that she smiled at him and he smiled back through the singing as if they were old friends. She got up and began to dust the Venetian blinds.

He sang two sad old songs, and one of them she knew. Her mother had often sung her to sleep with it when she was a child. It was about a young man who had stabbed his sweetheart because he thought she was unfaithful. The refrain was a slow lamenting:

"Oh, Edwin, I'll forgive you with my last and dying breath, For I know that I never deceived you," And she closed her eyes in death.

How she had loved that song and the vivid and terrible images she had been able to conjure for sleep!

"Imagine!" she exclaimed and hurried over to the piano. They sang together the mourning sentimental tale of ruined love through all the many verses and repeated choruses, and when they came to the end, he swung round on the bench and looked at her and they both laughed, so that he swung back and played another chorus. She stood behind him, singing and looking at his thick red hair, his masculine head that astonished her and made her feel lonely.

She should move away, but she could not, and as if he felt this, he played a happy song, not singing, and stood up. He looked at her so abruptly that she knew that he had seen her tender expression as she had seen his revealed by the singing and quickly concealed as she had concealed her own.

She turned away and lifted a metal pitcher filled with lemon leaves. The electric sting of contact snapped in the quiet room, startling her so that she set the pitcher down.

"Oh, a shock!" she protested. "I was just going to get some fresh water for these leaves."

"Now," he said, looking at her impersonally, his voice the tone of a lecturer, "take those sparks. They're the same sparks that fly between two people without a word of warning. Scientists will never figure that out."

"Oh, they might; it's nothing in the world but electricity."

"So! But everyone hasn't got the same frequency. Perhaps we've each our own delicate vibration level, our own cadence that simply doesn't harmonize with every Tom, Dick and Mary."

"Young people think it's love," she said, rash and frightened, "but we know it's untrustworthy."

"I beg pardon, ma'am, we don't know anything of the kind. Though," he added politely, "you're right in the sense you speak of." He watched her blush. "But there are many levels of response. Some very trustworthy indeed."

The wind was blowing fully. A sweeping rush made the big trees outside the windows sound like river water.

"I'm sure some industrial scientists are working on this right now." He struck a high black key in satiric dissent. "If they could just do away with all the waste motion caused by sparks flying, proper unions could be arranged, proper babies could be born, for, let us say, proper usefulness—practicality."

"Dear me," she said, grateful that he was aware of her discomfort and was changing the subject somewhat.

He looked at her gravely for a long moment and went right on as if she had freed his lonesome thoughts. "There'll be tables of human types at every post office. There'll be posters: MARRY YOUR TYPE AND ELIMINATE WASTEFUL PRIMITIVE EMOTIONS. OR, WASTEFUL SPIRITUAL QUALITIES. There will be laboratories where a person troubled with the impulses of love can have his surplus electricity removed!"

"Then you still do believe that electricity is a part of love?" she asked coolly.

"Certainly, ma'am, a part! But I've no clear idea what all of it is. Have you?"

Veering away, Carrie said with assurance, "One is afraid to say a word these days for fear science doesn't agree. But science itself is always changing!"

"That's our only hope! Now, ma'am, science is a fine thing—in its place. But reason and proof that once freed the mind may end up limiting it. No matter, though; in that case, someone or something will break the old mold. We'll need fresh concepts to make the new one."

"Oh, I agree! But where do you get all that?"

He tapped his forehead. "Then I'm also a bit of a one for reading. To sit in the quiet rooms of the public library of an evening with just the rustle now and then of a page turning—have you ever been there, ma'am?"

"Only once," she said, determined to go again.

Her housework by now was two hours late. She didn't even care. She wondered what she could say to start him again on this outrageous conversation which was so pleasant in some of its implications. Or perhaps he was the kind that simply loved to talk. This thought made her feel critical of him, almost angry. Why didn't he leave?

Instead he began to play again.

Without being aware of it, she was humming the melody. Suddenly he left the piano and faced her with the gayest approval she had ever seen in any expression directed at her.

"You were humming that!"

"Was I?"

"I was just making it up as I went along! I was thinking of something else."

"So was I," she said quietly.

"Remarkable!" He looked past her and spoke, excluding her. "That settles it. Indeed it does."

"Settles what?"

The sharp delight in his face became tender. "Now, isn't that a woman for you? How lovely!" His foreign accent was strong on these words. "'Settles what?' A very revealing remark. It gives me courage to overstep myself by asking—" He paused.

She waited. There was a coiled silence in which both were trapped. Carrie felt suspended, miserable, eager to say: "Yes, yes, come here again!" What possible harm? She glanced at him cautiously and saw that he looked ruffled and uncomfortable. How very nice! She wanted to laugh in giddy triumph, but she was afraid. She frowned and absently touched the metal vase. Electricity snapped in the air, and she was overwhelmed with guilt.

"—courage to overstep myself by asking—" His next words came out in a rush. "Are you married, ma'am?"

This unexpected question confused her even more, but she knew that her answer did not matter. She was fixed within the moment of acceptance. She must remain silent, and in this swell of harmony he would understand all she felt.

Dimly she realized that they were standing in the dusk and that he was waiting in a hurried and anxious way. The air between them was powerful with meaning. She wanted to reach out her hand and touch him for reply, but she could not move. Didn't he know the answer by their singing together? Wasn't the eloquence she felt apparent? Still he waited, and his expectant eyes revealed uncertainty. Still she could not speak.

Without meaning to at all, she looked down at the open case of aromatics and poisons, and as if it hindered her reply, she stepped back, back perhaps in an effort to break the circle of recognition that bound her voice.

"Oh!" he said with courteous pride. "Oh, I beg your pardon, ma'am!"

He jumped to close the case and pick up his hat. He was the stranger—rebuffed.

"We Welsh are great for singing," he laughed, and there was a slight, careless apology in his laughter. Then he was gone, out the door and into the street so rapidly that when she understood what was happening, she ran to the door, but his car was already zooming away.

If she had known his name, she would have run out and called to him, breaking the stranger's dignity, "Gareth Davies! Gwilym Morgan!" or whatever his Welsh name was.

She rushed back to the piano to look at the card, and it was not there. He had picked it up when she had glanced meaningfully, as he must have thought, toward his case of wares. How painful it was to have hurt him! She stood in the dusky room wondering if he had ever been, if any of this had happened at all. Then she touched the piano keys and they were still warm.

By nightfall the moody electric Santa Ana was blowing hard off the Mo-jave. There were great rushes and furtive silences. On her way to bed, Carrie stepped out on a balcony and gazed into the clear, alive night. A restless dog trotted past on his way to nowhere.

An empty can whipped down the paved hill road. Street lights glittered as beautiful as stars in the clean wind-swept air. Behind her the drying wood cracked like cautious, secret steps.

A delicate light from the moon permeated the dark and shone on her ringless hands curving tightly over the railing. Below, the large green leaves of banana trees, yesterday whole, were split like fringe along the leaf spine; and now they plopped against the house, making a hollow tattoo of shadow and sound. As the wind swung them one way and another, they exposed and concealed the determined, inedible fruit growing on the sterile trees.

In bed she could not sleep, bewildered in emptiness and despair. The dry mysterious fragrance of a strange land was borne on the wind. It entered her mind, prying up lids, shaking locks and trembling the doors of her unperceived wisdom.

She got up and returned to the balcony, looking down into the now deserted street sealed under the moonlight and dappled swinging shadows of the trees. The solemn darkened houses rose up like ancient cliffs along an unknown river; and feeling herself a part of this night, unknown and yet related, with strange thoughts stinging her mind, a wildness like the wildness of the sly archaic wind rose up in her.

She ran downstairs and found the jar of crystals with his name. She turned off the lamp and sat in the dark, unaccustomed to being beautiful and possibly in love—and even loved.

The Wild Flower

On Sundays they slept no later because the cow wanted to be milked on time, but they napped in the hot afternoons unless they went visiting and they rarely did. The distances were far, the car was not often inclined to run, being old and needing repair in too many parts, and they did not know many other farmers well enough to arrive without telephoning first and they had no telephone. The lines hummed along the road and Dale often placed his ear against a pole and listened to the pleasant and mysterious rhythm which he called "talking." He made a line of his own with a long wire and two tin cans, but there was no one for the other end.

This Sunday in late spring, while they were eating a breakfast of eggs and pancakes and corn syrup and coffee, a warm lonesome wind came in the window and made them all feel restless. Dale asked Homer for a spoonful of coffee in his milk and his father gave it without protest. There were only three small oranges and Betts brought one of them to the table and gave it to Dale as a surprise present. The orange made the day like Christmas, except that at Christmas they had been snowed in and had very little of anything to eat.

"Well," Homer said, winking slyly at his wife, "if you could pack up something, Betts, we might go a-visiting."

"Who'll we visit, dad!" Dale exploded, losing a piece of orange onto the oilcloth table cover.

"That depends on your mother."

"If you'll kill a chicken, Homer, I'll fry it, and make some potato salad and devilled eggs."

"Who, dad?"

"Dip."

"Oh, boy! Dip!"

"We ain't visited Ol' Dip in a month o' Sundays," Homer said forlornly.

"It's a nice day for the walk," Betts said. "I ain't over missin' Dip myself."

"One thing," Homer said, "We don't have to phone up Dip. We're welcome anytime."

"That's one of the pleasures of his state," Betts said, and her slow smile sent the corners of her eyes up.

"I'd like to be excused," Dale said, crossing his knife and fork on his plate.

"You may, son. Don't be in too big a hurry to set your chair in to the table."

Dale obeyed and ran out letting the screen door fly back with a soft thud against the piece of rubber Homer had tacked into the jamb.

"Beats all how excited a kid can get over a small thing."

"I'll bet you're kinda' excited yourself, Homer."

"I am that," he smiled at her. "Summer makes me want to ramble around."

"I'm glad to get out of the kitchen," she said, and began clearing the table. "I've got to step lively."

"Now don't get flustered. We got all day. I'll kill the chicken and pick him."

"Pick him, too?"

"I will."

"This is a rare day, Homer Delaney."

"Why, woman, I'm liable to lose my temper."

"Faunch away!" she laughed.

"No, my temper's restin' too."

"Get a move on you, Homer. Men are so slow."

"Some men and some women," he said gently, and went out.

She put the potatoes and eggs on the stove and got out the old grape basket and washed it, lining it with clean paper and a tea towel. Up from the cellar she brought a jar of pickles for the salad.

"Wish I had some lemons for lemonade," she grumbled. "Reckon there'll ever be a time when we got enough of anything?"

"Not likely," said Homer, coming in after the hot water.

"Don't come in on me like that!"

"Been comin' in this door some years now. Little late to start knockin'."

"I didn't mean that."

"Then you better stop talkin' to yourself."

She flushed. "It's natural when a body's alone so much."

"You said you didn't like to live in town."

"I don't. I just wish we had the money for a better car so we could go in oftener or go a-visiting."

"Well, we're going a-visiting today."

"And here we are, all excited. It's the limit!"

He went out with the steaming teakettle, and she moved quickly preparing the picnic lunch. When Homer came in again, he said, "I cleaned it, too!"

"Well, forevermore, Homer. I believe you're right down anxious."

They stood in the treeless yard waiting for Dale, who came running.

"Get a drink first," Betts said.

"Ain't we taking water?"

"A little, but you fill up now. We don't want to load ourselves down."

"It'll be hot walkin'," Homer said. "We'll take turns carryin' the basket. 'Course, since Dale's the littlest he won't have to carry it very far."

With the back of his hand, imitating his father, Dale wiped the water off his smiling face. "I'll bet Dip's been lonesome. Reckon he's changed much, dad?"

"Not much anymore. Last year was the biggest change."

The wind was pungent with the smell of sage. A row of thunder-heads like a street of white mansions curved round the big blue sky to the east.

"They just lay off there and promise and threaten and don't ever rain," Homer complained. "I declare, it tries a man."

"They look like big fat white cats sound asleep," Betts said accusingly.

"When it lightnings," Dale said, "they're opening their eyes."

"Blowing and yowling when they go on the rampage."

A meadowlark flew up suddenly from the grass, and Dale ran toward it.

"Don't bother her nest, son."

"I won't, dad; I just want to look."

"Better come away; she's worryin'."

The low tough grass was springy under their feet. The sun grew warmer and they went without talking over the treeless plain. In each of their minds was an image of their dog Bounce who had just last week run off over the prairie with a queer jerking gait and a queerer bark. He had got rabies from the coyotes or wolves and gone mad. Homer had come in for the shotgun and killed him "to get him out of his misery" and that night they ate supper in silence. Homer passed word along to the neighbors for a pup. Occasionally townspeople dropped unwanted dogs on the road and they wandered to the nearest farm. Bounce had come to them like that when he was small. Maybe they would be lucky again.

"I read where some old crank," Homer said, "wants to kill off all the dogs. Says their barkin' causes eight per cent of all nervous breakdowns."

"Must be that humans cause the other ninety-two per cent," Betts said. "Does he want to kill *them* off?"

"Wouldn't be surprised, if he's sour on an animal as good as a dog."

"What's a nervous breakdown, dad?"

"I can't rightly say, son, but I reckon that was what happened to that little coyote we had chained up. Remember how he would run out to the end of the chain all the time and get jerked up short. He lost confidence in himself. He couldn't live his life the way he ought to, and finally he just crumpled up and didn't care. Couldn't care, I reckon."

"Is that all?"

"Well, you ask your mother. I may be entirely wrong. Women folks have more such ailments than men folks."

"I doubt that, Homer Delaney! If men had to be women a little while they'd crumple up faster'n that poor little old coyote."

"Look out, now, Betsy, we're out for a good time."

"You're a good enough man, Homer, but I declare, that humorin' won't fit down very snug over the truth of such things."

"Well, the men folks have their troubles, too, but I ain't thinkin' of trouble today."

"I'm not, either. This is a quiet and peaceful day and my heart matches it."

Homer had been walking a few steps ahead and he dropped back beside her.

They came to a hollow which Dale thought was fun. He ran down the side, lay panting at the bottom and waited.

"Haven't seen any old rattlesnakes today," he called to them.

"Well, now, it's just beyond," Homer said.

As they came out of the hollow, Betts stopped and looked around. A mirage shimmered far ahead like a new dream. "This is a lonesome land, but I like it. As far as the eye can see, just space, and the biggest sky there is. Not one tree."

"Some folks wouldn't like it," Homer said proudly, "but I can't tolerate being shut in by a lot of hills and trees."

"A tree in our yard and one at Dip's would be nice," Betts said. "That would be enough."

"There he is!" Dale shouted. "There's Dip!" He ran ahead.

Dip was easy to see on the prairie. They came up to him and stood together looking down.

"Hello, old boy. We've come to pay you a visit," Homer said cheerfully.

"Hello, Dip," Betts said.

The bleached white skeleton of the horse lay as if asleep on the prairie. The wolves had at first torn him apart, but after the flesh was gone, Homer and Dale had rearranged his bones, and now that they were dry and odorless they remained unmolested.

"He was a good worker," Homer said, "and steadied that nervous Lollie."

"I'll bet he's been lonesome, dad."

Under the great bow of his chalky ribs a bull snake stirred and moved off slowly toward a soap weed.

"He's a grand horse," Betts said. And it seemed to them all for a moment that Dip was sharing the pleasant Sunday afternoon.

A few feet away Betts spread a cloth on the grey buffalo grass and set out the lunch. Looking out for the small round cacti which grew like cruel buttons on the earth, they sat down. The sun was warm but the wind that would blow hot in mid-summer was now cool, and tangy with the smell of the high arid lands. They ate leisurely, speaking quietly the random thoughts of their Sunday minds.

"Supposing we were the only people left on earth," Dale said, waving his arm around at the uninhabited plain.

"It's not unlikely," Homer said drowsily.

"Supposing," Dale said, paying no attention to anything but his imagination. "Supposing—"

"Supposing we got so lonesome we went calling on the bones of people?" Betts asked.

"Naw. Just supposing we had the earth all to ourselves."

"Wouldn't do us a bit of good, son. Though I swear there's a lot of grown men with the same thought."

"Can't we just imagine we're the only ones left?"

"Sure we can, but your imagination'll die off feedin' on such as that. Folks seem bent on destruction."

"More people are bent on living, I'd say. Look how they survive," Betts said sharply.

"Aw, you won't play," and Dale got up and kicked at Dip's skull. Then he bent over curiously. "There's a little blue-bell growing up near his head!"

"That's just a little reminder of the indestructibility of nature, including two-legged man. Kinda' like the hope weed. Can't kill it."

"Don't break your jaw, Homer. You showin' off before Dip, here?"

"No, woman. I could as easy say the plain stubbornness of life in everything, but I've come by a few words in my time, and I mean to whet my mind."

Dale was on his knees peering into the horse's skull.

"That flower's some of Dip's immortality, son. You been askin' me what immortality means."

"You mean a flower can grow from a horse?"

"In a roundabout way. Everything dies and goes back in the earth and helps something new to come up. In that way we live forever, and in no other, the way I see it."

"Could I be some wheat, maybe, dad?"

"Reckon so—unbeknownst to you. In that case you'd end up as bread and keep another man alive."

"Say!" Dale said, and picked the flower gently, twirling it between his thumb and forefinger.

"You see that flower puts a fine thought in us. Thoughts live too, son. Now, our thoughts, well—maybe I'm goin' a piece too far today, but it's in my mind."

"It's endless," Betts said. "One thing leads to another."

"Yes, it's endless."

"Does Dip know about the thought he gave us in the flower?"

"No, son, but it won't matter to him because he's dead and the thought is alive."

"I can't imagine dead," Dale said.

"That's because you can't imagine *nothing*. Ain't none of us can do that."

"I wonder," Betts said tartly.

"Be a better world on earth if men weren't saddled with future bliss," Homer grumbled.

"What's that, dad?"

"Well, heaven and such. It's a crime to make a mockery of life on earth. It's a good thing to feel wonder, but there's room enough for wonder in nature and man."

"Homer, ain't you sleepy?" Betts demanded.

"The thing is, son, to put your mind on your living life and other people's. I don't mean meddlin'."

Dale looked puzzled.

"What would you say to goin' round by way of the crick and all takin' a bath?"

"Whoopee!" Dale yelled, instantly shedding eternity.

"I didn't bring towels, Homer."

"Ah, we'll use the sun and the tablecloth."

The sun was halfway down the sky.

They went over to Dip and for a moment their sadness came back. Dale wore the flower in a buttonhole of his overall strap.

"Goodbye, old boy. We'll visit you again."

They started off south although there was nothing to be seen but the prairie. After two miles they came to a precipice. Far below, a small stream ran through a wide bed of sand. On the opposite shore was the pale bright green of cottonwood trees; beyond, a rise of rock and scrub to the level floor of the endless plain. They found a steep path and supporting themselves on the huge eroded stones, they reached the stream below. There a willow tree grew on the bank with part of its roots exposed. They placed their clothes on a rock and holding onto the roots waded into the shallow crystal water. Homer and Dale were naked but Betts wore her underskirt. They swam where the water was deep enough, splashed, laughed, rubbed themselves and dried in the cooling sun. Refreshed, they dressed and climbed up to the plain, starting the long walk home.

The red sun set on the horizon and then moved slowly down, sending great colored shafts into the sky. After the long sunset,

the dusk came up around their knees like the fields of night growing swiftly into a forest darkening overhead. They moved a long
time through the dusk and during the last mile they came into
the night, as if it had been waiting for them ahead, another place,
a world of night. The sky was black and tall and wide and pointed
with all the stars. No moon rose.

They walked steadily and did not speak, withdrawing into
delicately defiant separateness. Now and then Dale touched the
wilted tender flower in his overall strap.

Their silence was not sad although they were lonely. This was
not a loneliness for anyone, because the three of them had no acute
feelings for anyone else; it was merely aloneness, therefore it had
a largeness, an impersonal grandeur, which caused each to feel
in need of some special communication. They had felt it often,
especially at night when they stood in the yard before going to
bed and looked into the dark. This aloneness appealed silently and
familiarly to the big sky and the stars and the moon (never to the
sun), to the vast distances of the prairie, to the winds always blowing, and most of all to the night, because the night was endless
unlike the circled day, because the night contained many things:
reminders of the known, urges to the unknown; smells, of living
things and dead, of the weather; sounds, of animals, wild and tame,
of a motor on a far road, of distant thunder, of the high faint roar
of an airplane, the lonely whistle of a train. The wind made sounds,
although it blew unrestrained across the prairie over the low grass.
Along the roads it sang through the wires, a weird music, it whined
around the corners of farm buildings and moaned to itself. The
winds of storm blasted and roared and boomed and made them
afraid of its mindless fury. But the un-angry wind of tonight had
ears to listen to their wordlessness.

They entered the yard feeling reluctant and glad to be home.
When Betts lighted the lamp, they looked sheepishly at one an-
other and Homer said loudly, "We sure had a good time with old
Dip, didn't we?"

"We sure did!" Betts and Dale spoke at once.

Betts lighted the oil stove.

"That old cow must be thinkin' hard of us," Homer said. "We're late with the milkin'."

Betts placed the teakettle on the flame, scraping the bottom over the burner unnecessarily. Homer and Dale went out to do the chores. As she turned toward the pantry she saw Dip's flower lying crumpled on the floor.

"Wild flowers don't last," she mumbled, but she picked it up and dropped it into a jelly glass of water. She gazed at it remembering the indestructible and living day. Starting, she hurried into her tasks.

"One thing's clear," she said aloud, "I've got to put some food into our mortal stomachs."

Davy

avy heard the thud of the two weekly newspapers against the house, and a door was banged twice with the abandon of someone immune to all noise. That would be Mrs. Nelsen who lived in the other half of the old house and supported her four children with washing. Davy had been home from school an hour, sitting hunched with cold on her bed, reading a book. The house was quiet now. Papa was gone. She pushed her blonde straight hair back and rested her eyes on the dried morning glory vine still clinging to her window by its rotting summer strings. How lovely to again see its delicate purple trumpet! Would they live here then?

Davy tried holding her breath. Since Mrs. Nelsen, the odor of soapsuds came under the doors, overpowering all pleasant smells, even their memory. There was a brown swatch on the front yard where she dragged her tubs out and up-ended them onto the struggling grass. Papa had nursed that grass. He had a way with plants and animals. It was said he had a way with people, but that did not affect her and Mama. It was said he was handsome, too.

The first early snow had melted and even though all the grass was brown, on Mrs. Nelsen's trademark it was dead. This reminded Davy to get the newspaper. She unwound her long legs and stood up, feeling stiff and cold. Mama always urged her to build the fire after school on Fridays, and not to worry about the coal, but Davy was cautious and saving, afraid of the future. She had a small secret bank and old Christmas presents put away for that fine day when she could get away from home.

She went outside as stealthy as a thief. The other door led out of Mrs. Nelsen's kitchen and Davy loved peace; she was afraid of the woman and only nodded in a dim friendly way when she encountered her at all. The last dead leaves were falling down on the grass, whirling weakly as if trying to rise up to the tree again. Davy thought that Papa would have them raked up and burned by now; that was one of the few things he was good for but it was hardly impressive enough to qualify as a father.

She stepped off the low front porch looking for the paper just as Mrs. Nelsen came round the house carrying an armload of clothes from the line. The clothes were frozen into strange shapes and the woman's hands that held them were red and cracked with cold. Davy's pity went into a shy smile, and Mrs. Nelsen said pleasantly, "The weather fair bites, but I don't bar nobody, I got the whitest clothes in town!"

"They look nice," Davy said.

"Nice? That's a lame word for them!" She watched Davy poking around the dead vines under the window where the paper sometimes lodged. "If it's a snake it'd bitecha. There, right in the crack of the walk out front."

"Oh," said Davy, confused.

"Like as not, the Lord ain't meanin' yu to find it this day," she said meaningfully. "So help me, it's worse than I surmised."

"What is?" Davy said, holding the paper folded.

"Have a look for yerself, child, then go hide yer face for shame. The sins of the fathers—"

Davy closed the door quietly on the mawkish voice. An ash of loyalty for Papa burned in her for a moment, then the fear to open the paper, and after that the hate.

She laid the fire expertly in the kitchen stove and pushed the coffee pot forward, pouring water over the morning's grounds.

Mama wanted a cup of black coffee as soon as she came in from work at the store. Davy set the table carelessly with a wan thought for the monotonous meal. Then she unfolded the paper. Its usually quiet face which had nothing for a banner headline more than once a year had one this night: RAID NETS BOOTLEG RING. Davy looked with contempt at the list of names and her breath caught angrily. There was Dave Fitzgerald first of all, followed by three more. A ring! And Papa in it! "Fitzgerald was seized in the lobby of the Royal Hotel after he had obtained a pint of whiskey for an officer who cleverly posed as a thirsty acquaintance."

Davy stuffed the newspaper into the fire feeling sick of Papa and sick of the whole town.

When Mama came in it was apparent that she had seen the paper. Her smile was left safe in the cash drawer, put away like an artisan's tools. Her face was naked, revealing its tired humiliations.

"Hungry, little baby?" she asked, touching Davy's hair.

"Not yet."

"Then I'm going to rest a little." She carried her cup of hot coffee into the cold bedroom, and after a while Davy heard her blowing her tearful nose.

Papa was usually getting up about this time, teasing them with his high spirits until he gave up and sat at the table practicing: shuffling and dealing his cards, watching them seriously, reading their infinitesimal signs.

Mama and Papa had been separated three weeks, and the divorce was already filed. To Mama, her own decision was still blurred by its strangeness. Mama was not at home in decisions. She had hardly complained about anything for the whole twenty years, and then one day she got sullen and angry, and with the help of a lawyer, concisely listed in legal terms all the misery of her uncertain life with an irresponsible husband whose profession was gambling.

It was that last month which had stopped Mama's secret weeping and given her a stubborn, independent air as she came home from work and walked past Papa, sitting on the bed in his underwear, just having woken up. Davy thought Mama had clicked her heels hard on the floor in a sharp warning. The warning was about the rent. Papa had not won enough lately to pay the rent and all the expenses now fell on Mama, whose wages were very small, only a little cash and the rest in groceries at retail rates. That was the reason they had had to move out of the other half of the house and rent it to Mrs. Nelsen. Papa had a quarrel with Mrs. Nelsen right off about pouring soapy water on the grass. He had indicated that she was not as clean as she should be, and what Mrs. Nelsen indicated, although solely to the neighbors, was more interesting but also more damaging. All she said directly at the time was: "Sir, I can give you as good as you send. God help me, there's different kindsa' dirt." Papa came in the house because he had sure ideas about how much you could say to a woman. This did not include Mama.

Papa lay down for a nap. At first he couldn't fall asleep, and he said with derisive sadness to Davy, "You know, that dirty old woman insulted me."

"She had to call on God to help her do it," Davy assured him. Davy knew he was glad for this little crumb of a compliment; he was very fond of her and for three years she had shown him nothing but her hatred. Because they roamed from one little town to the next, and the people in them knew her father was a gambler, she was cut out of everything she expected to find while growing up. She was sixteen and lived like a hermit. Once in awhile someone was generous and invited her out, but just because they *were* generous, she couldn't go. On these evenings she hated her father very much.

One of the things she hated most was his sleeping in the daytime. He stayed up all night. Every night about eight or nine o'clock he would move restlessly about the kitchen for a few minutes and say, "Well, I have to hustle up a little game." He would kiss them both and go out the back door across the alley toward town and the Royal Hotel. The Royal Hotel was not the best, but it was the largest and the least dull. Travelers stopped there; the town luncheons and wedding parties went on at The Bella Brock.

Davy liked to hear the small cracking sounds of Papa's steps going over the crusty snow toward the Royal Hotel. She tied two sweaters over her shoulders and put her feet in the oven of the cook stove and sat back in peace.

She studied or read or planned. The only interruption was the necessity to fix the fire so that it would not burn up the coal too fast, and still keep them warm. Occasionally her mother asked her how to spell a word for the long letters she wrote nearly every evening to friends she missed in other towns. Once in awhile they went to a movie together, but Papa never took them anyplace except the Carnival, which happened only once a year.

It frightened Mama for her to hate Papa. Although Mama wasn't religious, she knew there was a Commandment against it, the number of which always failed her and weakened her argument with Davy.

Davy was deep in a fantasy of running away when her mother came back into the kitchen. She animatedly related the details of her day at the store before she mentioned Papa, and then she only said bitterly and soothingly, "He's trying to disgrace us some more because he's alone."

"I thought he wanted to be alone," Davy said.

"Well, he does and he doesn't. That's the way men are."

"What about women?" Davy asked innocently.

"Does it matter what a woman wants?" Mama grumbled.

"Of course, it does! Stop sounding like a worm, Mama."

"I only wish I were. I'd certainly go underground after today."

Davy subsided into her silent distaste for both of them. She day-dreamed another home and two new parents who were—

"Let's eat, Davy-honey. You know, if I wasn't so dumb and uneducated we could move and I'd get a job, but I'm afraid to leave this one now I have it."

Davy felt a little ashamed over the last day-dream.

"I see you've cleaned the house up spic and span," Mama said.

"Yes. Tomorrow's Saturday. I'll wash the windows. Sunday I have to write a study of Tolstoy's *Anna Karenina* for school."

"What's that about?"

"An unhappy woman."

"Look at your Mama!" she laughed.

"Would you like to read it, Mama? It's very good."

"When I get home from work I'm too dog-tired to read any-thing, Davy. The letters are different. I just ramble on. It's like talk-ing to someone, the way you do when you're thinking."

"It's like that with the books," Davy said, shyly, "—listening to someone I like."

Mama sighed. "I suppose we're all going different directions—all hunting for someone to talk to. Why is it such a mean game? I am a fool—everyone betrays me."

"I won't ever give anyone a chance to betray me."

"Then you'll miss something, Davy. I'll take my sorrows. See? I have you."

Davy did not understand. She felt guilty when Mama spoke of her life. She looked at Mama's bland face, feeling terribly afraid of the future. I won't be like that, she thought fiercely, I'll run away from it.

II

Davy walked hurriedly along one of the wide paths of the small wintry park leading to the new jail in the center. The earth was frozen hard and the cold stung her face and the tips of her fingers. The tall trees that almost hid the jail in summer were black skeletons now, baring the paths and the grey stone buildings to every eye. She was the only one walking on the path although people hurried along the sidewalks around the park, and it seemed to her that each person looked and recognized her and glanced away sheepishly, leaving her exposed to the next.

Papa had sent her a message by the young gambler who tagged after him. The message was that he had a bad cold and wanted his medicine. Davy put it in a paper bag and handed it to the boy, but he backed away saying, "I think he wants you to bring it." Papa had told her often, "Never associate with a gambler," so, although the boy had an incredibly innocent appearance, she thanked him coolly and closed the door. When she thought of going to the jail, she said aloud, liking the adult sound of it, "I hate sentimentality!" This private display of maturity had no effect whatever on the growing panic she felt at being alone with her father, actually faced with the necessity of a conversation. What had they to say to each other? The time of pleasurable childish talk with him was fallen away in her memory and so corroded with her sense of his betrayal that she could not yet remember any of it with tenderness.

How was it that Papa, who had no roots in anything, could have appeared such an anchor? Such a source of fun and delight? Such a warm and magnificent being whose wide shoulder held her head, whose arms protected, whose vibrant face and dancing voice made eagerness grow in her like an indomitable weed? Whose mere existence inspired her love? Why was she deaf to his adult words all around her? Sightless to the shabby ways of his life? Because he loved her, because he was her father, a simple fact?

One day, after a long time of shadowy emotions, without his having changed, without his having said or done one thing different, she looked at him with cruel and intolerant clarity, and silently accused him of failure, of betrayal. Disillusionment had ached within her for three years now, three years of withdrawal, with as few words spoken as she could manage. Although he was hurt, he was unbelieving and tried for a while to continue the playful expressions of their love. He had cheated her by his very identity with her. Today, how would they speak, when casual words were the most difficult of all?

She was unsure how to approach the jail and while she hesitated, more people saw her. Even her back grew warm with embarrassment as she turned away from the eyes in the street. The door opened easily and she was surprised to meet an old woman who looked like a Christmas grandmother. She came to the counter with a dust cloth in her hand and greeted Davy sweetly, as if this were a call at her home. Davy's blush that had begun outside as she turned toward the door now deepened and spread down her neck in fiery splotches. Her voice was being squeezed away from all speech. She stood dumbly at the counter.

"Do you want to see someone, child?"

Davy felt her face cooling, getting pale perhaps, and the skin along her cheeks pulling stiffly.

"I'm Davy Fitz—" she whispered, losing her name in her tight throat.

"I know, now, of course!" the old woman said kindly. "You just wait. I'll get my husband to bring him in. It's my husband who's the turnkey here, not I!" She laughed and pressed a button that made a buzz someplace else. "We live here, you see. Our rooms are very nice in this new building. I swear, I'm content, and my husband says that's unbelievable."

Davy began to feel herself smoothing out. She was curious now, but still afraid someone would come in and see her here.

"Would you care if I went there—where Papa is? Is it all right?"

"Indeed, yes, although it isn't customary. Papa—bless you! Your papa is a dear man. No harm will come to you with him around. I don't know what he's doing in here. I swear, I believe it's all a mistake."

"I'm afraid not," Davy said, coldly.

"Well, last night, my husband and I just let the rules go hang, and we invited him in to supper. I put a poultice on his chest, too, the poor fellow." She touched Davy's arm and whispered, "He's grieving over the divorce charges. He can't understand them. They're outrageous. I believe the lawyer made a mistake."

"I don't," Davy said. This time she saw the old woman's faith hesitate.

"The papers had to be served on him in here, and that, of course, was humiliating."

The old man came in and his wife rapidly explained. He beckoned Davy to follow him. He said nothing all the way along the cool passage until they neared the cells on the second floor. He looked sharply at Davy, whose blush had come up again, and said, "Your father is a fine man. This'll teach him his lesson."

As they came into the first section, she heard her father's voice in the familiar tone of mingled humor and anger.

"God damn, you fellows are dirty just because you're in jail. I get you to clean up your cells and now I smell socks. You've got nothing to do and you don't even wash your clothes."

"Pressing your new denim suit, Dave?" someone called mockingly.

"No, by God, but I washed it."

Someone began to sing.

"Cut it!" another called brutally, as if he had been interrupted.

"Let him sing," Dave shouted. "Sing my favorite, Hank."

"No bad talk, you fellows," the old man announced. "A lady's here."

Davy wanted to turn back. The quick silence made her feel as awkward as had the walk across the park. The old man turned the key in her father's cell, left the door ajar and went back downstairs.

"Hello, Papa," Davy said uncomfortably.

"Come in, Davy," he said. "You can sit on my cot. It's nice and clean."

"*Is it clean!*" someone called out.

"Shut up! My daughter's here."

"Didn't mean no harm, Dave."

Papa was smiling at her. "We have to have some fun. It gets lonesome in here."

She handed him the paper bag and he sorted the medicine and rubbed salve around his nostrils.

"I have a hell of a cold," he said.

"Who's cussin' now?"

Davy looked around at the neat cell and back at her father. He was thinner and this gave him an even younger appearance than usual. He was looking down at her slippers and his face was sober, touched with an almost-sorrow, she thought. He glanced up quickly, and his dark blue eyes filled up with light that came from some place back of them. His mouth turned in a subtle smile, as if he would not be caught and exposed in a deeper mood.

"I don't like him," she thought. "What is he hiding from me?"

"Why don't you talk to me?" he asked playfully.

"Why don't you talk to *me*?"

He said nothing, then he glanced at her slippers again, as if rescued. "Are those the best shoes you've got?"

"Yes."

"When I get out and make a winning, you can get a new pair."

"I'll bet," she said.

"Say, Davy, don't you like your dad?"

"No."

"Your mother must have turned you against me," he said easily, but the bitterness stayed on his words.

"She didn't at all."

"All right, then."

"Is your cold better, Papa?"

"Those damn divorce papers! She's charged me with everything except women."

"Would that be true?" Davy asked.

"You know damn well I never drink or chase women!"

"I guess you did other things," Davy said quietly.

"Guess is right. I don't even know what some of the words mean, and I'm damn sure she doesn't."

"That's the lawyer."

"Well, let her have her divorce. But I hate to be named such things in public."

"The lawyer said he will ask for a private one."

"Will you be the witness, Davy?"

"I guess so."

"When I get out of here, I'll go away so I won't disgrace you anymore."

Davy liked the cool, unemotional way he said it. "You needn't."

"You want to keep going to school and try to be something, Davy. I'll help you out whenever I make a winning."

"You know you won't, Papa."

"Well, now, I might. You can't tell."

That was better, almost an admission that he wouldn't, instead of the promises he meant and never kept.

"You ought to get away from both of us for awhile, Davy, and get some confidence in yourself. You've got to quit being so scared of people. You're a smart girl, and pretty good-looking, too."

Davy's amazement that he was speaking to her in a confidential way made her feel even more clumsy than she had felt at first, but she decided to tell him a compliment that had happened.

"The Prosecutor came to see Mama and me one evening and he said you should have been a lawyer. He said you have a mind as sharp and clean as a whip."

"Not so clean," her father said, but he looked pleased.

"He said," and Davy stopped and laughed. "He said he believed he could reform you, and it would be a shame to divorce you. But Mama said she had made up her mind."

"Did he say that! Well, he's a good fellow. I've nothing against him. But this other fellow, now, I'll punch him in the nose when I get out of here."

"Who's that?"

"That crook. That's what I call a real crook. We talked in the lobby and he kept asking me about a drink, said he had a cold. Finally I went around to Buehl's house by myself and bought him a pint with my own money. When I slipped it in his pocket he had the money ready and then he arrested me. That's what I get for living in a dry state. I told him he knew I wasn't any bootlegger, and he says, 'You are now.'"

"That's dishonest," Davy said.

"That's what I don't like about it. I said, 'Why don't you vag me?' No visible means of support. By God, Davy, I'm no bootlegger. I'm a gambler. Why don't they arrest me for gambling? Elections are coming up, and the damn crooks have to get some fines and jail sentences."

Davy was tired of this old talk. She said, "Papa, back to the Prosecutor, do you think you'll ever reform?"

"Hell, no Davy. You know better than that."

Davy glanced shyly at his direct, serious eyes. He is not afraid now to tell me the truth. Why? No love came back for him, no attachment. He seemed to her only a separate person, unrelated—a small, unfledged knowledge wound round with the strain of their meeting. She felt sorry that he had been tricked.

"I wouldn't like to reform," he said gravely. "I couldn't stand the gaff."

She plucked a hanging thread off the sleeve of his jail suit, and rolled it into a little ball.

He leaped up and squared away, shedding his mood instantly, inviting her into one of the games of her childhood. She felt startled and pained.

"Come on, Davy, let's spar a little. You've got to be such a damn girl lately."

"I *am* a girl," she said sternly. But she rose, facing him, feeling awkward and all wrong. She could not raise her fists; she could not be that little girl because it required love. He waited, like the statue of a boxer, proud and unwilling to accept his defeat. She saw that he left his guard open so that she could steal an easy blow. Finally she struck him softly on his arm nearest her, unable to take any pose but the one in which she stood.

He dropped his arms laughing as if it had all been a joke, but she saw that he was pleased.

The old man was tapping his keys on the iron door. "Old lady's got a little job for you, Dave," he said, and winked.

"You better go on ahead, Davy," her father whispered. "I don't want the fellows to feel bad."

On the first floor the odor of food cooking bandaged the hard smells of metal and linoleum and stone. The old woman was out of sight.

The knowledge of her father's separateness, un-momentous back there, gathered momentum.

The jail door closed after her just as people were walking along the paths going home from work. If anyone stared, and of course they did, it seemed to her now a reasonable curiosity. She was coming out of the jail. I'm myself, she thought rather grandly, and then she felt how absurd she must be, and added, whatever that is. It's I.

Cry of the Tinamou

P edro and the burros waited in front of the shop while I
bought twenty pounds of beans. This was a long transaction
because the shopkeeper was determined to gather the final
news of me on what he considered my final journey. Next to my
knife, *frijoles* were the most important. So I was told. He grumbled
a few warnings. As this would be a completely new experience,
I preferred the advice of old Juan, who seemed to me, in my ignorance, the only good man in Las Lomas, a Central American
town of spiteful Spaniards, living and behaving in the same cruel,
intriguing ways their ancestors behaved when they conquered the
Indians hundreds of years before. If it had not been for old Juan
and our rambling daily talks, I should never have heard of the
place up in the jungles. Once heard of, I could not wait to go.
Disapproving and alarmed as he was, he arranged with Pedro, an
Indian who owned a burro and rented two more, and he, Juan,
advised me what to take along. By the universal communication
system of the grapevine, he had even sent word ahead. I was glad
to leave.

A month in Las Lomas and nearly everyone knew me and
spoke ill of me because I was alone; Las Lomas still courted by
balconies and *duenas,* and all the women wore black and were not
permitted out except when accompanied back and forth to church
or other homes.

Old Juan had consoled me, "You have a pure face and a pure heart, and you cannot help it if you are not a Spaniard."

"But my grandfather Alonzo, doesn't he count?"

"No, no, he was an Irish 'Spaniard' and you are an Americana del Norte, and you have these strange ways. Also, you are a young woman of twenty-two and unmarried. Frail and unprotected. A beautiful child, and this is dangerous. Try to look more like an Indian."

The Indians were a beautiful people, with exceptions, of course, and I wished that by some magic I could look like them. Their velvet black eyes shone in their nut-brown skin. My white skin made me appear to have lived under a rock.

On market days the remnants of several tribes came down from the mountains in their white clothes and big bright stream-ered hats and black braids, walking erect in their beautiful bones.

Old Juan advised me to spend my small bits of money on items the Indians needed so that I could barter for their help. He had never been to my destination, few had, but he knew the very small tribe of Indians left there were friendly, could speak very little Spanish, using their own language, and that there was a good empty house which I had rented for a few *pesos* a month. At that rate I could live there a year, and still get back to the States by the cheapest way, find another job and earn enough for another adventure.

"You may not have another," *el tendero* said after such a reply to his questions.

"Why?"

"Because you are alone. That is for a man."

"*Si, si*, senor!"

"I forgive your tone to me. What will you do when your supplies run out?"

"Pedro or someone may go up again if I send word down the grapevine. Or, I may learn to manage."

The shopkeeper shrugged. He looked at the sandals tied together over my shoulder, and then at my bare feet, toughened now and almost as good as sandals.

"You have not the proper heavy boots? There are stones and poisonous snakes, two kinds."

Old Juan smiled his patience and pointed to my heavy boots tied to a burro.

"*Bueno!*" *El tendero* gave in, but he stared long at my Zuni Indian betrothal necklace of silver and turquoise, and said to old Juan that I could barter it if I ran out of trades.

"*Sacra!*" Juan said. "*Sacra! Only* if desperate!"

The necklace was the only thing of value I possessed, but aside from its worth, it had an almost sacred meaning for me, and old Juan somehow knew that. It had been given to me by a Zuni when I lived in Santa Fe.

El tendero shrugged again, as if to suggest my clothes were not up to the necklace. I wore an Indian cotton skirt and blouse I had bought last market day, but I had a pair of jeans rolled up in my extra clothes. I might have been stoned if I had worn the trousers in Las Lomas. Many old towns had their customs I wished to respect, but Las Lomas had a private set of intolerant judgments. Its handful of Spaniards, remnants themselves, inbred for centuries, were proud and polluted by their purity of strain, despised by the impoverished Indians who endured their abuse if they were not fortunate enough to live high in the mountains. Pedro was one of them, and if he respected me it was because I respected him.

We started, both of us hearing, with polite acknowledgment, the fearful predictions of *el tendero*, concerned with my solitary state. The road out of Las Lomas was as hot as the top of a stove, but the early morning air was clear and clean. As we climbed I looked back on the little valley with its tile-roofed white houses and the purple and cyclamen splashes of bougainvillea, and thought how innocent and peaceful it all appeared, how deceptive, and how happy I felt to be on my way to this unknown and nameless place in the high jungles.

Pedro and I rode and walked but we walked as much as we could to save the animals for the places along the trail when we most needed them. The tough little burros put down their delicate hooves with a sureness that soothed my fears, and their huge plush ears swung forward and back in a rhythm which would have lulled me to sleep if I had not been awed every moment by the grandeur of the scenery on all sides.

In the afternoon, I could look from the steep mountain trail we were climbing back to another range erupting wild and green into a grand sky mansioned with white clouds still and magnificent along the lanes of heaven. I ached with the terrible beauty of this violent land and with the inevitable loss of impressions that nearly overwhelmed me.

The burros set the pace, they rested when they needed to and would move on only when they were ready, but they invented no delays and before nightfall we came to a space of bare ground where Pedro said we would camp. He built a fire and made all the preparations for night and I watched him to learn these unfamiliar and necessary tasks. When he untied a pan and a bundle of food and placed them near me on a stone, I accepted my role and rather clumsily made our meal. We sat in the evening light, quiet and tired, enjoying the food for our hunger, hearing in the vast silence the intimate sound of the burros feeding. As there was no stream near, I cleaned the one pan with earth, and I saw Pedro's sly smile of acceptance or perhaps even approval.

He covered the fire with gravel and rocks, and without asking if I were afraid of the night, he stationed my burro near my sleeping bag. Dark fell down from the sky like a black cloud, sudden and dense, and when I heard the burro lie down near me and give a huge sigh, I was comforted. There was no moon and for awhile I gazed up at the stars in the blackness, asking myself for the first time if I had made a decision as foolish and dangerous as half of Las Lomas considered that I had; if I could live in this far wild place alone and survive, and come down the mountains again in well-being.

Morning reassured me; the thoughts of the night had been lost in peaceful sleep, and absorbed in the sweet animal ease of my burro's breathing.

After the second night and two hours riding in the crystal morning, we arrived at a strong mountain river and rode along it until we came to the clearing where all but two of the Indian tribe, a remnant sixteen, had gathered to welcome us. They had not only received word to expect us that day, but they had heard us long before we came to the river.

Pedro began at once his bartering for labor. I had brought a *machete*, several knives, needles, and from other Indians around Las Lomas, colored wool *cordones* to be worn in the hair, white cloth, embroidery thread, and two woven *horongos*. Part of my possessions I kept for future bartering. Pedro explained to me in Spanish that much of the talk aside from the bartering was about the two Indians, the head of the tribe, an "old man of forty," and a young girl of thirteen, who was the only single female left. The head and a young boy of seventeen were the only single males. Pedro gave me an eloquent glance that said I could easily guess the situation, and the reason for the excitement among the Indians. The chief had taken the girl away a week ago and it was very odd that they had not come down for the arrival of the stranger.

The Indians greeted me in quiet friendliness, mostly with looks and shy smiles. They were a handsome group, the men short and lean, the women delicate-boned, and all wore their black hair long. They were prideful walkers in their simple clothes, once white and now stained and green from the brush and jungle.

As no one had occupied the house for five years, a path had to be cut and the men set to work slashing rapidly with their *machetes*. When they came back, the fourteen Indians and Pedro and I, leading the burros, tramped down the new path. All the way I kept asking myself, where is the jungle? There were trees and brush growing thickly, but no jungle as I had imagined it, and no tropical fruit growing wild. I tried to let my disappointment dissolve in the good fortune of the Indians' acceptance.

The house was on a rise of ground in a small clearing much overgrown and I could see nothing but its cane roof. The men went ahead to cut more brush. When we came to *la casa*, I could not believe what I saw, and only by a huge effort of will was I able to keep from turning to run back along the path. The house looked all right and would be fine with a few days' repair, but it was nothing but a small roof upheld by six posts! This then was the fine house, and apparently it was, but how could I live alone in this strange wild place without walls? I was here, I had made up my mind to live here and write for as many months as I could without the added demands of a full-time job, which left me little strength for writing at night. I had had a few stories and poems published, and I was committed to my dream. I would stay in the house. I would get used to it as I had got used to many and various circumstances all my life, and with these thoughts my sense of life rose up again.

By gesture and Spanish of which the Indians understood little, I finally made clear to the men that I wanted them to build me a small alcove in one corner where I would sleep and work, keep my papers and books. I would do the rest of my living under the roof without walls. No one could understand why I wanted such an enclosure, but in a few hours the men had chopped equal lengths of cane, bound it together with vines and fashioned in one corner walls that touched the earthen floor and stood within a foot of the roof. One side was an open entrance and nothing I could say would convince them that I should have a door. Next they built a small, low platform for my *petate*, a straw bed mat. As these Indian women squatted at cooking and other tasks, chairs and tables were unnecessary, and quickly they seemed unnecessary to me.

I was beginning to feel much pleased with the prospect of my new life and walked about *mi casa* and the small clearing looking at the surrounding landscape. Then glancing down at the moist ground, thinking of planting a garden, I saw the clear and unmistakable and very large pad prints of a soft-toed beast!

"*What is this?*" I called out in fright, pointing at the fresh marks.

"Tigre," one of the men replied casually, and all the old stories I had read of tigers devouring the villagers of India and China flew obligingly into my thoughts.

I could not stay here; shame or will or desire could not make me stay now. I had never felt fearful of wild animals, and had slept out many years of my childhood, but tigers! Tigers in my house and yard! Tigers and not even a door!

I motioned to the men to stop work, to Pedro to reload the burros, and I was overcome by a sadness to leave as if I had been here all my life, but leave I must, without this good experience. The men and women spoke to Pedro and Pedro explained to me that the *tigre* was not interested in hurting human beings, and that as he had passed here last night, and habitually traveled in a large circle, this particular *tigre* would not be back by this spot for several months. No need to worry. No one here had ever been eaten by a *tigre*. But, if I wished to have a rifle, a .22, there was one, and it would be brought. Did I know how to shoot? I knew how to shoot, and I did not add that I was a good shot, but that I did not wish to kill anything ever. Nevertheless, I would stay.

The only harmful animals here, the men went on, were two poisonous snakes, and the wild boar that traveled in large herds and *would* attack human beings. This was far more frightening to me than the tiger as I felt assailed by the very appearance of the wild boars and their repulsive grunting, a horrendous sound in chorus. All work stopped again, to advise me that if I ever heard wild boar coming there was only one possible thing to do: climb the nearest tree and climb it quickly. I resolved to practice climb-ing trees the very next day.

II

I wonder if the next day and the next and the next will ever fall away in the dark of my memory. They were beautiful and terrifying, but the terror was of the unknown and the unseen, of the acutely heard. The Indians had made my room in a few hours and though Pedro had given me advice and directions, Pedro and the burros had gone down the mountain. Knowing no other place than this, save for the short moves they made as they wore out the earth and burned off a new patch to farm, the Indians perhaps did not know what it meant to be a stranger. Before sundown, they filed down the path toward home. For the next few days the men worked at my clearing and at cutting the grown-over path to join another which led to an abandoned tiny farm where fruit and vegetables continued to grow as they pleased in the garden.

That first evening when all had gone, I was so tired from the trip that I lay down at once on the clean grass mat on my hard bed and fell asleep. I awoke in the dark. Oh, what dark and what silence! Palpable, substant, primordial. I found that I was holding my breath, listening, waiting. My eyes seeking shape in the blackness saw only the rhythms moving away from me like the waves of the sea undulating toward the shore. My ears seeking sound heard the silence so deep that a grass blade touched by an insect slit the stillness. I sat up, leaped up and out of my enclosure to the freedom and safety of the outdoors. I stood in the clearing. The dark and the silence were immense. I felt as if the earth would give way and I should be in a void. Then I looked up and saw the stars! The sky too was dark but there were the stars! Red, blue and white fires! Planet Jupiter was blazing, and the Seven Sisters were clustered together in tender intimacy. Sirius, dear familiar dog-star, the brightest star in the heavens, was where he should be at the heel of grand Orion. Tears of recognition and reunion ran down my cheeks. I turned back to my roof, hearing now the small sounds in the grass and leaves, the nightlife of day-sleepers. I was cold. Without lighting a candle, I found my *serape* for cover and went back to sleep.

The next morning I woke at sunrise and looked over my green glistening world with delight. I unpacked and arranged my few belongings, rigged up a shelf for books and paper, improvising a crude table from the emptied baskets. When the Indians came, they put four posts on my bed platform over which I draped mosquito netting. They brought papayas, and I had a breakfast of melon and squash seeds. I built a fire in the earthen stove and set *frijoles* to cooking in an earthen pot. I felt very happy, but I wanted a bath.

Hours later when the beans were done, I took clean clothes and went down the long path to the river and bathed in a sheltered place the women had pointed out to me the day before. That night

I slept, at ease, a qualified ease; there was still the unknown black-night jungle.

Nevertheless my home was in a strange country, and I felt restless to explore my surroundings and to become better acquainted with my only neighbors, the sixteen Indians, the nearest living three miles away. After that, solitude would not be loneliness. Communication would be difficult but it is amazing how learning and imagination quicken with the need.

At the end of the week, one of the young wives, the one with whom, that first day, there had been a wordless exchange of liking, came to see me. She brought me a bowl made from half a large fruit with its pulp scooped out and its shell patiently dried. We shared a papaya, and then as I was about to seek her advice, she made me understand that she had come to show me where to wash my clothes. She had left her own bundle to be picked up on our way.

As we went down the path and along the river, I asked her where, and she answered, "*Distante.*" I had thought we might use the river along the way, but there was no place to get down the treacherous bank, and the tiny pool where I had bathed was not suitable.

She could not pronounce my name and I could not pronounce hers. To each of us, the unfamiliar juxtaposition of letters and sounds twisted our tongues. We laughed. Out of our fun and high spirits I suddenly sang, "La La, La La!" She giggled and pointed to herself, saying, "La La!" Then she pointed to me, saying, "La La!" These became our names to each other, and finally, in gentle ridicule, to all the others.

La La continued to repeat, "Far, far."

All week I had wondered in disappointment where the jungle was, and now we entered it, following the river, and at last after a journey of several miles, we came to a pool where the water was quieter and where we could wade into it and beat our clothes upon the smooth rocks until they were clean. At this time I had the magic aid of soap, but later only the water and the rocks. While our clothes were drying on the bushes, we bathed and washed our hair. Aside from care against the maddening sting of water flies and a lookout for lethal snakes, this was a lyrical time. Monkeys chattered in the matted trees, birds sang and shrieked, and I was acutely aware of the primeval forest and a time when man was slumbering, un-evolved, in other forms. Awe is exalted sorrow for the incomprehensible, as if we grieve for our brevity and small-ness, and sense our vast and endless potential. It is too intense to bear for long. I was glad when La La gestured to go. We must not be caught in the jungle night that came quickly into its daytime gloom.

That evening I forgot to wind my watch and after that I read the hours by the sun and lost the names of the days. I misplaced my knife and was frantic until I found it, and I longed inordinately for a length of string until I remembered the vine the Indians had used to lace the wall of cane together. Water was my only real problem. I could carry no more than enough for drinking up the long path from the river. This was my first morning chore.

When my fresh food ran low, I realized that I could put off no longer my first long journey alone to the abandoned farm. As this would be a weekly trip, I must learn to do it without help. I had been given directions. In this whole place there were a few major paths and one must stay on the path or risk being lost. Fruit was not growing wild on the trees, food was cultivated and scarce. The ancient land had been burned off and farmed for centuries; as the earth was impoverished, the Indians moved on, burned an-other patch and used up its elements. The old patches eventually returned to trees.

The good fortune of my house was that two miles away a tiny farm had been left before it was worn out and there in the ne-glected years the fruit and leaves must have fallen on the ground and rotted back into the soil. Tubers had remained with no one to dig them up. All had given back what it had taken away, and the garden flourished in solitude and splendor. I followed the path the men had cleared and had no trouble finding the farm and there filled my knapsack with papaya, *limones*, and fruit unknown to me, tubers and greens. I rested and ate and watched the monkeys wasting fruit by taking one bite, tossing the rest away, picking another and repeating their extravagance. Perhaps they were after all fertilizing the earth. I wanted a monkey for a companion but I was afraid of disturbing a family and I didn't know how to catch one.

I started back about noon and while passing through the densest part of the jungle, the sun shafts went out and a sudden deluge fell down, soaking me and beating upon me and darkening the way. I hurried to escape and when the rain stopped as abruptly as it had begun, I saw that I was no longer on the path. I urged myself not to panic, looking for familiar trees, but masses of vines hung from them all, and after the shower, the monkey chattering, the bird squawks and singing were wildly intense.

I could hardly press down my terror when I became aware of the sense, imagined or real, of *seeing* the jungle grow. The snap of a carnivorous flower at that moment would have caused me to cry out.

I had been told to leave signs along my trail if I were ever lost, small mounds of pebbles or rocks, knife cuts, anything recognizable. I went toward the path but it was not there; I left signs and went in circles for an hour or more. Then I worked out a plan like the spokes of a wheel, and after several more trips away from the rim to the hub, and out once more, I finally, joyously found the path! My tiredness disappeared, I walked as fast as I could to get home before the black of the unlighted night fell down. I thought of the thousands of important events taking place that instant in the world, of how small and unimportant would be my loss, but, oh, how dear and wonderful and beautiful was my precious life to me!

III

In the long walk in that high cold evening air, my wet clothes chilled me, my teeth chattered uncontrollably and the sack of food weighed more and more, but I dared not leave it on the path or animals would devour it before morning.

As I came under my roof, the tinamou, a grass bird, was crying its mournful evening song, such a heart-breaking cry that it roused in me that vast and arid loneliness that is not for anyone at all, but for something ineffable and far away and beyond all knowing. I had felt it in the jungle and on the plains, in certain bird songs and animal cries; in rare moments of music and reading and art, in that ache of inspiration and inability to express conception, and in those ethereal and poetic times of love. The tinamou cried evenings and mornings in that same high pitch of longing. In all the months I listened, that song asked and reached for the meaning of existence. It urged me to create, to utter my own small joyous and sorrowing cry in the wild silence.

IV

The tinamou woke me as it woke me every morning and set me to work. The sun was big and fiery rising over the eastern mountain range, the night-cooled heights were warming and a drowsy, harmless snake was sunning half in my house and half in the clearing, unaware of the unmarked line that was to have separated his domain from mine.

The trip for food had given me confidence, and although from the first almost everything had been more difficult than expected, I felt a growing sense of adventure and exultation, especially in the clean, sparkling mornings. While the Indians would barter *la leña* for the fire, still I should have to make long walks every week for bathing, washing my clothes and gathering food. But already there was a new rhythm to my days, time rediscovered, uncluttered, a shift of emphasis and a balance of physical and mental work and pleasure.

I missed discussion, but my few books gave back more for the deeper attention given them. Familiar, I roamed about in them, opening the novels to odd scenes in which these character-friends broke in without preamble like a friend continuing his confidence.

When I was desperately lonely for human contact, I walked to one of the farms of my Indian friends, or as if they felt my need from a distance, one or two of them would visit me. Their hearing was so acute that they heard me long before I arrived and often a child came to walk with me. The children were few and much loved; their race was dying with the dying soil, their own infertility matched that of the earth.

La La sometimes brought her work and sat embroidering colored flowers and birds on handwoven cloth to take down the mountain on market days. We sat quietly with few attempts to communicate aloud. Our exchange was heightened by the long silences. I could even write a poem in her presence.

One morning I saw two strangers coming up the path, and I knew they were the head of the tribe, the "old man of forty" and the girl of thirteen, missing that day a month ago when I arrived. Through curiosity and courtesy they had come to welcome me and I prepared to offer them the hospitality of my house and food.

The man spoke a little Spanish, but the girl kept silent and looked down. She was not pretty and her face was sullen. I saw her eyes only when her curiosity overcame her and she raised her lids for flashing moments. The man ignored her, but there was a bond between them.

I knew their story from La La; she had made it clear with our few common words and her pantomime when we met at the river pool. As I looked at this unmatched couple I felt that I understood and even pitied the man but I could not like him. He had the erect and graceful bearing of his tribal brothers, the fine features, the fine bones, and long back hair, but none of their ancient, eloquent beauty. Unlike the others, he had a desolate, desperate arrogance that glowed and dimmed in his face as if these emotions were lights that went on and off in his skull.

The girl was a tribal jewel because she was the only unmarried female, and she and the young boy were in love, La La had told me. No one knew whether the chief desired her, but it was imperative to him that he replenish his tribe, almost extinct. Before her time, so desperate was he that he went down the mountain to other villages and accosted strange women in the streets with an offer, a demand even, of marriage. Being of other tribes, they did not wish to leave their own, and besides, he was considered old. When he saw that the girl and the young man were in love, he was afraid to wait longer, and by authority of his chiefdom, he had taken the girl and gone higher into the jungles, and apparently had just returned. The others had not thought well of him for leaving when a stranger was arriving, as only one other had appeared here in all the years remembered. So, the chief had come now to pay his respects. I was glad when they went back down the path.

At any rate, the chief's slightly larger Spanish vocabulary made it possible for him to give me a bit of news. He said that a man and his wife had lived for several years farther up in the jungle, that they had come from a foreign land, and I gathered from his efforts to explain that they were making a scientific study of some sort and keeping records. Whether or not I should see these people seemed to make no difference, but the news had an odd effect upon me. I felt already as if I had someone to talk with, and that was a very comforting thought. The way up the jungle was perhaps impossible for me, but it was preferable to the precipitous journey down to Las Lomas because it would have a true destination.

Almost immediately I had no desire to see them, sensing the artificial and disinterested relationship with the Indians a study suggested. It was all right, perhaps important, but it was not for me and my friends who were simply living our daily lives unobserved.

The next morning when I was on my way to the abandoned farm for fruit, I met La La on the river path on her way to invite me to a festival. One of the young men had killed a wild boar as part of the welcome for the returning head of the tribe. The boar was presently roasting. I postponed my trip and went with La La to the clearing above which smoke was rising. The smell of roasting pig was in the fresh morning air. I had not tasted meat for over two months and was content, sure that no killing ever again would be involved in my survival. But my refusal to share the feast surely would cause my Indian friends to be offended and perhaps distrust me. Worse still, as we came nearer, my appetite rose. I could not bear to look at the whole boar roasting, but later when a piece of meat was handed me on a leaf, I hypocritically ate with relish. This troubled me as a serious flaw in my character, and while I was enjoying the gaiety, my mind was filled with questions. Relief came when I saw the young girl standing near the chief. As before, she said nothing and looked down, her face with but one sullen expression. When the chief moved about she followed him. At one point in the festivities the chief and several men went into the trees and at once the young girl came out of her torpor. The young man was looking at her and she at him—those shy, tense looks of first love. He walked past her and yanked one of her long black braids. She turned, giggled, gave him a push and ran, and he ran after her. They played this sweet game of pursuit and chase for several minutes and then before he caught her, they stopped abruptly and listened. I could hear nothing for several minutes, but they had heard. The boy drew aside, the girl became still, her eyebrows frowned, and she waited. When the chief appeared she followed him obediently. I watched the boy and saw that he was careful not to look at the girl or the chief. How grotesque was this pair, and how beautiful were the boy and girl in their love play. I longed to interfere, but there was no way, or I could think of none. Sympathy for the pair was obvious but all took for granted the chief's right to the only free female left.

V

Jungle bugs were eating away at my neglected manuscripts; the paper already appeared old. La La brought me some discouraging leaves to place among my papers and books. I gave her a poem about the tinamou—there was always a courteous exchange. After hearing it, having to intuit its nature, she folded it many times into a square and placed it in a tiny woven bag tied to her belt. Then she whistled a fragment of the tinamou's song and ran down the path.

After the dubious festival I was lonely as I had not been in long periods of work and solitude. I guessed that much of this feeling came from the little drama that now engaged my imagination and would not let go. In new love there is no other world; life has its being, intense and radiant, within the microcosm created by the attraction of two out of many. The girl and boy, only a few years younger than I, were dispossessed of that isolate ephemeral enchantment, surely love's due. Insignificant, infinitesimal in the world of all, that comparison could not lessen the pain of their separation. I could not bear to see the girl at the heels of the aging chief, her feelings no matter to him. Begetting was at stake. He did not leave her alone for a moment although he appeared unaware of the boy. Perhaps it was beneath his position to notice.

One afternoon they paid me another visit. The two of them sat without a word for some time, then he made me understand that he was leaving her there under my guardianship. Did he think there was too much sympathy among the others? She gave me a bitter look and assumed her now familiar stupid pose. The chief went off down the path.

Evening came, the tinamou sang its mournful song, and he had not returned. The girl ate only a little food with me, and that without even a glance, but she became alert and tense, listening for sounds my ears were not trained to hear. Entering my small enclosure to get some need, I heard her stir for the first time. I felt rather nervous if she should run away but I had no right to prevent her. How to explain to the chief when he had given me the dubious compliment of his trust was more difficult than I cared to consider. I waited, giving her the chance to escape, but she went only into the clearing a little way and gave a long high whistle like a jungle bird I had heard but did not know. She crept back and just as she was about to sit down under my roof, I came out. Startled, she looked at me, her eyes fully open, dark, liquid, their love surprised. I smiled at her, a secretive smile. She ran to me and threw herself on the ground. I sat down beside her and without a word, we embraced. That passionate instant of understanding between us broke her reserve. She began to cry in tight, barely audible little whimpers as if she were learning to cry. I imagined her crying this way in the nights up in the jungle, trying to accept submission, and disavow her longing persistent dreams of love— such a burden of emotion for this girl who was far more a woman than she appeared!

As we sat there on the ground with our arms around each other, rocking gently back and forth in deep instinctive harmony, we heard the whistle very near, low, almost like that of the mournful tinamou somewhere out there in the grass. She lifted her dark face, pinched and crumpled a moment before, suddenly smooth and illumined. She whistled, low and cautious. The boy came from the back, having circled the clearing, and when he hesitated in the shadow of the trees, she leaped up and beckoned to him, all shyness again. He came under the roof, shy too, confused at having to greet me.

The dusk was rising delicately, the far mountain ranges were shades of cobalt blue, and night was already in the valleys. The air around us was blue, growing darker, and that first evening stillness was on the world. A small wind sighed through the wilderness and passed by trembling the dry cane roof. Silence again. An unseen, intuited baton slashed the night and insect music vibrated the air.

I went into my room without lighting the candle. The girl followed, wanting me to stay, perhaps for a custom, perhaps from fear of the chief's return. Back in the open I sat down cross-legged and she sat near me. The boy had moved to the edge of the clearing. Soon we could see only the dark shapes of one another by the sheen of the stars. The tribal language, of which I had learned very little, gave them privacy, but their tone was that of a casual talk, with long pauses. He tossed a pebble and struck her and she tossed one back, and their low, excited laughter sang through this long game. They stopped abruptly and the boy was gone into the brush; the girl rose and signaled to me to stay where I was. She ran into the enclosure and sat down on my mat. She sighed once and I imagined her face sullen and closed again. I began to sing a song low as if to myself to continue the sound in case the chief had heard their quiet laughter.

He was not long in coming up the path. He saw me easily in the dark and asked where the girl was. Imprisonment in my room pleased him. He asked me to light the candle and showed me some colored hand-woven ribbons he had bartered from another tribe, ribbons to wear in her hair at the wedding. I watched her face. Not a quiver of despair revealed itself; only the sullen resignation to her lot. I asked him when; he held up the fingers of one hand for the days, explaining that the men must go hunting and the women must make her a dress. Poverty would cause her to wear this dress for as many years as it would hang together. Impulsively I took off my silver-turquoise necklace and fastened it around her throat. A flash of pleasure showed in her eyes before she looked down again.

The chief studied the necklace at a courteous distance and nodded slowly. He was curious about its origin but would not ask.

"Americano del Norte—Indio—Zuni."

He gave me a rather fierce, reserved smile as if his smiles had run out and he must take great care in sharing them.

"Ummmm—" he said in thanks, and handed me one of the ribbons. I accepted it as a token of our moment of understanding, the girl's and mine.

The girl laid her delicate brown hand with its ragged nails over the necklace's symbol of the womb, which she understood. She gave me a long, full look. I knew she was speaking in silence of the boy.

They went down the path into the night. The river below had a dark gleam, and I listened to its strong, steady rush of water, mindless, destined, drawn to a faraway sea.

I needed to look at the stars.

Acknowledgments

All of the stories, with the exception of "Cry of the Tinamou," originally appeared in the following publications.

"The Larger Cage" – *Antioch Review*, summer 1953.
"A Scandalous Humility" – *Northwest Review*, spring 1968.
"Reconciliation" – *New Mexico Quarterly Review*, summer 1947.
"The Meeting" – *Southwest Review*, winter 1982.
"Aslant the Moon" – *Yellow Silk*, spring 1986.
"Run, Sheepy, Run!" – *Kansas Magazine*, 1966.
"Love Be My Destiny" – *Southwest Review*, spring 1964.
"The Vine by Root Embraced" – *California Quarterly*, winter 1952.
"Matriarch of the Court" – *Southwest Review*, autumn 1955.
"William Shakespeare" – *Montevallo Review*, summer 1950.
"The Tea Party" – *Seventeen Magazine*, March 1956.
"The Santa Ana" originally appeared as "Night of Yearning" – *Saturday Evening Post*, November 26, 1959. Used with permission from the *Saturday Evening Post*, © 1959.
"The Wild Flower" – *Kansas Magazine*, 1949.
"Davy" originally appeared as "Snow Is a Promise" – *New Story* (Paris), July 1951

About the Author

Sanora Babb (1907-2005) is the author of seven books, as well as essays, short stories, and poems that were published in literary magazines alongside the work of Ernest Hemingway, John Dos Passos, Ralph Ellison, Katherine Ann Porter, Genevieve Taggard, and William Carlos Williams. She taught courses on short fiction writing in the UCLA extension program and had stories published in *The Best American Short Stories*. Babb's stories reflect her strong empathy with marginalized people and their daily lives, an affinity with the natural world, and the ability to elevate the ordinary into the extraordinary.